Another Sun

Also by Timothy Williams

Another Sun

Timothy Williams

This work was first published in French, as *Un Autre Soleil*, in 2011.

Copyright © 2011, Editions Payot & Rivages

First published in English by Soho Press in 2012.

English copyright © 2012 by Timothy Williams

Published by
Soho Press, Inc.
853 Broadway
New York, NY 10003

Library of Congress Cataloging-in-Publication Data

Williams, Timothy.
[Autre soleil. English]
Another sun / Timothy Williams ; translated from the French by the author.
p. cm.
"This work was first published in French, as Un Autre Soleil, in 2011."
HC ISBN 978-1-61695-156-6
PB ISBN 978-1-61695-363-8
eISBN 978-1-61695-157-3
I. Title.
PR6073.I43295A913 2012
2012027237

Map of Guadeloupe: © istockphoto

Printed in the United States of America

10 9 8 7 6 5 4 3 2 1

À la mémoire de Claude Ruette
Ils font toujours braire.

Another Sun

I

TIM TIM

It was past six o'clock and night had begun to fall.

The group of men moved aside as the Land Rover came down the track. The whip aerial swayed against the red sky. The yellow beams were like two eyes.

The Land Rover halted and the engine was turned off. The toads resumed their loud monotonous croaking in the grass.

Two white men jumped down. They wore kepis, neat khaki uniforms and black shoes. They walked toward the group of waiting men.

The driver remained sitting behind the wheel.

"What is it?" one of the gendarmes asked, turning to an old man.

The old man was holding a bicycle. He had one hand on the cracked leather saddle, and with the other, he pointed to the middle of the pond. The black water reflected the lingering light of day.

A dark, humped shape was caught among the reeds.

"A man?"

The old man shrugged.

The others stood in silence. Some wore rubber boots, several had narrow machetes that hung loosely in their hands. Their eyes followed the two white gendarmes.

"I've never seen this pond before."

"It comes with the rain." The old man spoke in Creole.

The fronds swayed and creaked. The pond lay in the hollow of the sloping valley. Grass-covered hills ran down to the edge of the white dirt track and its two parallel lines of coconut trees. To the east, against the darkening hill top, rose the gaunt silhouette of the derelict sugar refinery. A couple of hangars and a tall, crumbling chimney that pointed to the sky and the rising half moon.

The gendarme turned to his companion. "You'd better pull whatever it is out of the water."

"The water is infected—there's bilharzia." Anxiety in the eyes beneath the brim of the kepi.

"The cows drink the water." The captain pointed to the dark forms of an indistinct herd of cattle grazing on the far side of the pond.

As if in acquiescence, a cow emitted a single, mournful low. Elsewhere in the valley, another cow gave an answering call.

The third gendarme slipped from behind the driver's seat and began to undress. "I'll go."

The captain returned to the vehicle and leaned inside the Land Rover. He then clambered onto the rigid bonnet. A searchlight on the roof came alight, and he aimed the beam toward the dark water. A mist had started to form, dancing wisps along the surface.

The gendarme had stripped to his underclothes; he walked across the grass and stepped into the pond.

"A damn fool wanting to fish." Behind the searchlight, the captain lit a cigarette.

The old man said, almost under his breath. "No fish in that water."

The black gendarme stepped further into the pond. A circle of light followed his movements. He gave a curse, stumbled and began to swim, only his head above the water. A couple of strokes brought him alongside the floating object.

He stood up, took hold of the nerveless bundle and waded

2

back toward the edge of the pond, bright rivulets streaming down his face and body. He squeezed his nose and spat into the water. "He's dead."

Throwing away his cigarette, the captain jumped from the roof of the Land Rover while the crowd moved forward. Many hands helped drag the body onto the grass.

The corpse lay like a landed fish, transfixed by the single beam of the searchlight.

The captain crouched down and ran his hand over the bloated, pale flesh. In the light, the fingers cast spiderlike shadows.

"Gunshot wounds."

Red mounds against the white skin.

"Stand back," he ordered and, tugging with both hands, the captain pulled at the corpse.

It rolled over slowly, the body faster than the head. The mouth fell open and water ran from colorless lips. The throat gurgled.

The old man with the bicycle peered at the body. He clicked his tongue.

The captain turned, shading his eyes against the light. "You know him?"

The man nodded.

"Who is he?"

The old man did not answer and the captain raised his voice, "Who is this man?"

"They've murdered Monsieur Calais," the man replied softly, and with his gnarled hand, he crossed himself.

2

Twelve bore

The Mercedes pulled off the track and the driver opened the rear door. The *procureur* rose with difficulty from the seat.

The procureur could have passed for a white man, despite the short curly hair, now turning white. His skin was pale. He was overweight and he had to exert himself to get onto his feet. He was wearing a white shirt and a pair of pale blue slacks. His tennis shoes appeared exceptionally small.

The onlookers had come from the neighboring hamlets, on bicycles and *mobylettes*, or in battered Peugeot and Toyota pick-ups. There were several women, squat on their rubber sandals and shapeless beneath cotton dresses. One held a child to her chest.

Barriers had been put up and a gendarme held the crowd back.

Uniformed men and civilians moved within the radius of the converging floodlights.

The corpse lay beneath a dark blanket.

A van stood near the pond. Nearby, two men were talking. *Commandant* Lebel looked up and, noticing the crowd of onlookers draw apart, rose to his feet and saluted briskly.

The procureur was out of breath. He took a small cigar from his mouth. "This Calais?"

Commandant Lebel nodded. He bent over and lifted the edge

4

of the blanket. The procureur squinted, smoke in his eyes. He looked down on the face, now grey in death. "Poor bastard."

"You knew him, *monsieur le procureur*?"

"Who didn't know Calais?" Slowly the procureur turned on his small feet and looked at the stationary vehicles, the Jeeps and the Saviem van.

"Everything in order?"

Lebel let the blanket fall back on the dead face, "Everything in order, monsieur le procureur."

"I'll be needing an autopsy." He paused, looking at Lebel thoughtfully. "Gun wounds?"

"We've found the cartridge—twelve bore."

"Fingerprints?"

Lebel shook his head. "The cartridge had been trampled in the mud."

"When did he die?"

"The corpse must've been in the water for at least eighteen hours."

The procureur took a small packet of *Déchets de Havane* cigars from his pocket. "Twelve bore?" He lit another cigar with the burning stub.

"We've located the culprit."

"Fast work, Lebel." The procureur raised an eyebrow. "My congratulations."

"We need permission for a search warrant—and to bring the man in for questioning."

"Who?"

"An old man. A revenge killing."

"You're sure?"

"The man spent most of his life in French Guyana—in the penal colony. An ex-convict."

"How do you know he's guilty?"

"He'd been making threats against Calais."

The procureur sucked on the new cigar and looked upwards into the sky. For a few seconds the moon broke through the

5

low clouds. It soon disappeared again, leaving a blue aureole. Addressing no one in particular, the procureur said, "Calais must be disappointed."

"Disappointed, monsieur le procureur?"

"To be killed by an old convict." He raised his shoulders. "Calais who wanted to be a martyr, who wanted to die for a cause."

"What cause?"

"God knows." The procureur laughed again.

Commandant Lebel appeared embarrassed.

"You're sure it's the old convict?"

"Good evidence, monsieur le procureur. I think we can be sure."

"Hearsay is not evidence." The procureur's smile was bland.

"You want me to bring him in?"

The procureur nodded; his thoughts were elsewhere. "I can entrust the enquiry to *Juge* Laveaud." The floodlights caught his smile and revealed large, stained teeth. "Let's see what she can make of it."

"She's an intelligent woman."

"No doubt. Intelligent and ambitious."

3
Pointe-à-Pitre

"My God, it hurts."

Trousseau smiled from behind his small desk. His long fingers lay on the keyboard of the old typewriter. "Somebody's thrown a curse on you, *madame le juge.*"

The skin on the back of Anne Marie's left hand and fingers was swollen with white weals. She could feel the heat of friction as she rubbed. "Who hates me, Monsieur Trousseau? I haven't been here long enough."

"You're white—that's enough to get yourself hated."

There was a sink in the corner of the office. She got up and turned on the tap, then held her hand beneath the cold water. She rubbed again. "Must be something I've eaten. I never had an allergy before coming to this country."

The water had a numbing effect. She let it run for over a minute. Trousseau started to type.

Anne Marie looked out of the window. She liked her office—little more than a cupboard, just big enough for her desk and the *greffier*'s, a couple of filing cabinets, a floor of polished mahogany and a small sink. It was at the top of the Palais de Justice and the gentle winds came through the open shutters and pushed against the billowing lace curtains. Lace from Chantilly that she had bought in Paris before sailing out to the Caribbean. As the water continued to run, the pain ebbed and became a dull sense of heat. Anne Marie leaned against the sink and looked out over the vivid red of the corrugated roofs of the nearby bank and the old Chamber of Commerce. Ship masts, bare without their sails, rocked with the movement of the green sea within the small port.

Pointe-à-Pitre.

Along the quayside, only a few meters from the schooners and the rust-stained ferry for Marie-Galante, the stalls bustled with their early morning commerce: jars of hair pomade from Liverpool, ground corn from Suriname, anthuriums from Martinique, good-luck aerosols from Puerto Rico. Sitting on cardboard boxes, the fat smuggler women from Dominica had laid out contraband brassieres and minuscule knickers for children. And in the distance, standing out in clear relief against the sky, the Souffrière. The mountain range filled the horizon and the volcano, with all the intricate detail of its eroded flanks, its gullies and its tropical vegetation, rose up above everything else until its summit was lost in a dark crown of clouds.

"Get somebody to cast a spell for you," Trousseau said, pointing at her hand. "A spell against the curse."

"These curtains are dirty. They need changing."

"I know an old man—a *gadézaffé*—part Indian, part Carib—who lives down at Trois-Rivières. He knows all the remedies. He'll cure you."

Anne Marie turned off the tap.

"He also does sacrifices."

With a handkerchief, she made a tight bandage around her left hand. Then she returned to her desk.

"A letter for you, madame le juge."

She took the letter—it was from Papa—and placed it in her handbag. "What's on the agenda for today, Monsieur Trousseau?"

"The old people know about these things. They had their own medicine—the Caribs and the Arawaks—long before Christopher Columbus set foot on this island." He added, disparagingly, "Christopher Columbus and the white men."

Anne Marie looked at the chipped varnish on her damp fingers. "The agenda for today, Monsieur Trousseau?"

"We're booked for the seven thirty flight for the Saintes tomorrow."

"The Saintes?"

"The girl who smothered her baby."

"And today, Monsieur Trousseau?"

He pulled the day-to-day calendar from behind the typewriter. "Lafitte will be here soon—in about ten minutes."

"Which dossier, Monsieur Trousseau?"

"The Calais killing." He pointed to a folder on her desk. "It's all there—Lafitte brought it round last night."

Anne Marie picked up the beige folder.

The cover, made of cardboard and cloth, with a loose buckle, smelled of glue. *Calais, Septembre, 1980,* had been typed on the label. Above it in neat printing, *Ministère de la Justice, Département de la Guadeloupe.*

"The old man says he's innocent," she said.

"What proof is there against him?"

"The accusations of a few villagers. He'd been making threats against Raymond Calais. The gendarmerie found the cartridge on the scene of the crime—twelve bore. Then yesterday they found the gun."

"Where?"

"Buried, madame le juge. A hunting gun. A pre-war model, probably an Idéale. Buried about two hundred meters from where the old man sleeps. He denies ever having hidden his gun, but that's where the gendarmes found it—in a field where he keeps his goats. It had been wiped clean of all prints and wrapped in an oily cloth. Then put in a plastic bag." Trousseau paused. "His name is engraved on the butt."

"His name?"

"Hégésippe Bray." Trousseau frowned, his dark eyes watching Anne Marie's fingers as she started to scratch again at her left hand. "He harbored a grudge against Calais. Hégésippe Bray

9

claims a lot of Sainte Marthe, the Calais estate, belongs to him by right. As it is, he's been living in a hut on the edge of the estate."

"When did he get back?"

"Get back, madame le juge?"

"From French Guyana. When did Bray get back to Guadeloupe?"

"Last Christmas. Calais—with his racing horses as well as a couple of villas—generously agreed to let Bray have the hut. No water, no electricity—just a dilapidated hut on the edge of the estate."

"The Sainte Marthe plantation?"

Trousseau nodded, "Forty years in equatorial America can't have done Hégésippe Bray's brain much good. That and rum." He tapped his temple. "When Bray came back, he hung around the shacks where they sell cheap liquor, and once he'd had a few glasses of rum, he'd start to make threats."

"Against Calais?"

"Threatened to kill him."

"Why?"

Trousseau nodded toward the dossier. "Calais' father had sold at least ten hectares to Bray—and Hégésippe Bray maintains that in his absence, Calais took everything for himself."

Anne Marie squeezed her hand. "Paraffin tests?"

"Positive." A shrug. "Bray admits to having used his gun that morning."

"Why?"

"To kill a goat with scab. He owns several goats—and a garden, where he grows tomatoes. And yams and string beans."

"A revenge killing?"

Trousseau shrugged again. "You'll find everything in the dossier. Lafitte's been very thorough, as usual."

Trousseau returned to his typing and Anne Marie opened the file. She glanced through several pages. Twice she nodded. Looking up, she was surprised to see the door open.

"Lafitte's outside, madame le juge."

She took a fifty-franc note from her handbag, "I'd like to have a better look at the dossier before seeing Lafitte. Perhaps you could get some sandwiches—and something to drink."

Trousseau stood up.

"And see if you can get something from the chemists—something to stop this itching."

4

Lafitte

"Why was he sent to French Guyana?"

"He murdered his wife."

"Why?"

"He thought she was a *soucougnan*."

"A what?"

"A voodoo witch."

"So he killed her?"

Lafitte nodded. He was a few years older than her. His skin had taken a slightly yellow tint, with the wrinkles of years spent in the tropics. Yet he remained boyish in appearance. The sandy hair was short and brushed back. He spoke with the hint of a northern accent—from Roubaix or Lille. He had entered the police after a brief career as a professional cyclist. In his spare time, he captained a cycling team.

"How old is Bray now?" she asked.

"Nearly eighty-three." He pointed to the desk. "Madame le juge, it's all there in the dossier."

"I'd rather you tell me," Anne Marie said honestly; it was always a good policy to flatter a man's professional pride.

"There hasn't been time to check through all the archives. The trial was in Basse-Terre in 1940, and most of the records were destroyed in the fire of '55. Yesterday I saw his half sister—she wasn't too helpful."

"Where did Bray grow up?"

"He was illegitimate." Lafitte leaned forward and opened the file. "Never knew his father. His mother worked on the Calais estate—first in the fields and then later in the main house. She was a Carib and that is where he got his looks from."

"What looks?"

"The thin nose and those high cheekbones—they're Carib rather than African features."

"Who is this sister you mention, Monsieur Lafitte?"

"Half sister," he corrected. "A retired school teacher. Twelve years younger than him. She says it was Bray who helped toward her education. She passed her *certificat d'études*, and she got to be headmistress in a school at Pointe-Noire."

Anne Marie nodded and looked at her hand.

"Now lives in Morne-à-l'Eau with her son. They were responsible for getting the old man back from South America."

"How did they know he was still alive?"

"When he was deported, she sent letters but never got a reply. Then later she made enquiries and wrote to the Ministry of Justice in Paris. This was after the war, about the time they were shipping home the last of the convicts, and she wanted to know for certain Hégésippe Bray was dead."

"Well?"

"Paris replied that he'd died of malaria in 1946."

The lace curtain danced with the wind; somewhere along the docks a car hooted angrily.

Lafitte continued, "Salvation Army found him. They thought he had syphilis—it was endemic among the convicts. They picked him up, lying on the banks of one of the canals in Cayenne. Local people'd seen him around for some time, scavenging in the dustbins, hanging around the restaurants and the bars near the Place Grenoble. Probably came in from the country—there are still ex-convicts living among the Indians in the rain forest. Bray would beg for a few coins from the children on their way to school. A few francs to buy tafia."

Anne Marie raised an eyebrow.

"Cheap rum—made from molasses. Should have killed him years ago. But once the Salvation Army got him to the hospital where they could wash and clean him up and give him regular meals—food and not just alcohol—his memory came back. The Salvation Army's used to these cases. Arabs, West Indians as well as the Europeans—dross from all over the French Empire, ex-convicts who'd landed up Guyana. Deportation effectively destroyed most of them. Even once they'd done their time, they had to stay on and do an equal number of years in French Guyana. The hope was they'd help the economy."

"When were the penal settlements abolished?"

"At the end of the war but before French Guyana became an overseas *département* in 1946. There was nothing for the ex-convicts to do. They weren't allowed to own land or set up shop or have a business. Most drifted into petty crime. Either that or working as a domestic in the house of one of the prison officers. And working at virtually slave labor rates."

"They weren't sent back to France?"

Lafitte looked at the ceiling. "The bill to do away with deportation was voted before the war —because there was growing pressure in France. In the press."

"Albert Londres?"

"Madame, why do you want me to tell you when you know about these things?"

Of course she knew about these things. At magistrate school she had specialized in punishment and recidivism. She gave him a friendly smile. "Continue, please, Monsieur Lafitte."

"Newspaper articles shocked the public—at a time between the wars when there was a growth of interest in the colonies. The penal settlements in French Guyana would probably have been done away with by the time Hégésippe Bray was sent there if it hadn't been for the war. French Guyana—like Martinique and Guadeloupe—came under the control of the Vichy government. So it was there—Devil's Island and the Moroni—the collaborationists sent all their political undesirables—Gaullists and Communists. Useful because it was out of the way."

"Bray wasn't a political prisoner."

"A murderer, but the court decided there were extenuating circumstances. So he was condemned to seven years in French Guyana. *La guillotine sèche.* Dry guillotine. No dripping knife edge and a lot slower—but just as effective."

"Why wasn't Bray sent back here? After the abolition of the *bagne?*"

"Like everyone else he was offered a free passage back to France. He'd been to France during the Great War and had almost died of flu there. He didn't want to go back—he wanted to return to Guadeloupe. For that, he says, there was no arrangement. He had no money."

"Strange."

"And perhaps he was ashamed."

"He could have contacted his sister."

"Half sister." Lafitte shrugged. "Possibly he didn't want to."

"He owned land in Guadeloupe."

The door opened and Trousseau entered carrying a couple of sandwiches wrapped in brown paper. Without a word, he set the sandwiches and two bottles of Pepsi Cola on Anne Marie's desk.

"And your ointment, madame le juge." A green box with a red cross that Trousseau placed before her.

Anne Marie turned back to face Lafitte. "What do you know about Hégésippe Bray's past?"

"We've telexed to Paris," Lafitte said.

"I'm quite sure you're following up all the lines of investigation with your habitual thoroughness," Anne Marie said. "Please tell what you know about Bray's past. What did the half sister tell you?"

Lafitte stared at the dossier that he had opened on his knees.

"His mother died when he was in France. During the first war, when he was a soldier in the infantry. He was sent to the front where he ended up building the road that carried arms and men to Verdun. Verdun was under siege from the Germans."

"Really?"

The yellow skin of Lafitte's face seemed to tinge with a blush. "He worked alongside the Senegalese. He even shook hands with Pétain once—which made him a life-long admirer of the *Maréchal.* A quarter of a century later he was indignant about being sent to prison alongside people who denigrated the Maréchal."

Anne Marie smiled.

"Wounded in the first war. And decorated. Possibly that's what helped him get off the death sentence in 1940. Above all, what stood him in good stead with the judges was the fact he was Calais' favorite employee. At the age of twelve he'd started work on the Calais estate—first as a stable boy, then in the fields. Later he was put in charge of the horses. Very good with animals and the old man Calais was impressed by him—at least, that's what the half sister says."

"She's told you a lot of things, Monsieur Lafitte."

"Back from the trenches, Calais gave him a job as a foreman. With horses, a house of his own, a maid—and the responsibility of going round the plantation, seeing everything was in order. And paying the workers at the end of each month. Hégésippe Bray got on well with the coolies."

"Coolies?"

"The Indians. At the end of slavery—after 1848, the Negroes didn't want to work in the fields any more—the planters brought over indentured laborers from India. Good workers." He smiled, turning in his seat. "I'm sure Monsieur Trousseau'll agree with me."

Trousseau looked up. "Negroes, mulattos, Indians, whites—all the same to me."

"Negroes and Indians don't always get on very well."

Trousseau sucked his teeth noisily.

"Go on, *monsieur l'inspecteur*."

"There was . . . there appears to have been a bond of loyalty between the old man Calais and Hégésippe Bray. According to the half sister, Calais considered Bray a son. By 1937, Bray was able to buy land from Calais, and he started growing his own sugar."

"He continued to work for Calais?"

Lafitte nodded. "And he took a common law wife. This was in 1939, so he was already fairly old."

Trousseau said, "Forty-two."

"She was from Saint-Pierre in Martinique. A maid who worked in Calais' house—a mulatto woman of considerable beauty. However Bray must eventually have decided she was a soucougnan because of the curse she put on him."

"What kind of curse?"

"She took away. . . ." Lafitte blushed again. "She took away his virility."

"Many witches still about," Anne Marie remarked.

"There was a child," Lafitte said. "A boy. The boy was found drowned in a rain pond. Bray claimed she killed the child to spite him."

"Bray killed his wife out of revenge?"

"He killed the woman because she was a witch, a soucougnan. She was young and beautiful, whereas he was old. She wanted a vigorous young man. One night he cut her throat—with a machete. Then he burned the corpse."

"And he was sentenced to a mere seven years?"

Lafitte's smile was apologetic. "In those days, courts were more sympathetic to jealous husbands."

"And they knew all about witches."

"Bray had the good testimony of Calais. He got life—more than life. Thirty-eight years in a tropical prison."

Listening, Anne Marie kneaded the back of her bandaged hand.

"When the Salvation Army contacted the half sister, she went down to Cayenne, and she persuaded Hégésippe Bray to return

17

to Guadeloupe. He agreed on the understanding he would live in the country—on his own. The years of solitude had made him something of a hermit. Bray lived on the edge of the Calais estate."

"Then why kill Calais?"

"An old grudge." Lafitte shrugged. "Really there was no reason for Calais not to have taken the land back, even supposing that it'd once belonged to Bray. Like everybody else, Calais must've assumed Bray was dead."

"You believe Bray killed Calais?"

"The motive was there. Hégésippe Bray had made threats." Lafitte ran his hand through his hair. "And if it wasn't Bray, who could it have been?"

Drops of condensation had formed on the bulbous glass of the Pepsi Cola bottles.

"Always possible that it was somebody completely different."

"Such as, madame le juge?"

"Such as terrorists."

5
Hégésippe Bray

Bray had blue eyes—bright blue eyes as clear as polar water.

The old man shuffled in like a man who had forgotten how to lift his feet. He advanced very slowly, guided by the prison officer who held his arm. Hégésippe Bray's hands hung loosely before him; they were chained together.

"Unlock those cuffs." Anne Marie spoke curtly to the officer. "And then kindly wait outside."

When the officer had left, Anne Marie pointed to a chair. Lafitte took a couple of steps forward and placed it behind the old man.

Hégésippe Bray was wearing a faded prison uniform. The top buttons of the shirt were undone, revealing tight curls of white chest hair. He had not shaved. The skin of the jaw—a matte black like leather—was partially hidden beneath white stubble that gave him the look of an escaped convict.

Hégésippe Bray had once been strong; his chest was deep and his shoulders broad. Now as he lowered himself carefully into the wooden chair, putting his weight on Lafitte's arm, he winced with pain.

Trousseau remained behind his desk, watching the old man.

In silence, Anne Marie and Hégésippe Bray stared at each other. Anne Marie had never seen a black man with blue eyes.

The innocent, clear eyes of a child.

"I am Madame Laveaud—the *juge d'instruction*—and I've been charged with the Calais dossier—the murder of Raymond Calais." She tapped the beige folder. "There'd appear to be a prima facie case against you, Monsieur Bray, and you're temporarily being held at the *maison d'arrêt* in Pointe-à-Pitre so that you can help us in our enquiries."

There was no reaction.

"It's my job to see whether the accusations that the gendarmerie of Sainte-Anne has made against you are sufficiently founded for you to be sent for trial before a court of law." She paused. "Do I make myself clear?"

The eyes stared at her.

"Do you understand, Monsieur Bray?"

The old man turned, moving his head with his shoulders. He looked at the greffier.

Anne Marie said, "I want to help you, Monsieur Bray."

Lafitte coughed. Behind the typewriter, Trousseau was silent.

The old man's forehead formed long ridges. Slowly, very slowly, he looked about the office, at the lace curtains and the filing cabinets. He looked at the photograph of the president of the Republic, Giscard d'Estaing.

"Please tell me if you understand."

Lafitte gave the old man a reassuring nod.

Hégésippe Bray spoke in Creole. His voice was higher and thinner than Anne Marie had expected.

Trousseau grinned.

"What's he saying?"

Trousseau rubbed at his moustache and his dark eyes twinkled. Glancing at Lafitte, he tried to smother his smile behind his hand.

"Well, Monsieur Trousseau?"

Hégésippe Bray saw the smile on Trousseau's face and nodded.

"Kindly tell me what Monsieur Bray's just said."

"You're a woman."

"Of course I'm a woman, Monsieur Trousseau."

"He'd like to speak with Monsieur Lafitte—alone." Trousseau wiped his mouth with the back of his hand. "He doesn't wish to talk with you."

"Tell Monsieur Bray to remember how he was treated by men." Anne Marie had to stop herself from bridling. "How men deported him, men put him in prison, men sent him to work in a foreign country. Remind him how men punished him and then forgot all about him. And when it was time for him to return to Guadeloupe, those same men couldn't be bothered to send him home. Kindly tell him that, Monsieur Trousseau."

Trousseau shrugged. "I think he knows."

"Kindly do as I say."

"He can speak French."

"Then why doesn't he speak French with me?"

"Perhaps he doesn't want to."

"I'm not going to send him to rot on Devil's Island. Or on the Moroni."

It was Lafitte who then cleared his throat to speak. "He's not used to dealing with women."

"More's the pity." She took a deep breath and turned. She gave Hégésippe Bray a reassuring smile. "I'm not going to send you away to die in prison. You've already suffered enough, Monsieur Bray." She stood up and moved round the desk. Today Anne Marie was wearing her Courrèges skirt. The blue eyes followed her.

With a movement of her hand, she gestured to Trousseau to stop his typing. She approached Hégésippe Bray—he smelt of carbolic soap—and bending down, she placed a hand on the worn cotton of his shirt. "I'm your friend." She could feel the bones of his shoulder. "I want to help you."

The old face remained impassive.

"There are things I need to know, and I can't help you if you won't help me." She spoke slowly. "You must tell me what happened, Monsieur Bray."

The silence was broken only by the brush of the curtains against the wood of the window and the distant sound of traffic.

"Please help me."

Lafitte coughed.

"For your own sake, you must help me."

Hégésippe Bray shook his head, and at the same time, he shrugged her hand away from where it lay on his shoulder. "*Une greluche*," he said defiantly.

The slang word for a woman. He used the intonation of Paris. Of Pigalle and Belleville, beyond the boulevards. Paris—the cheap pimps, the dry smell of the *métro*, the weasel-faced gangsters, the painted whores, the *gonzesses*. Paris—a soulless world of asphalt and despair.

"The penal colony doesn't exist anymore—you know that." Anne Marie returned to her seat. "Nobody wants to send you there. You will not leave this island—even supposing you're found guilty."

The old man lowered his head.

"If you want to live in peace with your goats and your garden, then you must help me—help me by telling me the truth. Monsieur Bray, the gendarmerie at Sainte-Anne believes you're involved in the death of Raymond Calais. In his murder."

"I didn't kill no one."

He spoke in his throat, guttural and tough. He must have picked up the accent from the riffraff of the penal colony—the murderers and gangsters who were sent out to Cayenne at the time of the *Front Populaire*. And before.

"You wanted revenge."

A ship—a cruiser, perhaps bringing American tourists—sounded its horn in the harbor.

"You wanted revenge because Raymond Calais took your land—land his father had sold you forty years ago."

"Old man Calais was just."

"You wanted to get your revenge on his son."

"Monsieur Calais was good to me. I was his foreman for more than twenty years."

"His son is dead." She folded her arms. "You're accused of killing him. Of shooting him point-blank through the chest."

Hégésippe Bray shook his head.

"You told everybody you wanted revenge." She leaned forward. "Did you kill Raymond Calais?"

He did not speak.

"Did you shoot him?"

He waited before shaking his head slowly.

"Then who did, Monsieur Bray?"

The blue eyes stared at her.

"Who killed Raymond Calais?"

He spoke slowly. "I didn't kill the son of my employer."

"Who killed him? Who shot Raymond Calais in the chest with a gun?"

"You are a clever woman. You have studied. You speak French. You can read. You've been to school." A wrinkled finger pointed toward the pile of well-thumbed Dalloz texts. "You've studied many things. And you have soft hands."

"Answer my questions."

"Very clever."

"Did you willfully murder Raymond Calais on the Sainte Marthe estate on September 7, 1980?"

"Clever." The leather of his face broke into a watery smile. "But you don't understand nothing."

"It was your gun."

"I know whites," Hégésippe Bray said. "People like you. With your skin. I have known many whites—criminals, hard men who did bad things. Men who murdered their mothers. With some, I even became a friend—if you can be the friend of a white man." He spoke very slowly. "Hard men. They understood what they could touch. Things they could touch and see. Things they could kill." He stopped. "What they could not see they never understood."

Tired by the exertion of speaking, the old man fell silent.

"Did you murder Calais?"

With a crooked thumb, he tapped his chest. "What a black man sees a white man can never understand. We are not the same. We are different—like cats and dogs. We were never meant to live together." He pointed at her chest, "You're white and you have your books and your soft white skin. But a black man"—he made a gesture toward Trousseau, whose hands were now motionless on the Japy typewriter—"A black man sees things no white man will never see." A grimace that extended the old, cracked lips. "White man, white woman."

"What do black men see?"

"He had to die."

"You murdered him?"

"I did not kill Raymond Calais."

"Sunday morning and there was nobody in the fields. You saw him and you pulled the trigger. After thirty-eight years. You killed Raymond Calais, you shot him in the chest. It was your revenge."

"You don't understand nothing, white woman."

"I understand only too well."

"He had to suffer."

"So you shot him dead."

"To suffer as he had made me suffer."

The blue eyes were now cold and small, and they stared at something beyond Anne Marie.

"Like a cockroach that flaps and kicks. You hold it in the candle flame and it knows it has to die. It kicks and its flaps its dirty wings." He looked at her sharply. "You don't understand."

"Understand?"

"Raymond Calais was going to die. He'd lived enough and now it was his turn to suffer. Not shot with a bullet through his heart." Hégésippe Bray showed her a toothless smile. "Die like a cockroach. In torment, endless torment."

6

Pâtisserie

A bicycle had been padlocked to the parking meter.

"What would you like to drink, madame?"

There was no door or front window. The cake shop gave directly onto the sidewalk. Anne Marie turned her glance away from the street to face the girl.

At this time of the morning, the Pâtisserie Prudence—the letters in red and white paint above the entrance—was hot despite the large revolving fan that stood on the refrigerator. Paper napkins fluttered on the bamboo tables when they were caught in the artificial breeze.

"Any fresh juice, mademoiselle?" Anne Marie enquired.

The girl shook her head. A crescent of starched cotton was pinned into her hair. The hair had been straightened but a couple of unruly strands rose from behind the white cotton. She wore pink lipstick. She held an order pad in one hand, a pencil in the other. She did not look at Anne Marie or Trousseau but stared out into the street as if fascinated by the padlocked bicycle.

Then she shrugged. "Only cane juice."

Anne Marie said, "Two glasses, please, with ice and a slice of lime. And a couple of cakes."

The girl nodded and moved away, scarcely lifting her feet. The rubber sandals flapped against the floor. Her dark legs were badly blemished. Anne Marie turned to Trousseau. "There is never any fresh juice."

"It's all imported. Madame le juge, if you want fresh juice—real fresh fruit juice—you must come out and visit me in the country. Guava, passion fruit, bananas, pineapple, star apple, custard fruit." He gave a short laugh of pride. "I grow them all."

A few minutes later the girl placed the drinks on the table.

"Visit me. Bring your husband and come to Trois-Rivières."

The girl left a piece of paper, torn from her pad, beneath the plate and returned to her stool behind the counter, where she continued to stare at the mid-morning sunshine and the bicycle.

"I thought you lived in Pointe-à-Pitre, Monsieur Trousseau."

"On the weekends, I go down to Trois-Rivières. I like to work in the garden." His face suddenly darkened, and he spoke with unwarranted vehemence, as if in answer to a personal attack. "I'm an Indian, madame le juge. I am not like the blacks. I'm not ashamed to work with my hands, to get them dirty turning the soil. For me, slavery is nothing to be ashamed of. The blacks don't want to get their hands dirty. They don't want to work in the fields because they think it's beneath their dignity. That's why they all come flocking to Pointe-à-Pitre." He added, "Just because I have a black man's name and because my skin is dark, madame le juge, don't think I'm afraid of hard work."

She gave him a broad, friendly smile. "Would you care for some *doukoun* cake?"

"You whites think we're all the same. The only thing that counts for you is the color of our skin." He stroked his moustache. His eyes seemed unnaturally large. "I've worked in France, madame le juge, and I own a flat in the Seventeenth Arrondissement. Not in the suburbs of Paris where all the Arabs and the foreigners hang out. In the Seventeenth Arrondissement. One of my daughters goes to boarding school in Saint-Germain-en-Laye. You think I have to stay in Guadeloupe?"

Anne Marie said nothing.

Trousseau picked up his glass and drank. "If France is forced into giving independence to Guadeloupe, believe me, I'm going to be on the first plane out. If ever the MANG. . . ."

The girl at the counter turned her head.

"If ever the independence people, the *Mouvement d'Action des Nationalistes Guadeloupéens*, get their way, please don't worry about me. I don't give a damn." He laughed through his nose; his voice was angry. "Like Haiti, with Papa Doc and *Tontons Macoutes* running around with machine guns—that's what this island'll be like." He pointed at Anne Marie. "You think my family will want to stay on here when the French move out?"

Anne Marie wiped her fingers on the paper serviette.

"You know my wife is a highly respected tax inspector? And you know she is white?" The accusatory eyes looked at Anne Marie, waiting for an answer. "Highly respected."

Anne Marie rubbed at the back of her hand, then said, "That ointment of yours just makes the pain worse."

A derisive laugh. "A curse, madame."

"You really believe in all that witchcraft? Just like Hégésippe Bray?"

"Why not?"

"I must see a doctor tomorrow."

"Tomorrow we're going to the Saintes. If you want to see a doctor, you must get an appointment." The dark eyes twinkled. "This isn't Africa, you know. A civilized country and you'll need an appointment."

"Perhaps I can go on Friday."

"I can fix you a meeting with a gadézaffé in Trois-Rivières."

A man entered the pâtisserie—against the morning light, he formed a tall silhouette with broad shoulders and a narrow waist. He approached their table. He held out his hand to Trousseau. "Le juge Laveaud?"

"I am the greffier."

27

The man was embarrassed. He turned to Anne Marie. "You must be. . . ."

Anne Marie nodded. "The investigating judge."

"I was expecting a man."

A tight smile. "I trust you're not too disappointed."

7

Suez-Panama

"My name's Marcel Suez-Panama." He held out his hand, "I wonder if I could speak with you for a moment."

"It's nearly eleven." Anne Marie looked at her watch— a cheap Kelton with droplets of humidity clinging to the inside of the glass. "I must collect my son from school."

"Just a few seconds of your time, madame le juge."

Not trying to hide her lack of enthusiasm, Anne Marie invited him to take a chair.

Marcel Suez-Panama was wearing beige trousers with a sharp crease. He pulled at the light fabric before sitting down, then crossed his legs, an ankle on his knee. Expensive shoes of thin leather, Bordeaux red, and ankle socks of fine cotton. Dark eyes and long lashes. His skin was café crème. Good looking, Anne Marie decided approvingly. Where he shaved, the skin formed a darker, uneven surface.

Trousseau said, "I think we've met."

"Possibly."

"You are from Morne-à-l'Eau?"

Suez-Panama nodded.

"You teach at the *collège?*"

"My cousin Fulbert. I work at the university."

"You studied at Toulouse? A degree in mathematics?"

29

"Biology."

Trousseau said, "I know your cousin well."

"Guadeloupe's a small island." Suez-Panama turned back to Anne Marie. "It's about my uncle—my mother's half-brother. I was hoping I could speak with you for a few minutes. About Hégésippe Bray."

Anne Marie frowned. "What about him?"

"You know who I am?"

"You have just told me."

"It was Mother who brought Hégésippe Bray back to Guadeloupe."

Anne Marie nodded.

Trousseau straightened his tie before standing up. "Work to do." He shook hands with Suez-Panama. "Nice to have met you. My regards to Fulbert when you see him." He went over to the girl. In silence she took his money, and Trousseau stepped out into the street.

Suez-Panama looked at Anne Marie. "He's innocent."

"Trousseau?"

"You must let Hégésippe go."

"He murdered his common law wife forty years ago. I don't see why he couldn't have murdered Raymond Calais."

"Hégésippe never harmed anyone."

In the street, a postman on a yellow mobylette went past and the screech of the exhaust was echoed off the church wall. The sound reverberated through the bar, drowning the gentle hum of the fan.

Anne Marie asked softly, "Can I offer you a drink, Monsieur Suez-Panama?"

"Please."

"Please what?"

"Let Hégésippe Bray go."

She raised her shoulders. "I must do my job."

"My uncle's an old man."

"Old or not, he is the prime suspect for the murder of Raymond Calais."

"Let him live out what remains of his life in peace."

"Perhaps you're not aware of what I can do and what I can't do." She tapped the top of the table with a chipped fingernail. "I'm simply the juge d'instruction. It's not me who wishes to accuse your uncle of murder—that was the decision of the *procureur de la République*, acting upon evidence given to him by the gendarmerie of Sainte-Anne. It's not for me to impute innocence or guilt to anyone." She rubbed at the back of her hand, which now smelled of eucalyptus.

"My uncle's suffered enough in his life."

"To impute guilt or innocence is the role of a jury. By comparison, my job's simple. Hégésippe Bray's not been arrested—at least, not yet. No formal charges have been brought against him. I've been called upon by the *parquet*—which is to say the Ministry of Justice in the person of the procureur—to look into the facts relating to the untimely death of Raymond Calais. Your uncle's helping us because there would appear to be evidence pointing to his involvement."

"Evidence, madame le juge?"

"Repeated threats against the person of Raymond Calais. A murder weapon which was wiped clean of all traces of finger prints—and then hidden. Paraffin tests carried out on your uncle—tests which proved the use of firearms."

"Paraffin tests more than a day after Calais' death."

"I have the job of looking at the evidence collected by the gendarmerie. I must decide whether this evidence will stand the scrutiny of a court of law. I must be the guarantee that Hégésippe Bray is treated impartially—and not merely by police officers who may be more interested in prosecuting your uncle, regardless of the facts. Do I make myself clear?"

Suez-Panama nodded uncomfortably.

"If I have reason to believe the accusations against him are founded, I will draw up a dossier that will be handed over to the parquet. And Hégésippe Bray in time will pass before the *Cour d'Assises*. Should the evidence on the other hand appear to be of a dubious nature, I will inform the procureur that there can be no justification—or wisdom—in Bray's being sent for trial. He will be set free, and I shall continue my enquiries into the death of Raymond Calais."

"He is innocent."

"Perhaps you'd care to share those details upon which you base your conviction." Anne Marie glanced at the Kelton watch. "Share them with a good lawyer."

"My uncle's poor. How can he afford a lawyer?"

"If necessary, the Tribunal will appoint a lawyer to defend him."

Suez-Panama took a bunch of keys from his pocket and banged them jarringly against the palm of his hand.

"Have a drink, Monsieur Suez-Panama."

Suddenly he relaxed. "I am sorry, I'm being rude." He smiled and turning in his chair, he called the serving girl. "A Vichy, mademoiselle. And another cane juice for the lady."

8

Convent

Suez-Panama looked around the pâtisserie, at the low-slung bamboo chairs, the wall lighting and the large mirror advertising Fanta. "We used to come here after school, some friends and I." A shy smile. "The girls from the convent school at the back of the church used to frequent the place. Out of bounds for them—and sometimes a sour old nun would come looking for her wayward flock. Not too happy to see her little lambs taking cigarettes from kids like us." He took a packet of Craven from his shirt pocket.

"Perhaps the nun was jealous."

The maid came over to the table, dragging her plastic sandals, and placed the bottle of Vichy on the glass top. Anne Marie made use of the opportunity to study Suez-Panama's face.

He caught her glance as he poured his drink. He smiled, a trace of moisture on his lips.

"Any success with the little lambs?"

"They weren't really interested in us, madame le juge. Not old enough for them . . . and we were too black for their tastes. They didn't want us—but they were glad enough to share our cigarettes." He frowned, "Thirteen, fourteen years old—but even at that age, women already know what they want."

"You're married, Monsieur Suez-Panama?"

"What is wrong with your hand?"

"My greffier tells me this itching is the result of a curse."

He laughed. "We like to tell the world that this little island in the middle of the ocean is a corner of France. We're told we're Frenchmen, and we genuinely get to believe it, but when it comes to superstition and strange religious beliefs, we're still a lot closer to Africa than to Europe."

A car went past in the street.

Anne Marie rubbed between her fingers where the skin was swollen. "Probably something I've eaten."

"Rubbing only makes it worse." Suez-Panama reached out and separated her two hands. "Stop it," he said softly. His hand was cool. "You must see a doctor, madame le juge."

Her hand lay in his.

Anne Marie noticed that he had long fingers.

Suez-Panama looked up at her from under his eyelashes. "You will help him, won't you?"

With a sharp movement, Anne Marie extricated her hand. She frowned as she wrapped her handkerchief about her fist. "My son will be waiting for me."

Anne Marie started to rise but he placed a hand on her forearm.

"An old man who spent most of his life in a penal colony." There were wrinkles at the corner of his mouth, "You did that to him."

"Me?"

"France. You crippled him emotionally and physically. And then you threw him away. *France*," he said again, and laughed coldly. "Hégésippe Bray didn't matter." He paused. "A weaker man wouldn't have survived. But my uncle did survive and now he's back. Old and quite harmless. He can hurt nobody."

"Your uncle's gun hurt Calais—hurt him a lot."

Suez-Panama threw his cigarette to the ground and squashed it beneath his heel. "Hégésippe Bray didn't kill Raymond Calais."

"On his own admission he hated Calais."

"Everybody hated Calais." He had started playing with the keys again.

"Only one person shot Raymond Calais point-blank. And then left him to float in a rain pond."

A shaft of light caught the iris of Suez-Panama's eye. "A lot of people knew my uncle held a grudge against Calais. A justified grudge. Perhaps the real murderer wanted to make use of that. Using my uncle as a scapegoat."

"Possibly."

"He's come back from the land of the dead." Suez-Panama looked at her. "Back to where he belongs, where he's wanted and loved." A hesitation. "Don't send him away from us now."

"Why does he not live with you?"

"Only normal Hégésippe should want to live at Sainte Marthe—away from the noise of the cars. There he's happy—with his goats and his garden. It is quiet. That's where he grew up. Don't you understand that in prison, locked away in jail, without the sky and the sugar fields and his animals, Hégésippe Bray'd go mad?" Again the handsome face looked at her, "You will kill him."

Anne Marie asked, "How old are you?"

"You are very indiscreet."

"Did you ever meet your uncle before?"

"I'm not that old." A dry laugh and again he jangled the keys. "*Maman*'d already left for France when Hégésippe was sent to French Guyana. Papa'd been called up into the navy and Mother followed him. That's why I was born at Le Havre in 1940. We didn't get back to Guadeloupe until 1946, until after the war. Though I never met him, in a way, Hégésippe Bray was a father to me. Maman idolized Hégésippe. Like a husband."

"Hégésippe Bray murdered his own wife."

"Hégésippe Bray's a good man." The shoulders sagged beneath the fabric of the shirt. "Even if he's always had a bad temper."

9

Rue de la République

"Nice morning in school?"

Fabrice climbed into the car, threw his bag onto the back seat, kissed his mother and collapsed into the passenger seat. "I'm hungry."

Anne Marie moved the Honda back into the traffic. "What did you do this morning?"

"Nothing much." Then he grabbed her arm. "Maman, how long would it take to get to the moon?"

"To the moon?"

"If I walked all the way?"

She looked in the driving mirror. "Depends how fast you can walk."

"Very fast."

It was difficult to keep up with Fabrice. He talked rapidly and Anne Marie was concentrating on the traffic. She drove back into town, around Place de la Victoire, and parked on the rue Alsace-Lorraine. Fabrice yanked up the satchel with its battered stickers of *Obélix* and *Sainval Vecteur*. He jumped out before her.

"Look before you cross the road!"

Anne Marie locked the car, followed her son across the road. She pushed open the iron door of number 31, and the bolt scraped against the stone tiles. Grateful to be out of the sunshine,

Anne Marie went up the stairs. There were a couple of poisoned cockroaches on their backs, kicking their legs as they slowly died.

Fabrice had already started eating. He grinned at his mother over a full spoon. His satchel lay on the plastic table cloth.

"Have you washed your hands, Fabrice?"

"Yes, Maman."

She gave him a stern look. "Go and wash your hands, Fabrice. This minute."

He shrugged, slid from the chair and went to the corner sink. His trousers had been clean that morning; now the corduroy was thick with dry mud. He washed his hands, but his eyes remained on her, and he smiled. She handed him the towel, and theatrically he threw his arms about Anne Marie's neck and gave her a kiss that smelled of boiled bananas. "I love you, Maman." He left a patch of dampness on the back of her neck and returned to his lunch. "But I did wash my hands, I swear."

Mamie was in the kitchen. She was standing over the cooker. She brushed a wisp of grey hair from her eyes and leaned backward so that her daughter-in-law could kiss her.

"Hello, Mamie."

"Good evening, *chérie.*"

Instinctively Anne Marie looked at her watch; it was a little after midday.

"Hungry?"

"Been eating all morning, Mamie."

The radio was playing local music, loud and repetitive. *Douk-oun-aw dou.*

"You must eat some meat—it's good for you."

"I'm really not very hungry."

The older woman was pushing at slices of steak that cooked in a flat, aluminum pan. For a brief moment, the two women looked at each other in silence.

"Anne Marie, you must eat."

"I'm taking Fabrice to the beach this afternoon."

Mamie prodded the meat and the sliced garlic. "Fabrice can stay with me—he's no trouble."

"I've taken the afternoon off specially. Jean Michel said he would come."

"Jean Michel was here about half an hour ago. He said he'd try to join you, but he could not make any promises."

The battered transistor radio, the dial dusty and held together with a piece of black adhesive tape, stood on the window sill. It emitted noisy cadence and lyrics of sexual innuendo. "*Machiné ka machiné.*" Outside, the sun danced on the open patio and the spotless white sheets drying on the line.

"He knows I want him to come."

"He might have found a job."

"We hardly see each other anymore." Anne Marie could feel tears prickling at the corner of her eyes. "I so much wanted him to keep this afternoon free. For Fabrice's sake. I told Jean Michel that this morning. The job can wait—at least for another day."

"Poor boy, he's been looking for a job ever since you both got back from France."

"Fabrice needs to spend time with his parents."

"Then you should keep more regular hours, Anne Marie."

"I can't dictate the hours. I can't tell people when it suits me for them to get murdered." Anne Marie had raised her voice. "That's why this afternoon's so important. For once I am free."

"For once Jean Michel's busy."

"It could have waited another day, this wretched job of his."

"My son didn't think so."

"But his wife did."

"Jean Michel is a man," Mamie said as she turned off the gas. She also turned off the bronze knob of the gas bottle. "It's not right that a wife should give orders just because a man's out of work." She shrugged and placed the meat onto a large, chipped plate. Quietly, she added, "A man must have his self-respect."

Anne Marie did not reply, but blinked away a hot tear.

IO

Morne-à-l'Eau

They entered Morne-à-l'Eau. The flamboyants were not in blossom; pods hung idly against the empty branches.

Anne Marie parked near the main square.

"Wait in the car."

"I don't like it when you leave me alone." Fabrice pouted in self pity. "You always take ages."

"I'll only be a minute."

"You always say that."

"If Papa had come to the beach with us, you would be in bed by now."

Fabrice retorted, "Papa always takes me with him."

"Papa doesn't have to ask people a lot of questions. He's not a magistrate."

"When we went to see Auntie, I was as quiet as a mouse."

"Auntie?" Anne Marie asked, but chose not to wait for a reply. "If you come with me you must be quiet as a mouse."

Fabrice nodded sagely. "I promise."

Stone benches, a fountain and elegant lampposts that could have graced any provincial French town. Evening was falling. The lights had been turned on, their tinted blue gaining in intensity against the encroaching darkness. As Anne Marie climbed out of the car, she caught the wafting odor of ylang-ylang.

39

Fabrice clambered out beside her. There was still sand in his hair. He grinned happily.

She tried not to smile and for a moment stood quite still, breathing in the luxurious scent. She was happy to be where she was. Then the scent was lost to the smell of car fumes and the evening cooking from a nearby restaurant.

Music came from a record store—a hut whose walls had been painted red, green and yellow. A boy with an army beret and Rastafarian locks was swaying to the rhythm. The whites of his eyes caught the light of the street lamps. A toothless girl stood beside him. She was pregnant. Orange peel, little islands of intense whiteness, lay on the sidewalk.

"Madame Suez-Panama, please."

The policeman wore a kepi. He looked at Anne Marie with watery eyes and hesitated before speaking. His breath was tinged with rum. The directions he gave her were long, unclear and unhelpful.

Anne Marie thanked him and went down the side street that led toward the market. The smell of rotting fruit was strong here and the air was humid. Her body was damp with perspiration.

"I'm looking for Madame Suez-Panama's house."

A man in besmirched overalls and a peaked cap—the peak the wrong way and pointing down his neck—stared at Anne Marie and Fabrice from the far side of the road. A monkey wrench peeked from the pocket on the side of his leg.

"I'm looking for Madame Suez-Panama," Anne Marie repeated, squeezing her son's hand in hers.

The man pointed. He gave a large grin and automatically she smiled.

The man winked at Fabrice.

The house was on the far side of the market. It was colonial in style, part brick and part wood. A rusting enamel advertisement for Alsace potash—a stork standing on one leg—was smeared with the black and grey stains of frequent rain.

Anne Marie entered the doorway and found herself in a cool hall.

"Anybody home?"

Wooden steps and a wrought iron banister led upward through the planks of the ceiling. The steps were steep and creaked unhappily as Anne Marie started to climb. Fabrice followed her, his hand clutching hers.

Anne Marie climbed the last stair, slightly out of breath, with Fabrice close against her leg.

A large room.

A feeble breath of air rustled at the hanging potted plant. A smell of moth balls and kerosene. Circles of light came through the half-closed blinds, cast by the street lamps.

"What do you want?"

Startled, Anne Marie spun round.

II

Witch

The white head was lower than the backrest of the wicker arm-chair.

"Who are you?"

The woman was dressed in a cotton nightdress. There was a scarf about her neck and a blanket over her knees and chest. Slippers on her feet.

"I'm sorry."

"What do you want?"

"I am looking for Madame Suez-Panama."

The voice was peevish. "I am Madame Suez-Panama."

Anne Marie moved forward. "I am Madame Laveaud." She held out her hand but the old woman kept her arms beneath the blanket.

"I spoke to Marcel this morning and he suggested I speak to you. He says you rarely leave the house and I happened to be passing through Morne-à-l'Eau." Anne Marie spoke apologetically. "I have just come from the beach with my son. . . ." She added foolishly, "It is Wednesday today."

The woman said nothing.

"I thought I could drop by for a few words with you."

The leaves of the potted plant rustled. A cat walked over the planks of the wooden floor. Fabrice was silent, his body pressed against Anne Marie's leg.

"About Hégésippe Bray. I am the juge d'instruction. I have the responsibility of preparing the enquiry."

"What enquiry?"

"The murder of Raymond Calais." Anne Marie coughed. "I should really have asked you to come to Pointe-à-Pitre. I've already seen Monsieur Suez-Panama. And since I was passing through Morne-à-l'Eau. . . ." Again she coughed. "There are a few questions that I should like to ask about your brother—about your half-brother."

"Hégésippe will die if he's kept in prison."

"I have come to see you personally here because there are certain things that I need to know, Madame Suez-Panama."

"Raymond Calais was an evil man."

"Did your half-brother kill him?"

"Of course not."

"Then who did?"

"I am not a policeman."

"It would appear Hégésippe Bray had a motive."

"A lot of people had a motive." A harsh, rasping voice. "Raymond Calais deserved to die."

"If Hégésippe Bray didn't shoot Monsieur Calais, why weren't there any finger prints?"

"Why have you arrested him?"

"Monsieur Bray has not been arrested. He's merely helping us by answering a few questions."

"If he hasn't been arrested, why isn't he free? Why can't he go back to Sainte Marthe?"

"I hope to be able to send him there very shortly."

"Headstrong."

There was a long silence and then the woman sighed. "Even when he was young, Hégésippe was headstrong. Like all men. Proud and so sure he could look after himself. Never wanted help from others. Never sought our advice. A fool like all the rest of them." The old woman sat back and the rocking chair creaked. "An innocent fool—and a good one. Good to his mother and good to me. We were the only women Hégésippe ever really loved—and Mother and I were certainly the only ones who ever really loved him . . . loved him as he deserved to be loved." She sighed again, the cold voice now less unsympathetic. "Hégésippe sent money from the trenches so that I could go to school. The *certificat d'études* and then my job as a teacher—I'd never have had all that without Hégésippe." The chair creaked. "Always so kind—but that never stopped him from being a fool." She clicked her tongue. "The woman from Martinique—he should never have had anything to do with her. At his age. Scheming and evil. All she ever wanted was his money."

"What money?"

"She wanted the money from the land. The land he'd bought from Calais."

"The same land that Raymond Calais took?"

Madame Suez-Panama retorted, "Just because Raymond Calais took it doesn't mean Hégésippe murdered him."

"Your half-brother was sent to French Guyana. Why did you never stop Raymond Calais from taking your half-brother's land?"

A short, bitter laugh. "By the time I returned here in 1946, it was already too late. Raymond Calais had taken everything. There was nothing that I could do. What proof did I have? Me against a powerful *Béké?*"

Fabrice had buried his face into Anne Marie's side. She ran her hand through the hair thick with sea salt.

"I went to see him, you know."

"Who?"

"It must have been last year. Calais never liked me—but I managed to get him to agree to giving back some of the land. Not everything—Raymond Calais was very careful. But that's how Hégésippe got the hut at Sainte Marthe."

Car beams danced on the low wooden ceiling. Anne Marie noticed a single flex and a light bulb hung from the crossbeam. Hanging in parallel were two sticky rolls of flypaper.

"Who was the woman from Martinique?"

Madame Suez-Panama did not reply. The thin lips were tightly drawn.

"What was her name?"

"I don't know."

Fabrice whispered, "I want to go, Maman."

Anne Marie asked, "Your half-brother married her?"

Another laugh. "Hégésippe nearly married a white girl. She'd been his *marraine* during the Great War, and she wrote him letters when he was fighting on the front. He would have married her, but she died of influenza in '19. You think my half-brother'd have married a serving girl like her?"

"But he lived with this girl from Martinique."

"I've never understood men."

"Were there any children?"

"She gave him a boy. I was at Pointe-Noire, and I was busy. Running a school single-handed with my husband. I don't think I saw the child more than twice before she killed him."

"Who?"

"The girl from Martinique. She murdered the little boy."

"Let's go, Maman," Fabrice whispered hoarsely, his chin against Anne Marie's thigh. She caressed his hair, knowing she should never have allowed her son to come with her.

"Why on earth did she kill the child?"

"She wanted to wear nice clothes—but Hégésippe never had much money. He gave it away, the poor fool—he gave it to me, to help me. And then he bought the land from Calais' father. But he never spent anything on himself. He wasn't the kind to indulge in unnecessary luxuries—and she couldn't stand that. Nice things, that's what she wanted—gold that glitters and pretty shoes for her *métis* feet. She just couldn't understand why Hégésippe continued to work for Calais. She jeered at him, told him he was a peasant. Nagged him to spend more money. She had a nice house, and she'd probably known nothing better than a shack. You know what they're like, the people from Martinique—they think they are better than us."

"Why?"

"They look down on us because they think we're all peasants. With their arrogance and their French manners. Fort-de-France—they call it the Paris of the Caribbean, and they laugh at Guadeloupe."

Another car went past, the lights dancing across the ceiling.

"No better than us, believe me. For all their put-on airs."

"Why did she murder the child?"

"The war came, that's what happened. It was hard for us all. Fewer ships getting through and there was less food. Land became important and there was money to be made. On food—on the black market. That woman wanted Hégésippe to transform the land he'd bought. She wanted him to grow corn and other things—even rice." A laugh. "All she really wanted was money—money for her cheap finery."

"Why would she want to kill her own son?"

Madame Suez-Panama said, "She was a witch."

Fabrice's hand was cold.

"What happened to the child?"

The old woman chose not to answer. "He'd be over forty now," she said. "If he were alive. And Hégésippe would now have a son to look after him." In the penumbra, Anne Marie could see the corners of the thin lips turn down. "You see my brother now, old and burned-out. But in those days, he could have had any woman he wanted, but like a fool, he fell in love with a witch." Beneath the blanket the woman's chest rose in a long sigh. "And now there's no one to look after the old fool."

"He has you, madame."

"What can I do to help Hégésippe? I am old. He was too proud to come back when I was still young, too proud to return from that terrible place."

"How did the child die?"

A television came alight across the road.

"He was drowned in a pond."

"A coincidence?"

46

"What coincidence?"

"Like Calais."

Madame Suez-Panama was silent.

"How old was the child?"

"Two years old. The mother never cried. I remember because there was a phone call for me at the school, and in those days there weren't many cars. We were all poor then, except for the Békés. I couldn't wait for the bus. So I had to borrow a bicycle. And I cycled all the way from Pointe-Noire. The roads weren't surfaced in those days. It took me almost a day to cycle to Sainte Marthe." She allowed herself an amused grunt at the recollection. "Nothing that I could do. The little boy was already dead."

"Why kill her own child?"

The old headmistress was lost in her memories. "I sat there through the night at the wake, and Hégésippe wept like a woman, burying his large head in his hands. Hégésippe who'd spent two years at Verdun—he wept like a silly woman. I can remember his hair was already turning white. If only I could have taken some of the pain. But that little métis woman. . . ."

Madame Suez-Panama fell silent.

"Please go on."

"Not one tear."

"She didn't love her own little boy?" Anne Marie asked, her hand on her son's head.

A snort of ancient resentment. "I don't think I ever saw her pray even though we lit candles and set them round that poor, cold little corpse. She was pleased with herself. That woman was pleased with herself. Woman? She wasn't a woman. She was a devil."

The smell of rotting fruit in the market drifted through the blinds.

"It was that witch who put a curse on Hégésippe Bray."

"You really believe in those things, Madame Suez-Panama?"

"A spell on him and Hégésippe Bray became like a dog, with a chain around his neck."

"You're an educated woman."

"She bewitched him. She ruined him."

"How could she do that?"

"By getting him sent to that terrible place."

"Hégésippe murdered her—transportation to Cayenne was his punishment."

The woman nodded slowly. "I was in France—but if I'd been at the trial, Raymond Calais wouldn't have got away with it. Old man Calais' son—of course he wanted Hégésippe Bray out of the way so that he could get his hands on Hégésippe's land. All Raymond Calais ever cared about was the land."

"So your half-brother had good reason to hate Raymond Calais?"

"Anybody with any sense hated Calais."

"Who killed Raymond Calais?"

The gentle hum of the evening traffic along the *route nationale* and the confused sound of the neighbor's television. Fabrice tugged again at his mother's arm.

"Madame, who killed Raymond Calais?"

A harsh noise. Anne Marie felt the cold finger of fear running down her back. And that debilitating sense of fear remained with her even once she realized that it was merely the sound of the old woman sobbing.

Anne Marie hurriedly took her leave. She left, going down the creaking stairs with Fabrice pulling on her arm, urging her on, his face small and pale.

"Send Hégésippe Bray back," the voice called hoarsely from above. "Do you hear? Send him back before it is too late."

12

Alfa Romeo

Jean Michel's Alfa Romeo was there.

"Papa's back," Fabrice cried excitedly.

The garage, with its series of unlit concrete compartments and the puddles in the ground smelled of urine and stagnant water. Somewhere a pipe was leaking. The sharp, unpleasant smell was compounded by that of the refuse bins overturned and scattered by foraging dogs.

Anne Marie took the beach equipment from the Honda and walked toward the stairs. Fabrice pressed against her side.

Light from a naked bulb overhead was reflected on the cream paint and the chrome of the Alfa Romeo.

"Female intuition," Anne Marie said and with the palm of her hand, she touched the car's bonnet. It was still warm. She smiled grimly to herself.

"What does intuition mean, Maman?" He did not expect an answer. Once out of the garage, Fabrice released her hand. He was tired, and wearily he trudged up the stairs of the Cité Mortenol. There were lifts, but they frequently broke down, caught between two floors. Only the foolhardy or the handicapped would trust them. Anne Marie was terrified of being stranded in a lift during an earthquake.

Cité Mortenol.

Two apartment blocks facing each other. Two cubes built on the concrete pillars of the garage, five stories high and united by a couple of stairwells. There were small shops at terrace level. The last shops were now closing—it was nearly eight o'clock—and the iron blinds were being pulled down, their metallic rattle echoing against the canyon-like walls of the apartment blocks. Teenagers were playing basketball with an impromptu hoop attached to the first floor balcony.

Anne Marie knew that she had been lucky to get the flat. It was thanks to Freddy—one of Jean Michel's brothers who worked in the housing department at the town hall. Without Freddy's help, they would have been forced to stay at 31 rue Alsace-Lorraine with Mamie.

Anne Marie was out of breath by the time she reached the top floor. Fabrice was a flight of stairs behind. As she waited, she looked up at the sky where clouds hid the moon. A white haze lay over Pointe-à-Pitre—the glow of the street lamps.

Fabrice caught up as she was taking the keys from her handbag. He panted like a puppy. Anne Marie opened the door and Fabrice pushed past her.

"We're back, Papa!"

Fabrice ran forward and kissed Jean Michel.

Anne Marie's husband was wearing shorts and a tanktop. He lolled on the sofa with his eyes on the television. A newspaper lay at his feet.

"How was your day?" Anne Marie set the beach equipment on the floor and then went over to Jean Michel, bent over and kissed him lightly on the forehead. His cheeks were smooth and he smelt of bay rum.

"I drive all the way to Basse-Terre where I wait two hours for the editor. And the bastard never turns up." Jean Michel clicked his tongue. "He'd left a message with his secretary and the silly cow forgets to tell me."

"Why didn't he turn up?"

"He was called to the Dutch part of St. Martin—had hired

a private plane to fly up there." Again her husband clicked his tongue. "My whole day wasted."

"I was hoping you'd come to the beach."

He appeared surprised. "I told Mamie to tell you not to expect me, Anne Marie."

"It would've been nice to spend the afternoon all together."

"I need a job." His brown eyes glinted as he turned back to look at the television. Then he smiled. "If it materializes, this could be the job I've been looking for. The man's bringing out a magazine."

"And what are your chances?"

"Pro-Giscard, pro-government, pro-status quo. With all the latest news on Guadeloupe, Martinique and French Guyana. Plus Réunion. He's hoping to reach the West Indian market in Paris. With me doing the cultural page. They need people with journalistic experience." He laughed. "*Le Domien.*"

Fabrice asked, "What does Domien mean, Papa?"

"Inhabitants of the DOM's—the *départements d'outre-mer.*"

"Go and get ready for bed, Fabrice." Turning back to her husband, Anne Marie asked, "When will you know?"

He shrugged.

"Fabrice," Anne Marie said, her voice suddenly stern, "I told you to get ready for bed."

"But. . . ." The fear of the evening and of the old woman had disappeared. "I haven't eaten yet." Fabrice had clambered onto the sofa and was now snuggling down against his father in front of the television.

"Get ready for bed. This minute. And just for once, do as you're told."

Jean Michel said, "He can sit with me for a few minutes."

"First he must get undressed and take a shower."

The young eyes looked at the television. Fabrice frowned in simulated concentration.

"Hurry up, Fabrice."

"I'm clean, Maman. I was in the sea."

"Hurry up. You don't want me to lose my temper, do you? So far you've been a good boy this evening."

"I'm not dirty."

"Take the shampoo and get that awful sand from out of your hair."

Fabrice removed his thumb from his mouth and gave an exaggerated sigh. He slid from the sofa.

"And you can put that T-shirt in the wash, Fabrice. It's filthy and it smells of old sweat. You're worse than a Creole goat."

Fabrice went bleating up the stairs, his grubby hand reluctantly moving up the wooden banister. Anne Marie watched him, unblinking and unamused. Halfway up the stairs—the flat was on two floors—he stopped for another sigh.

"Wash, Fabrice."

He disappeared into the bathroom.

"You're too hard on him, Anne Marie."

"That's what comes with dealing with professional criminals." She grinned. "Fabrice's an amateur."

"Give him time."

On the screen, the news anchor was talking about the cane crop. The camera moved from Michel Gurion's pale face, almost hidden behind steel-rimmed glasses, to shots of new harvesters arriving at the port of Pointe-à-Pitre. The television picture was bright; against the wharves, the sea was an improbable royal blue.

Jean Michel tapped her knee. "I'm hungry, too."

"And I'm tired."

"You're going to prepare something?"

"The girl said she'd make a quiche lorraine."

"Béatrice is a lazy cow."

"She may be lazy—but I can't do all the housework. I'm a busy woman."

"Of course, chérie."

Anne Marie ignored the hint of irony. "I'm tired," she said.

Anne Marie did not want to argue—not again, not tonight. She flopped down onto the settee beside him. She had kicked off her shoes and their legs touched. The Courrèges skirt was now very grubby.

"Get a Dominican, Anne Marie. They work harder than these Guadeloupe girls." Jean Michel sucked on his teeth. "All Béatrice can think about is her boyfriend and money to buy new jewelry."

Absent-mindedly, Anne Marie stroked his hair. Her eyes looked at the image on the television screen but her thoughts were elsewhere.

"I'm very hungry." Jean Michel yawned.

A white man, his bald head catching the unflattering studio lights, was talking about the rainfall and its effect upon the sugar content of cane. It was as if he had difficulty forcing the words from his mouth. He spoke with the local accent—an accent that Anne Marie was finding increasingly irritating. He appeared unhappy.

"What's in the fridge, chérie?"

"I don't know." She stood up and padded barefoot into the kitchen. "What would you like?" She scratched her hand. "I really don't want to cook tonight."

"What is there?"

Anne Marie opened the refrigerator.

Tomato puree in a battered tube, a few eggs, sterilized milk, an avocado pear sliced in half and the green flesh now turning black. There was also a quiche lorraine on a glass plate; the glass had misted over.

A short silence. "What?"

"The girl made a quiche."

Jean Michel did not reply.

Anne Marie went to the kitchen door to look at him. "When did you get back from Basse-Terre?"

"About half past three." Jean Michel glanced at his wife. "Perhaps a bit later."

"Half past three?"

"When I realized the bastard had stood me up, I came straight back. Half past three—four." A shrug. "Too late for the beach."

Briefly they looked at each other—he was stretched out on the sofa and Anne Marie was leaning against the cold wood of the kitchen door.

"In four hours you didn't think to look in the refrigerator, Jean Michel?"

"I wasn't hungry."

Anne Marie knew that her husband was lying.

"Would you like me to make you an omelet?" she asked softly.

13

Le Raizet

"He's a maniac."

"Who?"

"The driver—the man they sent to fetch me."

"Jean Gabriel? Been like that ever since he lost his wife—and she was only seventeen." Trousseau shrugged. "Indians marry young."

Anne Marie stretched out against the backseat.

"How's your hand, madame le juge?"

Trousseau had been reading. There was a book on his thin knees. When Anne Marie did not answer, he picked up the book and continued his reading.

Way above her head, large fans—three of them—were revolving slowly. She could feel the gentle draft and the sweat on her body began to dry.

It was going to be another hot, humid day in Pointe-à-Pitre. Outside, cars traveling in front of the terminal entrance threw their reflections against the interior wall.

Shops were opening up. At the bookstore a girl was pulling a rack of postcards out into the main concourse. Elsewhere, there was the sound of iron shutters being cranked up.

The Laveaud family had come to greet Jean Michel and his young wife at the airport, and the newlyweds had spent a couple of nights in Pointe-à-Pitre. That first night in the Caribbean, Anne Marie had showered several times because of the oppressive heat and stickiness.

This morning, most of the airline desks were still closed. An Air France hostess in uniform and blue shoes headed toward the departure lounge. She carried a small clipboard beneath her arm, and as she went past, she gave Anne Marie a sharp glance. The glance went from Anne Marie to Trousseau and back again.

It was too early for the 747 from Paris. The next flight would be the Miami plane, calling in at Pointe-à-Pitre on its way to Caracas. That would be in a couple of hours' time.

In the departure lounge, there were few passengers waiting to be called—just a small group sitting on the row of armchairs or standing around, looking at their watches. Businessmen—probably from the English islands—wearing old-fashioned pastel-colored shirts and big shoes. A group of tourists, conspicuous with their pale faces and their canvas holdalls. And a couple of large women, flying home with their bags and cumbersome cardboard boxes. The women spoke pidgin English in a high lilt, and their matronly chests heaved. They were waiting for the short, inter-island hop to Dominica.

"My hand itches less this morning, Monsieur Trousseau—and thank you for asking," she said finally. "What've you found out about Raymond Calais?"

Trousseau tapped the case of his portable typewriter. "I brought the file."

Anne Marie turned to look at him. "I didn't ask you to."

"I know how punctual these flights can be."

"Where would I be without you?" Their eyes met and she tapped his arm. "You're very thoughtful."

The face seemed to grow darker; the eyebrows moved together. "Just because I'm not white. . . ." He put the book down and Anne Marie noticed that it was a comic. "You really mustn't think I'm like all the other people in this island. I've lived in France, you know. I've got a flat in Paris."

"In the Seventeenth Arrondissement, I believe."

Trousseau hesitated a fraction of a second before pulling at the skin of his arm. "I don't behave like them. West Indians, mulattos, Indians—don't expect me to be like them, madame le juge. To dance like them, to laugh like them, to talk like them, to have their women. I've lived in Paris, and I know what it means to have to get up at five o'clock to catch the métro."

An old man in faded dungarees was pushing a cleaning machine across the concourse floor. The bristles of the revolving brushes turned rapidly, and the machine made a quiet hum. A cigarette hung from the corner of the man's mouth; his eyes wrinkled against the rising smoke.

"My wife's from France."

"So you once told me."

"You see me now, madame le juge, and I'm an old man. But once I was young. And women found me attractive. I had my choice of women, you know—but I chose a white woman."

"Monsieur Trousseau, I'm very grateful to you for the way you always try to help me. You—more than anyone else—have taught me how to adapt to life in the département."

Trousseau appeared mollified. He sat back and folded his arms.

Anne Marie scratched lightly at the back of her hand before asking, "You still think he's guilty?"

"Who?"

"Hégésippe Bray."

Carefully, Trousseau folded down the corner of the page and closed the comic book. It was only then that Anne Marie saw the pink and yellow cover. The New Testament in pictures. "I'm merely a greffier, madame le juge. It's not for me to give my opinions."

"But I do respect them."

"No, you don't."

They looked at each other; then a voice—and Anne Marie, turning her head, saw the Air France girl talking into a microphone behind the glass window of her office—announced the imminent departure of flight AF 627 to Fort-de-France. Trousseau listened, his finger raised from the backrest of the seat.

Anne Marie turned away and looked at the man behind the machine.

He walked slowly. Like someone carefully mowing the lawn, he moved along a stretch of fifteen meters at a time, leaving behind damp, clean parallels and clear prints of his own worn shoes. Apart from the curling wisp of blue smoke from the cigarette, the man could have been asleep on his feet.

A sleepwalker. A zombie.

Then after those first two days in Guadeloupe Anne Marie and Jean Michel had flown down to the Saintes for their honeymoon. At last together alone. Three weeks in a tropical paradise.

"He was dying of cancer."

"Who?"

"Hégésippe Bray was right." Trousseau allowed himself a faint smile. "Calais was going to die anyway—according to the autopsy from the *Institut médico-légal.* Cancer of the stomach."

The airport, with its clean, tiled floor, its banks, its shops, the anthuriums and orchids now on display—it was modern and reassuring. European, civilized—what Anne Marie was used to. Reassuring and tangible.

Anne Marie shuddered. A sudden cold fear of death.

"The autopsy report arrived yesterday afternoon."

"How could Hégésippe Bray have known Calais was going to die?"

Trousseau laughed. "He didn't need to know."

"He'd put a curse on Raymond Calais? That's what you're saying, aren't you?"

The old man had come to the end of the stretch of floor. He turned the machine round and the rotating brushes tipped sideways. Then he stood quietly smoking. For a moment the old man looked at Anne Marie. There was a look of reproach in the brown, bloodshot eyes.

"Madame, you prefer not to believe in these things," Trousseau scolded.

14

Raymond Calais

Raymond Calais was born on January 8, 1919 on the Sainte Marthe estate, the son of Gérard and Laure Calais. At the time of his sixtieth birthday, he was a large man, weighing eighty-four kilos, one meter seventy in height, stocky and completely bald. With a protruding jaw and a large forehead, he resembled Benito Mussolini. Raymond Calais felt flattered by the comparison.

The first attempt on his life was made on Wednesday, March 5, 1980.

He drove his car down to the main dock area of Pointe-à-Pitre. It was 6:45 in the morning, and the sidewalks were still wet after a brief rainfall. Normally at this time of day, Raymond Calais had breakfast—two boiled eggs, a couple of croissants and a pot of coffee—in a bar at the corner of the Quai Lardenoy and the rue Achille René Boisneuf where he would spend half an hour in the company of friends— two of whom were believed to be on his payroll. On the morning of March 5, several people were waiting for him inside the bar—La Sirène du Sud—and the serving girl had already started to prepare Monsieur Calais' breakfast.

Raymond Calais parked his car—a Renault R30 with a tax-free registration plate, issued in the département of Gironde—against the curb outside the ironmonger's in the rue Achille René Boisneuf. He turned off the engine, got out of the car and opened the rear door in order to pick up his attaché case that lay on the back seat.

According to two witnesses—a municipal employee and a Dutch sailor returning to his ship—gunfire was heard at 6:48 A.M.

Raymond Calais lost consciousness and fell, with blood pouring from the left side of his head and trickling across his temple into the rainwater of the gutter.

He regained consciousness at 7:53 A.M.

Friends and associates had been able to pull him from the gutter where he had nearly drowned. The Police Secours *was contacted, and Calais was taken by ambulance to the Clinique Venise in the Assainissement.*

The bullet fired from a .22 long rifle had penetrated the skin behind the ear, had been deflected by the bone of the skull and had exited through the temple. The scar on the left side of Mr. Calais' head was eight centimeters long.

The projectile was later found inside the Renault. After bouncing off Calais' head, it had ricocheted off the roof and buried itself in the upholstery of the back seat.

Analysis of the bullet's trajectory was not sufficiently precise to indicate the place from where the shot had been fired.

Three photographs:

A photograph of Calais' head, with two white arrows indicating entry and exit point of the bullet.

A photograph of the back seat of the car, with a white circle drawn about a slight tear in the fabric.

A photograph of the flattened bullet.

Anne Marie looked at the photographs carefully. Apart from Calais' dark eyebrows, none of his face was visible. His ear was small, like a child's.

Anne Marie continued reading the report.

After an initial period of shock, Calais was soon sitting up in bed. His mind appeared to have lost none of its clarity. On enquiring where he was, he was informed that an attempt had been made on his life. The news did not appear to surprise him; he accepted it with grim satisfaction.

*Raymond Calais immediately denounced the political nature of the attack. Medical staff had difficulty in calming him. While his bandage was being applied, Raymond Calais insisted upon speaking loudly and gesticulating. To the police officers present, he announced that the previous day he had submitted conclusive proof of municipal corruption to a local magazine. The magazine—*Le Pointois—*was left-wing in sympathy and favorable to the national independence movement of Guadeloupe (MANG).*

The written evidence that Raymond Calais had handed over to the magazine concerned the Communist mayor of Pointe-à-Pitre. As proof of his own objectivity and as proof of the reliability of the evidence, Raymond Calais had submitted it to a paper whose political viewpoint he clearly did not share.

"They're calling our flight."

Anne Marie looked up. "Mmm?"

The old man was nearer now, still pushing the whispering machine across the airport.

"They've just announced the departure of our plane." Trousseau clicked his tongue and carefully took the file from her. "Only forty minutes late."

15

Town Hall

The airport, the city, and the encroaching mangrove swamps grew smaller as the Twin Otter banked. Skyscrapers and slowly moving traffic along the Pointe-à-Pitre bypass appeared like a picture from a geography book. The plane flew over the hospital and then evened its angle of flight, and there was a high-pitched ping as the safety belt and no smoking lights were extinguished.

Anne Marie relaxed slightly. Her palms were moist, and her left hand was itching again. "What municipal corruption?"

Trousseau was reading. "Look at the file, madame le juge."

"I can't understand it."

"Pichon dealt with it."

"Who's Pichon?"

"With *Renseignements Généraux*." Trousseau nodded. "Pretty thorough for a local. Not afraid of a bit of hard work. He looked into it and decided there was nothing political."

"In what?"

"The attempted murder on Raymond Calais."

"What were the allegations that Calais was making?"

"Something to do with a contract being handed out to a friend of the mayor's."

"And that's a crime?"

"Raymond Calais wanted to think so." Trousseau put down the

book and laughed. He ran a finger along his moustache. "Nothing came of it. Just another excuse for Calais to attack the mayor of Pointe-à-Pitre."

"Why do that?"

Trousseau replied, his dark eyes now liquid with amusement. "Raymond Calais always wanted to be mayor himself."

The plane banked again, and a bright row of sunbeams poured through the portholes. Anne Marie blinked and turned her head. Most of the seats were empty. A young man was sitting in the row behind. He was listening to a portable stereo headset. The thin strip of metal cut through his afro hair.

"What were his chances?"

"Of being elected mayor? Virtually nil."

Anne Marie looked sharply at Trousseau. "Why?"

"Raymond Calais was a Béké—and that alone excluded him. We don't like whites, you know." He shook his head. "They've always exploited us. Exploited us and despised us. The whites from France—the whites like you—you're bad enough." He turned and gave Anne Marie a long, thoughtful look. "You pretend to be broad-minded—after all, you're from the mainland. You're from France where people have got no time for stupid, old-fashioned prejudices." He snorted. "Doesn't stop you from thinking you're better than us. We're a lesser breed—and we all look alike."

"You generalize, Monsieur Trousseau."

"You're better than the Békés." He tapped his chest. "Otherwise I'd never have married a French girl. My wife's from France."

"A tax inspector, I believe."

"Her skin is fairer than yours, madame le juge."

"I had the misfortune, Monsieur Trousseau, of being born— like you—in the colonies." She made a gesture of impatience. "Tell me about Calais."

"The Békés hate us—they always have. They speak our Creole, and when they speak French, they have our accent. But they are ashamed of that, and they don't want to have anything to do with us. They despise us because they are rich and we're poor, because

we're nothing but simple-minded folk whose ancestors were cap-
tured like animals in the dark continent and brought across the
Atlantic to work as slaves."

"You're not Indian?"

The smile of amusement had disappeared from Trousseau's
lips; the eyes now gleamed coldly. "They speak Creole like us,
but they send their children to the private schools and the white
priests. In the three hundred years that they've been living here,
as slave traders, as masters and now as respectable businessmen,
they've done everything to keep their skin as white as the first
day they came to Guadeloupe." A tight, hard grin as he ran his
finger along the moustache. "Oh, don't worry—they'll screw our
women—they always have—and they'll leave their half-breed kids
for the mother to bring up. But when it comes to marriage," he
held up a thin finger, "when it comes to all their fine ideals and
their Catholic values—then they forget the steatopygous black
women and they marry among their own."

"Steatopygous?"

"Got to keep the fair, Béké skin—even if it means marrying
within the family and getting their pure chromosomes all mixed
up. Better incest than black skin, better a deformed child—
blind, deaf or retarded—than having the stain of black blood in
the family."

"What does steatopygous mean?"

He made a slapping gesture, and then the cabin grew dark as
they went through a cloud.

"I don't understand, Trousseau."

"The Békés will defy God's law rather than marry someone
with black skin, madame le juge."

"Who did Raymond Calais marry?"

"A stuck-up, arrogant English woman." Trousseau looked down
at the book, then at Anne Marie. He did not hide his irritation.
"Raymond Calais had no chance of being elected because he was
a Béké. That's all. We don't like Békés—nothing more subtle than
that. And he was too stupid to realize it."

"But he was a member of the *Conseil Général.* He represented Pointe-à-Pitre at a departement level."

"He could get a few friends to vote for him." The book slid from Trousseau's knees onto the grubby carpet of the passageway.

"Who?"

"Traders and shopkeepers who hate blacks as much as he did and who are terrified one day we might take over. Being voted *conseill général* is one thing—being mayor of Pointe-à-Pitre is something quite different. Calais had absolutely no chance."

"I was here during the riots."

Trousseau frowned. "Against the English?"

"Against the immigrants from Dominica. Calais was one of the ring-leaders—and he had popular support."

Trousseau shrugged. "Just another way of attacking the mayor—and nobody here likes the Dominicans. The pedestrian zone—he accused the mayor of letting it become a marijuana trading post for Dominicans and Haitians—a place where no self-respecting Frenchman would dare go. And when fighting broke out in the street and the rastas from Dominica were being hit over the head by angry demonstrators, Calais was making good political mileage."

"How?"

"Calais liked violence—that's why he had his band of armed men. That's why he often hung around the port. But people aren't stupid, madame le juge—not even my compatriots. You really think the people living in the slums—and even more so, those who have been recently re-housed into the new estates—you really think they had any sympathy for Calais? For a fat, wealthy Béké who modeled himself on Mussolini? A man who could buy any silly little girl into his car—and into his bed? They couldn't stand him. But Raymond Calais was too stupid to realize even that." Trousseau bent over sideways and picked up the book. "Calais always was stupid. A cocky, arrogant bastard, a womanizer—and everybody laughed at him. His father wanted to disown him. Old man Calais knew his son Raymond was incapable of running the Sainte Marthe estate."

"Raymond Calais was rich."

"Because he sold off a lot of land. Sainte Marthe was one of the oldest and most successful of the plantations—there are even people who maintain it existed before the English came here during the Seven Years' War. Perhaps if his brother Jacques had been in charge he might have made it into the biggest sugar plantation in the French Caribbean."

"Who did Raymond Calais sell the land to?"

"His father had started selling—but not on a large scale—to other planters. Raymond Calais sold to people who wanted to build. The only real economic boom in Guadeloupe's been in the building industry. Over the last twenty years, there's been a shortage of housing—of decent houses that will stand up to the hurricanes and earthquakes. Which explains why even a high-ranking civil servant like you—with the whitest of skins—is living in a city housing project. With all the money France pumps in, there are a lot of people who can afford to build. Hand in hand with the decline in sugar, there's been a boom in agricultural land transformed into real estate."

"Raymond Calais still grows sugar?"

"Sure."

"Why?"

"So that he can take the subsidies that France hands out so generously." Trousseau looked at the palms of his callused hands. "Sugar's a lame duck—but France gives money so that there is not total unemployment. Our sugar's not competitive—twice as expensive as the sugar coming out of Barbados or Jamaica." He shrugged. "France subsidizes an ailing industry—and of course, the money goes straight into the pockets of the Békés. With the connivance of the local politicians—and the government in Paris which doesn't really care one way or the other, provided Guadeloupe votes the right way at the time of the general elections. Or perhaps you have forgotten that de Gaulle's margin in 1967 was equal to the number of votes cast in Guadeloupe. And all the while sugar continues to slump."

"That's why he wanted to be mayor?"

"Raymond Calais missed the boat. Most Békés saw the change coming—like his brother Jacques Calais—and many moved into commerce. Sugar's dead. It will never be competitive again. Raymond Calais was just too stupid to see that."

Anne Marie grimaced. "But why mayor?"

"He wanted power."

The Twin Otter banked sharply, and glancing through the porthole, Anne Marie saw sunlight dancing across the surface of the sea.

"And his brother?"

"Too clever to want to hang around his older brother. A couple of years younger than Raymond, and like most Békés, Jacques Calais had got into import-export. In the early fifties, he managed to obtain the importer's license for American General Motors. Now one of the wealthiest men in Guadeloupe."

"The two brothers got on well?"

"The Békés form a caste. From the outside, they always appear united. And impenetrable."

"Then Calais' wife has nothing to worry about?"

Trousseau repeated sharply, "To worry about?"

"About money."

"During the war, when old man Calais died, she brought all her wealth. There are some people who say that was why Calais married her. She comes from a rich family—one of those white families where you never know if they're French or English. Families that have roots and relatives—and a lot of money—in all the islands. Not just in Martinique and Guadeloupe—but in the English islands as well. Trinidad and Dominica and St. Kitts."

"Where's she from originally?"

Trousseau shrugged. The cotton of the white shirt had been darned where the points of the collar had worn the fabric thin. "Who knows?"

"She works for Air France, I believe."

Trousseau laughed. "She works in the central office of Air

France on Boulevard Légitimus—it gives her social security, it gives her the overblown salary of a civil servant. . . ."

"We're all civil servants."

"At least we work." He looked at his palms again, then folded his arms. "A job at Air France gives her tickets at ten percent of their real price—for her and for all her family. So that they can fly regularly up to Miami and stash their money away safely in some American bank—thousands of kilometers away from the uncertain future of Guadeloupe."

The plane lost speed. The warning lights came on above the cockpit.

Anne Marie did not feel well. She was sweating.

"The Békés look after themselves," Trousseau said as he tightened the clasp of his seatbelt.

16

Honeymoon

On their honeymoon, the young couple had spent most evenings in Terre de Haut. After the stifling heat of Pointe-à-Pitre, Anne Marie was appreciative of the cool winds that blew across the Saintes. And she felt healthy. Not since leaving Algeria had she felt so well, so fit. Nor had she been so attractive.

At first sight Anne Marie had fallen in love with the Saintes, with the flowers, with the lemon trees, the café bâtard and the wild cinnamon. They formed, these forgotten islands, a terrestrial paradise, a corner of another, long-forgotten France, old-fashioned and peaceful, existing on the far side of the globe.

The newlyweds had stayed at the Hôtel Fontainebleau in a bright, clean room that looked out over the vast bay, the precipitous sugar-loaf mountain and the green-covered hills that reminded Anne Marie of her Mediterranean, of Algeria.

People walking backward and forward along the main street, the girls hand in hand, the men quietly smoking.

A television had been placed on the sill of the town hall, and when evening fell, the set was turned on and the Saintois watched the programs with innocent pleasure. Frantically they applauded the French team in Jeux Sans Frontières just as they applauded the arrival of seven gunfighters in the dubbed Western.

Jean Michel, however, soon got bored. He grew more and more restless

*at the Hôtel Fontainebleau. "If I had wanted to watch television," he
remarked when Anne Marie suggested they sit down among the children,
"I could have stayed in Paris."*

He spent a lot of time phoning his mother from the hotel.

17

Reconstitution

In the bright sunshine, she looked like a little girl.

"A lost child," Anne Marie thought, and she felt an unexpected sense of empathy for Cinderella.

Anne Marie hated crime scene *reconstitutions*. She hated seeing the accused re-enacting the past and reliving those moments which had led to arrest. Necessary and often useful, the playacting was also painful and very sad.

The woman from Dominica wore a painted dress made of cotton with an elasticized waist that had moved upwards, accentuating sagging breasts and poor posture. Her hair was coarse; it had been combed and woven into plaits. Her scalp was marked off into irregular squares, and from each square there hung a plait, anchored by an elastic band.

Thin arms hung loosely in front of her body, hands clasped. Anne Marie did not notice the handcuffs at first. They pinched slightly against Cinderella's blemished skin. Another, longer chain went from the handcuffs to a bored gendarme.

The brown eyes watched the gendarmes and the movement around her. Cinderella appeared distant, almost unconcerned, as if what was happening about her—the white men in their uniforms, the cameras, the crowd—had nothing to do with her.

"Coconut radio." Le Bras, the gendarme from Tréduder with the Breton accent, pointed to the large crowd that had gathered. People stood by the edge of the road and on the dry, white sand of the beach. "They saw you coming from the aerodrome, madame le juge." He shrugged. "Cheaper than the cinema."

"And we're the bit part actors." Perspiration had formed along the skin of Trousseau's forehead and on the sides of his nose. He mopped at his face with a handkerchief. He had undone the top two buttons of his shirt.

Anne Marie rubbed gently at the back of her left hand.

The crowd grew larger. Children had begun to appear, working their way toward the front. They had the features of the Saintois—yellow hair, brown or hazel eyes and a golden tan.

Anne Marie raised her voice, "Give her the doll."

The order was repeated, and a gendarme stepped forward to unlock the handcuffs. Cinderella rubbed at her wrists and the crowd fell silent. Another man approached her and placed a pink doll between her hands.

Trousseau was sitting beneath a sea grape tree where he balanced the typewriter on his narrow knees. He was looking at Cinderella attentively.

She did not move.

Her lawyer, a man in a suit that was too short for his legs, brushed past Anne Marie and took Cinderella gently by the elbow. He spoke in her ear, in a calm, reassuring voice, using carefully enunciated Creole, while his intelligent eyes remained on the juge d'instruction.

Cinderella nodded.

She began to walk. With small, hesitant steps across the sand, the doll held to her breast, she went to the entrance of the wooden hut that she had once inhabited. Her feet left indistinct footprints in the hot sand. She wore plastic sandals; on the right foot, the strap was broken.

Nobody spoke. There was just the gentle murmur of the sea

as it broke against the beach beyond the hut. Anne Marie, Trousseau, the lawyer and the gendarmes—they watched in silence, spectators to the play that the girl was about to re-enact.

In his hand, Le Bras held a notebook.

Cinderella put her hand to the doll's mouth and made the gesture of smothering it. The doll seemed to move. It jerked slightly. Cinderella did not look at the pink face but stared directly ahead. Her face was devoid of expression.

The crowd waited.

Like an automaton, Cinderella stepped from the threshold of the shack—the grey planks were rotting and covered with black lichen—and headed toward the crowd. People moved aside, opening a momentary passage for her as she walked toward a fence beside an uninhabited hut.

Eyes wide, a little boy stared at her. He was naked except for a dirty pair of old swimming trunks.

The gendarme followed Cinderella closely.

There was a tree—Anne Marie could not recognize the round, almost rubbery leaves—and in its shade, Cinderella knelt down. A few dried leaves lay on the sand. She brushed them away.

Her legs and feet were marked with dark scars. She had pale, prominent heels. For a moment, she was motionless; then she turned to look round at the lawyer.

The lawyer nodded, smiled reassuringly. He was sweating in his dark suit.

The woman from Dominica began to dig. Excavating with her bare hands, the doll now lying face down on the ground, Cinderella made a hole. The crowd emitted a low murmur of disapproval.

"Tell them to be quiet," Anne Marie said.

Le Bras walked away, and a few seconds later, the crowd fell silent.

When there was a neat pile of sand beside Cinderella's hole, she stopped. There was no tenderness in her action as she set the doll in its shallow grave and as she started shoveling sand over the pink plastic. The white shawl, the golden hair and the chubby, pink limbs disappeared beneath the handfuls of dry sand.

A swell of anger rose from the onlookers.

"Silence," Le Bras shouted.

Trousseau ran a finger along his moustache.

The girl stood up and stared at the ground. She had finished. A shy actress waiting for her applause.

No one moved.

The lawyer was standing beside Anne Marie. His breath smelt of garlic. Anne Marie had to lean forward to hear him because he was whispering. "She says the man kept watch."

"What man?"

"Lucien Savon." Drops of sweat had formed at the corner of his eyes. "It was his idea to do away with the child." The lawyer turned his head. Out to sea, there was the distant sound of beating. It was growing stronger.

"Why kill the baby?"

He turned back to face Anne Marie. "He couldn't afford to look after it—or her. He's married."

"The girl could have kept the baby—her baby."

"She can scarcely look after herself—and she's got no family here to take care of the child." The face crumpled with vicarious suffering. "She's not very bright. What little money she earns, she spends. She wouldn't have been able to look after a child properly."

"Most women are quite capable."

The lawyer seemed upset by Anne Marie's judgment. "Madame le juge, the girl's retarded."

"It was her child."

"She came to the Saintes after the hurricane in Dominica. She can't speak French—just her own patois." He shook his head. "To stay alive she had to sell her body. A poor child."

The crowd was now breaking up, moving toward the sea. Le Bras raised his hand to shield his eyes.

An Alouette was coming in fast from the sea, its nose down like an insect and the circle of its rotor blades a grim halo.

Anne Marie looked at the heap of sand where the doll was bur-ied and remembered her first pregnancy.

The noise grew louder as the helicopter, like an angry insect, began circling the beach. The wind kicked up the sand and scat-tered the dry leaves, the flotsam, the forgotten sponge and the seaweed.

In the bulb of the cockpit, his head submerged beneath a hel-met, the pilot gestured downward with his thumb. He was hover-ing at about ten meters, and sand blasted against Anne Marie's face and legs. She squinted, covering her nose and mouth with her hand.

The skids touched the sand, the pilot cut the engines, the high whine lost its deafening intensity. White letters that announced gendarmerie on the side of the machine.

The pilot jumped out and bent double, came scurrying toward Anne Marie.

"Le juge Laveaud?"

She nodded.

He gave a brief salute. "You are requested to come with me to Pointe-à-Pitre." He handed her a slip of blue paper.

Cinderella still stood beneath the tree, the bored gendarme beside her. She was staring at the ground, as if she had never noticed the arrival of the helicopter nor the wind of the rotor blades that pulled at her shapeless dress.

"Immediately, madame le juge."

18

Maison d'Arrêt

The chauffeur got out of the car and rang a bell.

A wooden peephole opened and then closed again, as if activated by a spring. There was the rattle of a bolt being drawn back and the large door opened inward.

The chauffeur stepped aside, and Anne Marie went past him into the cool air of the building. Her eyes adjusted to the gloom. A red tiled floor, several posters, a memorial stone buried into the wall and a long, bare desk.

"Your allergy, madame le juge—remember to rub it with green limes. Green limes and rum." The driver gave a friendly wave, and his boots made a soft tattoo as he disappeared down the sunlit steps.

"You must sign here."

The prison officer handed her a pen, and she placed a signature in the large book.

"This way."

Trousseau and Anne Marie followed the officer along the stone corridor, down several steps to a door where another man was sitting on a stool. He stood up and removed the earplug of a radio from his ear. The smile was sheepish.

He nodded to both visitors and tapped lightly on a door that opened immediately.

A man beckoned them to enter. His nose had been broken; his hair was the color of sand and lay in thin streaks across a domed head. He wore dark trousers, a white shirt and a loosened tie. He was also wearing a gun in a shoulder holster.

He closed the door behind them. "Identification."

Cold, professional eyes that moved unceasingly. They went from Anne Marie to Trousseau and then back again. They ran over her body, but without pleasure or male interest.

"Le juge d'instruction, Anne Marie Laveaud."

"And him?" A nod toward Trousseau.

"Monsieur Trousseau's my greffier."

He took Trousseau's card and compared the younger, less wrinkled face in the photograph with the blank face before him.

"Monsieur Trousseau's my greffier."

"Trousseau," the man said.

"Monsieur Trousseau. Jean Alphonse Ayassamy Trousseau. But educated people call me Monsieur."

There was no reaction in the eyes. The man with the gun pointed his finger at Anne Marie. "You can go in." With his thumb he indicated Trousseau. "He stays."

"Monsieur Trousseau comes with me."

The man shook his domed, graceless head. "I've no orders to that effect."

"Change your orders."

"Let me see that case."

Trousseau lifted the typewriter.

"Open it."

Silence.

"Please open your case."

Trousseau unlocked the small clasp; the bible picture-book lay on top of the portable Remington. The man touched it gingerly. "And this?"

"Dossier on Raymond Calais."

"Either of you carrying a fire arm?"

Trousseau said, "I left my flame thrower in the helicopter."

"Jokes like that can get people killed, pal." He turned and opened the steel door. The rivets were hidden by several layers of coarse paint.

19

Cell

A smell of cigar smoke and human suffering.

A blanket on the floor.

Instinctively, Anne Marie put her hand to her throat.

The procureur was sitting on the narrow bed, talking to another man. He stood up, getting onto his small feet with difficulty. He panted slightly from the exertion as he greeted Anne Marie. They shook hands. He nodded toward Trousseau.

The procureur was holding a cigar between the fingers of his hand. His face had lost its childlike joviality. In the feeble light he appeared anaemic. "May I present Dr. Bouton?"

Anne Marie and Dr. Bouton shook hands. The doctor's grip was dry and firm.

The procureur ran a hand through his hair. Despite the coolness of the cell—one wall of stone and two sidewalls of parallel iron bars—he had taken off his jacket and tie. He patted at his forehead with a red handkerchief. "You'd better take a look at that," he said, gesturing with the cigar at the blanket.

Anne Marie knelt down, and even as she did so, she realized the action was quite pointless. She knew what was there, waiting for her.

It was Trousseau who interceded. He unceremoniously pushed her aside and pulled back the edge of the woolen blanket.

Pale blue eyes, now protuberant and sightless.

The eyes seemed to stare at Anne Marie. The leathery jaw lolled open and revealed a few yellow teeth and a tongue that stuck out—as if in one last, hopeless gesture of defiance.

Anne Marie forced herself to look at the face.

"Why?" she whispered.

Trousseau let the blanket fall back into place, hiding the pink triangle of the tongue.

"Why?" Her body had begun to tremble.

"Why indeed, madame le juge?"

"How did this happen?" She turned to face the procureur. She wanted to control her voice but it seemed distant, strange—spoken by someone else. A cold rage had begun to swell up inside her.

"With the shoulder strap of his overalls." Dr. Bouton wore steel-rimmed spectacles. His face was thin, pale and angular. He had a small mouth. Dr. Bouton was like a fish—like a shark—at the bottom of a murky sea. "Somehow managed to attach his overall to the bars."

Anne Marie felt giddy. "How could he have done that?" The bars of the cell seemed to be moving.

"Hégésippe Bray wanted to die."

A bitter taste of bile rose from the back of her throat. "I don't believe that."

"Believe what you choose, madame le juge," the procureur replied. He sat down on the bench, his fat thighs apart. "I can only tell you what I know to be the truth. The only possible truth."

"I don't believe Hégésippe Bray. . . ."

The procureur jabbed with his cigar. "This is an old colonial prison. The architecture here doesn't come up to the requirements of French penitentiary establishments. With a modern infrastructure, there is no way Bray could have killed himself. But the old man wanted to die—and without too much difficulty, he's succeeded."

"No."

"Bray told the guard he did not want to live any more—not in a prison."

"No."

"Lower your voice, madame."

Anne Marie felt sick—stunned and sick. The dingy cell seemed to sway. Then the door opened, and the white man with the pistol stood aside to let a woman enter.

"Ah!" the procureur said.

Dr. Bouton stood up. He shook hands with the woman.

"Maître Gisèle Legrand—who was appointed Bray's lawyer yesterday."

Trousseau said softly, "Lawyer? Bray'll be needing an undertaker."

The procureur swung round, opened his mouth to say something, but his features relaxed as he attempted a smile.

Maître Gisèle Legrand wore sober clothes; a jacket with a hint of pinstripe, a silk shirt that opened low on her deep, freckled chest. A grey skirt that ended below her knees. Exclusive shoes—bought in Paris.

"We have already met." Anne Marie shook hands.

Maître Legrand had fair skin, and there were freckles on her cheeks. She wore red lipstick and a lot of rouge. Her hair had been straightened and it now formed a thick plait—like a bread loaf, it seemed to Anne Marie, who could distinguish between the natural hair and the finer, more lustrous hairpiece.

The eyes were glassy. "Pleased to meet you, madame le juge."

The procureur pulled back the edge of the blanket. Again the dead man's stare and his loose jaw held Anne Marie's attention. She leaned on Trousseau's arm.

"Hanged himself," the procureur said.

Maître Legrand nodded.

The procureur stood up, briskly rubbed his hands, straightened his shoulders and looked around the cell—at the scratched bars, the wall, the small bed attached to the stonework. "We should go somewhere else to talk."

There was graffiti on the wall—a few initials, a few sprawling obscenities.

The procureur replaced the cigar in his mouth. "Somewhere a bit more congenial."

20

Chair

She felt sick.

"Something to drink perhaps?"

Anne Marie rested her weight against the edge of the desk. "Hégésippe Bray did not kill himself."

"Please sit down, Madame Laveaud."

"No reason at all for suicide."

"Evidently Hégésippe Bray thought otherwise." The procureur shrugged. "He told the guard he didn't want to return to French Guyana."

"I had made it quite clear there was no question of his being sent back." She nodded to where Trousseau sat on a folding wooden chair. "My greffier is a witness."

Trousseau remained immobile, staring at the wall and at the calendar that had been pinned there.

Maître Legrand sat in a low armchair, her legs crossed and her chin tucked against her neck. Her eyes remained on the procureur. "Perhaps he didn't believe you, madame le juge."

The procureur had taken the comfortable armchair behind the desk. The dead cigar was stuck in the corner of his mouth like a morbid excrescence. "Please sit down, madame le juge."

"Hégésippe Bray believed me. I explained he'd soon be set free."

"The old man hanged himself."

Everybody—including Trousseau—turned to look at Dr. Bouton. "Hégésippe Bray hanged himself, madame le juge," the bloodless lips repeated with precise conviction.

"I know he didn't."

"Can you explain how Hégésippe Bray was found hanging from the bars of his cell?"

"He was put there."

Maître Legrand sighed.

"That is a very serious accusation." Dr. Bouton spoke softly—like a professor at the faculty of medicine.

"The only possible explanation."

"Hégésippe Bray wanted to die. Psychologically, it makes sense. You may have explained the temporary nature of his incarceration. You may have made it clear he'd never be sent to French Guyana. But that is not the point." Dr. Bouton tapped a pen against the side of his nose. "How old was Bray? Eighty-two, eighty-three? Clearly no longer in his prime. Clearly debilitated by the rigors of French Guyana. And totally unprepared for the new Guadeloupe." The voice was calm, reasonable, persuasive. "Social, psychological changes—all the changes that have taken place here since his departure for South America. Hégésippe Bray was lost. It was only normal he should feel. . . ."

"Hégésippe Bray had a place in the country—at Sainte Marthe—and he was happy there."

"Then who killed him?" Maître Legrand asked. Her sweet perfume mixed with the bitter odor of the cigar.

Anne Marie said, "I could make a guess."

The procureur placed his hand on the desk. "I'm pleased to see your reaction, madame le juge. I admire you. You show you're a warm person."

Maître Legrand gave a small nod.

"But are you not allowing yourself to be too emotional?"

Anne Marie remained silent.

"Please sit down." He gestured, then with the same hand, he

put the cigar in the ashtray. "This death is very embarrassing." The procureur leaned back in the leather armchair and ran two podgy hands though his hair. A button on his shirt was missing, and the fabric had drawn back to reveal pale flesh. "What we need is a drink." He thumped the desk. "Platon!" he shouted.

A man opened the door and stuck his head through the crack. "Monsieur?"

"Drinks—and fast." The procureur raised his hands, hospitable but slightly bewildered. "Bring us something. I don't know." He looked at Maître Legrand, who nodded. "A bottle of mineral water and some fruit juice, perhaps, if there is any—but none of that awful imported stuff. And for me a cup of coffee, Platon. A cup of very strong coffee."

The head nodded obediently and disappeared.

"Poor Platon's filling in while the prison director is in France, and he's not too happy to be chased out of his office—and it's air conditioned." The smile faded as the procureur took another cigar from the small packet. "You really must sit down, madame le juge. You seem to think this is a confrontation. We're not in a court of law, I assure you." He placed the cigar in his mouth and lit it. His lips were moist and flecked with a couple of shreds of tobacco. He watched the sinuous movement of the rising spirals of smoke. "A human life lost for nothing. After all those years in the wilderness. I understand how you feel, madame—and in your position, I'd be behaving just like you."

Anne Marie lowered herself into a canvas armchair.

21

Sin of Omission

"Enquiry?"

"Into the death of Hégésippe Bray. There shall be an enquiry, monsieur le procureur."

"I don't think so."

"Why not?"

"There's no call for any enquiry," the man said, raising one shoulder, "as I see it."

Silence—broken only by the steady hum of the air conditioner. Smoke formed grey curlicues that danced toward the ceiling.

He added, "Unless there's reason to suspect foul play."

Maître Legrand nodded. "An open and shut case of suicide."

"Bray'd lost all desire to live," the procureur said. "That doesn't excuse the guard. He should've kept his eyes open—he'd been warned. Nor does it excuse Platon. Platon's standing in for Rinaldo who's in France for a conference on security in prisons, of all things." He removed the cigar from his mouth and looked at the smoldering tip. "Rinaldo won't get back from Rouen until the end of next week. Which puts us all in a nasty situation—at just the wrong time. First the murder of Raymond Calais. Even if very few people regret his departure, the fact remains he was murdered. Murdered in an overseas département. And now this." He raised his hands. "Just to make things more intolerable."

The door opened. A man in uniform entered to place a tray on the desk and distribute the drinks.

The cold water chilled Anne Marie's teeth. She realized with grim satisfaction that she had forgotten about her itching hand.

Maître Legrand held a glass of passion fruit juice, and as she raised it, the corner of her mouth moved upwards, causing the freckled cheeks to wrinkle.

"Nobody's going to like it." The procureur drank his coffee in two gulps. He winced, brushed the corner of his eye with the back of his hand, then replaced the damp tip of his cigar in his mouth. "Nobody other than the political troublemakers." The procureur smiled at Anne Marie. "Try and understand what's at stake."

"Justice."

Maître Legrand gave a little laugh.

"Bray was not involved in Calais' death. There's no real evidence. The gendarmerie have based their case on hearsay—on the threats of an old man who'd drunk too much."

"And his gun?"

"There's no proof he pulled the trigger," Anne Marie said.

"Who else knew Bray had a gun?"

"It'd been my intention to liberate Bray within the next twenty-four hours."

"Pity then you didn't." The procureur sucked thoughtfully on the cigar. "Who, in your opinion, killed him? If you're so sure it wasn't Bray, you must tell me who killed Raymond Calais."

Anne Marie turned from the procureur to Dr. Bouton to Maître Legrand. They were looking at her attentively.

Anne Marie shrugged.

"You must have your theories, madame le juge."

"I don't know who killed Calais."

"Could it have been Hégésippe Bray?"

"It could've been anybody." Anne Marie glanced at the Creole calendar that Trousseau was still staring at. September 1980 and she had just turned thirty-four. "It could've been anyone at all."

"Precisely what I was afraid of." The procureur took a last suck on the cigar. "A decisive lie can at times be a lot better than a hesitant truth."

"Not in a democracy."

He stubbed out the cigar. "We should never have allowed the man to die. Platon and Rinaldo of course'll be able to shift the blame. They'll show that the real responsibility's in Paris. Not enough money—they're understaffed." He paused. "I feel just as bitter as you do, madame le juge. After all Hégésippe Bray had to go through—a life of exile for some crime committed years ago— at a time when in other parts of the world, men were slaughtering each other by the million." His eyes did not blink, but held her glance. "A sin of omission. Worse still, from my point of view, a sin of organization. However. . . ." The procureur took a deep breath. "However, we've no choice but to make use of this death, unfortunate and distasteful though it may be. Political use." A few threads of dying smoke managed to writhe upward from the ashtray. "A little payoff for all our pains."

Trousseau coughed.

"Hégésippe Bray killed Calais—or he didn't. Either way, both he and Raymond Calais are now gone. And there's no way of bringing them back." He paused. "If it wasn't Bray who killed Calais, there can only be one alternative."

Maître Legrand said, "Mouvement d'action des nationalistes guadeloupéens."

22

Renseignements Généraux

The procureur laughed, genuinely amused. "Guadeloupe is a powder keg—and Paris is terrified of the smallest spark, at the slightest hint of terrorist activity. As soon as Raymond Calais was found dead—within an hour of my getting back from Sainte Anne—Paris was screaming down the phone."

"There's no reason to assume Calais was assassinated for political motives. That was his own theory. It suited him. Calais liked the idea of martyrdom—but that doesn't mean it's true."

"Guadeloupe's little more than a colony—or at least, that's how it appears to other nations in the Caribbean."

Maître Legrand said, "Nations such as Cuba."

The procureur went on, "You see, madame le juge, Paris's terrified by the prospect of unrest here. They still haven't forgotten the riots of '67, and the last thing Paris wants—that Giscard wants—is bad press. There is no surer way of catching the international headlines than with killings. Political stability—that's all that France asks for. Next May, France votes for a president, and Guadeloupe votes, too. Terrorist activity—particularly a political killing—is extremely dangerous and unwelcome. Other countries start to ask questions, and a spot in the Atlantic suddenly becomes a suppurating abscess. People want to know how an old slave island with an African population can be part of the French

Republic. In the United Nations, the decolonization committee starts braying—and the corrupt governments of South America can divert attention from their own problems by denouncing France's intolerable colonialism."

Trousseau yawned.

"And here, there is the danger of an immediate radicalization. Like in '67. Everything becomes either black or white. Either you're for France—or you're against her. That, madame le juge, can bring about a very nasty backlash."

"Situations can be manipulated," Maître Legrand added.

"Paris wanted to send their own men, madame le juge." The procureur lowered his head. "I informed Paris you'd been given the dossier, and that I had complete faith in your competence. I said there was no need to send any of their own men, but there are people in Paris who consider Calais a very important man. People who are far from happy about this turn of events."

"Their own men?" Anne Marie asked. "Whose own men?"

"If Raymond Calais's murder's political—he was, let's not forget, a member of the Conseil Général—it's no longer under the jurisdiction of the parquet—under my jurisdiction. The integrity of the State's threatened, and the affair becomes the responsibility of the *Cour de Sûreté de l'Etat*. Paris wanted to know whether they should send men." A slow smile. "Detectives who are specialized in crimes that affect the integrity of the State. Political crimes." The smile was soon replaced by a frown that wrinkled the procureur's features. "You know the Cour de Sûreté has its own investigating magistrates?"

"Three of them."

"Some people believe the Cour de Sûreté de l'Etat should be abolished. Including Monsieur Mitterand and his Socialist friends." Maître Legrand adopted the tone of a lawyer addressing the bar. "The existence of a specialized court—and a court that can be convened in camera—goes against the Republican ideal of equal justice for everyone." She tapped her hair. "Regrettably, these same people forget the Republic has a long tradition of unrest—at home and in the colonies. A long tradition of turmoil and political violence." She folded her arms. "Such a court is a necessity."

The procureur nodded. "It'd be best for everyone concerned to wrap up the Hégésippe Bray affair here and now—without outside interference."

The perfume and the tobacco smoke were oppressive, despite the chill air. Anne Marie poured another glass of water from the Evian bottle. "Wrap it up in what way?"

"Either that or have it taken out of your hands."

"You want me to say Hégésippe Bray murdered Calais?"

The procureur and Anne Marie looked at each other in silence.

"Why not, madame?"

"It's not my job to attribute guilt where it's politically suitable—where you, monsieur le procureur, believe it's politically suitable."

Maître Legrand moved her shoulders to face Anne Marie. "Madame le juge, how long have you been in Guadeloupe?"

"Since August last year."

"In that time—just over a year—do you think you have learned all you need to know about Guadeloupe?"

Anne Marie could feel anger pricking at the corners of her eyes.

"Answer the question, madame le juge." The procureur leaned forward and his hand touched hers. "Please."

"How long I've lived here cannot affect my appreciation of justice. Justice does not differ from one country to another."

The procureur held up his hand. "You're European—a very attractive woman—and very intelligent and dynamic."

"You're most kind."

"But you didn't grow up here," Maître Legrand said. "Although you have a husband who is from Guadeloupe—whom I had the pleasure of teaching at the university—there are certain things that happen here in this département—things you really don't understand."

"We're a strange people, and in its funny way, Guadeloupe's

a world of its own, with its own peculiar mix of cultures—of Amerindian, African and European." The procureur plucked at the inside of his wrist. "My skin is pale as you can see, but in my veins, I have the blood of a slave." He laughed. "I never worked on a plantation or toiled in the fields of cane. I also have French blood—but my origins are in Africa, where my forebears were snatched away so they could toil in a white man's land. Africa's where I am from—but it is not where I am going." He tapped the armrest of his chair. "My future is with France. Guadeloupe and France have more than three hundred years of shared history—so why should we want to go back on our past? We're what our history has made us. Inextricably, France and her Caribbean islands are tied together. We're married, for better or for worse." A soft smile. "It is a marriage that works."

Maître Legrand nodded.

"Madame le juge, here in Guadeloupe we speak French, and we admire the French people—because we are the same people, with the same culture and the same civilized heritage." He held up his finger. "Don't smile. These are things which I believe sincerely—not only with my reason but also in my heart. There are so many things that cannot be forgotten. The men from this island who died in the Great War. And in the second war, too, we rallied to the flag, we rallied to de Gaulle." The procureur lowered his voice. "In thanks, when the last Nazi enemy had been defeated, the last outsider chased from the soil of France, the French people, in a genuine gratitude, transformed this old sugar colony into a département. An overseas département."

23

Algeria

Once, Anne Marie had seen a young Arab—fourteen or fifteen years old—in the middle of Boulevard Foch. It must have been in 1957, a year before Papa decided to leave Algeria for good. The boy had unfurled a French flag smeared with excrement. Then, relying on the protection of his young age, he had soaked it in petrol and set it alight.

On a nearby balcony, a Frenchman had taken a gun and had shot the boy through the head. Anne Marie could recall the sound of the man's laughter. She could remember the headless child lying on the road.

It was perhaps that dead boy which made Anne Marie decide she would one day become a lawyer, that she would fight to protect the weak.

"Madame le juge, I don't want the future of my island to be jeopardized."

"You're asking me to manipulate the course of justice simply because France and Guadeloupe share a common heritage?"

Maître Legrand shook her head. "Monsieur le procureur wouldn't ask anyone to manipulate the course of justice."

"Good."

"He's merely asking you to be reasonable."

"I can accept no interference into the course of my enquiry."

"Madame Laveaud,"—the *procureur* allowed a sigh to escape, his breath bitter with the smell of coffee—"you seem to forget the old man's dead."

Anne Marie wondered whether she was going to cry. Anger, frustration, and a sense of guilt. And the smell of the woman's perfume getting more sickening by the minute. Anne Marie needed to leave. To breathe fresh air. She said, almost in desperation, "Hégésippe Bray's dead because he's been killed."

A sharp flash of anger: then the procureur's eyes softened as he brought his emotion under control. "If Raymond Calais was just a man—an ordinary man—and if we were in France and not in this tropical island, I'd be glad to witness your indignation. Unfortunately, madame le juge, we're not in France but in Guadeloupe, where the situation's critical. We belong to France—but there are times when that lifeline is very delicate and it can easily be snapped. Which," he said, prodding a finger in the air, "could be fatal for all of us who live here."

"People in Guadeloupe should see France as a source of justice."

"Without France there is nothing. Sugar's a dead industry, and without outside aid, there'd be nothing for us to live on. No work. My compatriots have no delusions; they know the wealth of this island comes from the mainland—the money that pays your salary and mine. My compatriots don't want independence. They want Guadeloupe to remain a part of France—and they want France to remain what she's always been—a good and wise friend. Like a wife."

Anne Marie drank her third glass of water.

"We can't allow the MANG that kind of liberty. MANG wants terrorism for its backlash. For the way it'll divide this island into two rival factions—opposing, fighting factions. Which is precisely what you and I don't want several months before the elections. If this island is to progress, to develop, Guadeloupe can only progress within the framework of the French Republic. Democratically.

By denigrating the police and the system of justice, you're playing into their hands—into the hands of the people who're willing to risk everything for some utopian independence."

"You're asking me to attribute to Hégésippe Bray the murder of Raymond Calais just for the sake of all the good, hard-working people out there?" She gestured to beyond the window.

"They're Frenchmen."

"Liberty and equality—that's what the French Republic stands for—and if it doesn't stand for those things in the département of Guadeloupe, then the independentists are probably right. Your kind of republic is not a republic at all."

Maître Legrand tilted her head. "Are you a Communist, madame le juge?"

Anne Marie stood up and moved toward the door. Trousseau joined her.

"You forget one thing, madame le juge."

Anne Marie stopped, her hand on the door handle.

The procureur's face had hardened. "You wanted this case. You're an ambitious woman. You're tired of dealing with petty thefts and juveniles. You wanted a murder because it means you're moving up the ladder. A very ambitious woman, but you forget one thing."

"What?"

"Clear an old convict who was going to die anyway—clear him and before you know it, the Cour de Sûreté de l'Etat will be sending its own men—to take your job out of your hands. They'll be stepping out of the next Boeing."

Anne Marie hesitated.

"Rest assured that, as far as I'm concerned, your diet will be more juveniles, more petty crime and more cases of shoplifting. Until it's time for you to leave the département and return to France."

"Sounds very much like a threat, Monsieur le procureur."

The handle moved in her hand.

The door was opened. The man with the long head and the

shoulder holster entered. His face was drawn. He glanced hurriedly at Anne Marie and went straight to the procureur, placing something on the desk before him. A piece of crumpled paper. He whispered in the procureur's ear.

The procureur nodded.

"Bad news for you, madame le juge." The procureur pushed the crumpled piece of paper across the desk. "Just found in the old man's overalls—a suicide note."

24
Sainte Marthe

Anne Marie stared at the pool. The reeds swayed and frogs croaked.

Eight hundred meters to drag Calais' inert corpse—from the hut down to the pond, crossing the road. Anne Marie rubbed the back of her hand. Hégésippe Bray could not have dragged the body that far. Too old and arthritic. If he had killed Raymond Calais, he must have done it near the pond.

Ripples ran across the surface. Anne Marie had taken off her moccasins and the mud was cool between her toes. She was lost in thought for a few moments, then she shrugged and returned to the Honda.

Hégésippe Bray and Raymond Calais must have met by chance. Bray hunting birds and suddenly the white man before him. After all those years—large, white, sweating and without a gun. Defenseless.

The report from the gendarmerie had been precise. They had dredged the pond, they had scoured the ground—but had found no other spent cartridges. As for footprints, the ground had been too wet to preserve anything. For three days it had not stopped raining. By the time the first gendarmes had arrived, the ground had been trampled over.

Anne Marie stopped.

She had seen something out of the corner of her eye. A moving man.

He was at the top of the hill, a thin silhouette a few meters from Bray's hut. Caught against the reddening evening sky, walking between the cement hut and the Sainte Marthe villa, the silhouette carried a rifle, open at the breech.

Long legs that moved slowly.

Anne Marie ran back to the Honda, let out the clutch and the car jumped forward onto the road. And stalled.

She cursed.

A yellow post van came round the corner at speed and braked fast, almost going into a skid. Beneath his cap, the postman looked at Anne Marie in surprise. He just managed to avoid the Honda.

She put the Honda into first gear, crossed the road and went up the narrow cart track to the Calais villa. An old track—two lines almost lost beneath the grass and pitted with stones. The car bumped mercilessly on its springs, and twice the exhaust pipe hit the ground.

On either side of the track, there was hibiscus and oleander, forming a low hedge. She pulled on the steering wheel and came to a halt outside the deserted villa on the sloping lawn. The grass was short and had recently been mown. She banged noisily on the horn and then got out of the car.

The man was in a field that was staked off by a series of wooden posts and two strands of barbed wire. He was calling to the goats that seemed reluctant to give up their meal—grass that was less green than the lawn.

He wore large boots with lace holes but no laces. The tongues of his boots flapped against the ankles. The man had a strange walk, as if afraid to set his heels firmly against the ground. One hand held the rifle. In the other, he held several ropes to which the goats were tethered.

"I want to talk with you," Anne Marie shouted against the wind.

If the man heard her, he gave no sign. He did not turn, but continued walking downhill, past a rusting cauldron.

"I am from the police."

She saw the head nod, and the man lifted the rifle in a sign of recognition. He disappeared over the brow of the hill. The goats bleated, and the man reassured them with animal-like sounds. His voice was carried by the wind.

Soon the sun would be setting. The blue of the sky was washed with red.

Anne Marie stepped round the car and went up the concrete steps that led to the villa. A squat building, a flat roof and a large, iron door that had not been open in months. The villa was surrounded by a broad, open veranda made of concrete. Grass had begun to grow along the winding cracks of the surface.

Anne Marie crossed the veranda and peered through the grimy glass of the closed shutters. The wall was still warm with retained heat. The wind whistled along the isolated electricity cable that sagged from successive poles. The wind also pulled at her hair, blowing strands into her eyes.

Through the glass, she could see the interior was dingy. Armchairs of wood, a dusty table, a crucifix on the far wall and a large dresser, with a dreary parade of bottles of rum and liquor. An ancient television cabinet.

"Madame?"

Anne Marie swung round.

A thin nose, dark matte skin, narrow lips and a broad forehead. In a different context, he might have been a teacher or a priest. He was wearing a battered hat, made of soiled cloth, with several haloes of sweat along the band and a large brim that partly hid his eyes. Long, scraggy hair, streaked a greasy black and grey, lay upon the shoulders of a khaki shirt. Thin chest and long, slender arms.

"Who are you?"

He raised his head slightly. A smile ran along the protruding, toothless jaw. Glinting dark eyes.

"Who are you?" Anne Marie asked again. She stepped back.

In one hand, dangling loosely at his side, was a long machete—the type of machete for cutting cane. The edge had been sharpened to a scarred silver.

25
Tetanus

"I live here."

"This is Monsieur Calais' villa."

An affirmative nod. "I work for him."

"Calais is dead."

The smile disappeared but the narrow head continued to nod. "Dead," he repeated sadly.

An idiot. Anne Marie glanced at the machete.

As suddenly as it had disappeared, the smile returned. He shrugged lopsidedly. "I work here."

"Work?"

"I look after the animals. The goats that belong to Monsieur Calais. And several cows. And chickens. And the pig. I have to feed them." Beneath the sagging brim the eyes clouded. "I'm going to lose my job? She won't let me keep my job?"

"Who?"

The odor of rum was heavy on his breath. "She can't get rid of me, you know."

"Who?"

He moved toward Anne Marie. "I've always worked here—Madame Calais knows that."

"I never said Madame Calais wanted to get rid of you." Anne Marie's eyes remained on the machete.

The tip of the blade tapped against the cement. "A thousand francs—even the Haitians ask for more. A thousand francs a month—it's not a lot to ask for." The machete went from one hand to the other. Then all grievance disappeared and he held out his hand. "My name is Michel."

"Madame Laveaud, juge d'instruction."

Michel looked at her admiringly. They shook hands.

"Would you like an avocado pear?"

Anne Marie remarked, "A thousand francs is certainly not a lot of money."

"A thousand francs and a place to sleep—next to the pig." His skin was unwrinkled and the texture smooth, though he was well into middle age. His features were Indian. "I work for it. I look after the animals." He scratched his chin with the hand that held the machete. "And the vegetables. Monsieur Calais refuses to pay for any insecticide and then tells me off when the tomatoes are shriveled and green."

"You could go elsewhere. You'd earn more—a lot more."

"No." He pointed to the distant Souffrière, now a darkening line against the angry red sky. "My woman is over there." In a conspiratorial whisper he added, "In Basse-Terre."

"Go and live with her."

"I can't."

The evening wind rustled through the leaves of the tamarind tree. "Why not?"

"They're jealous."

Anne Marie noticed that he had long eyelashes.

"Look," he said, with sudden excitement, "look." He rolled up the bottom of his trousers. He did not crouch but bent over awkwardly to show protuberant veins that pushed against the dusty skin of his foot. The tongue of his boot lolled over the edge of the laceless eyelets. He pushed the point of the machete against the skin.

"Don't do that."

He laughed happily. "It doesn't hurt."

"Please." Anne Marie held his wrist—thin and strong. "You can catch tetanus."

"In my legs." He rolled up the other trouser leg and tried to prod at the foot with the machete.

Anne Marie tightened her grip.

There was pride in his voice. "My feet are numb."

"You must see a doctor."

"A curse. Because of the women." Michel nodded. "All the women."

Anne Marie shivered. "In the hospital they will be able to give you blood tests. They'll give you x-rays."

"I'm not insured."

"You can still go to a hospital."

He shook his head, grinning broadly. "Because of a curse. That's what the man told me."

"What man?"

"He knows about these things—he's studied them. A Haitian. He knows how to cast curses—and how to get rid of them." The Indian sighed. "Somebody hates me." Then he laughed, putting a hand to his open mouth. "They hate me because I enjoy the women too much. Somebody's jealous—some husband who's growing horns like a goat." As an afterthought, he added, "Pretty women—Métis and Negroes and," he raised his eyes, "white women."

"You must see a doctor."

He held out his arm—lines of muscle and vein stood out beneath the skin. "Numb." His fingers opened and closed. "Sometimes I can't even hold the knife. It jumps from my hand—like a devil."

"I can get you money for the doctor."

"I went to the hospital and there was a white doctor. He was white like you." Michel nodded. "He took my blood with a needle, and I went again the next day, and he gave me pills. They were red."

"Did they work?"

He shook his head. "I wanted the green pills." His face lit up. "You can get the green pills for me?"

"I'll see what I can do. First you must answer some questions, Michel."

The Indian frowned and moved away from her. He walked awkwardly, the weight of his body on his toes.

"Some questions about Hégésippe Bray."

"He's not here." Michel approached the concrete steps of the veranda. "While he's away, I look after his goats."

Anne Marie followed him down the steps, smelling the odor of rum, unwashed clothes and rancid sweat. "Where does Bray live?"

"He is in Pointe-à-Pitre now."

"He sleeps over there, doesn't he? In the hut?"

Together they moved toward the concrete hut; it stood on the ridge but was lower than the villa and at a distance of about two hundred meters. A grass path led toward the closed, wooden door. The outside walls had been painted white but were now covered with a series of black patches, rain stains and lichen.

Michel tapped the ground with the machete. The grass was already damp with evening dew.

"Does Hégésippe Bray ever go into Monsieur Calais' villa?"

"They say he's not coming back."

Anne Marie frowned. "Why not?"

"They say that Bray's going to die in prison."

"Does he ever go to the villa?"

A nod. "To get water. There is a cistern at the back."

The hut was built on a cement foundation; the surface was chipped and, in parts, overgrown by grass. Near one wall stood a large oil drum, its surface scarred by rust. Beyond it, the regular neatness of vegetable beds. A single plant of lady's finger was pointing to the red sky.

Michel pulled the bar that closed the door and they stepped inside. A single room, three meters by six. It was dark and the air was still warm.

Michel opened the blinds and the evening light entered the somber space; a couple of lizards darted across the ceiling and hid behind the cement rafter. Flakes of blue paint lay on the floor. The mattress was placed by the wall.

"No bed?"

Michel shrugged "The man spent years in prison." He had left the machete outside.

A portable gas stove, the paint rusting, a few utensils, a plastic plate, and some cutlery had been neatly arranged on an open sheet of newspaper. Beside the mattress, there was a jar containing a half-burned candle. A crucifix, a bottle of hair oil, and a photograph in a tortoiseshell frame.

Anne Marie picked up the photograph, wondering why it had been left by the gendarmes. With it in her hand, Anne Marie approached the window.

The photograph showed a woman wearing traditional matador—the madras, lace and finery of the national costume. Three tips rose like feathers from the back of the head. The woman looked at the camera diffidently. A Creole woman with an intelligent face, unafraid of the passage of time. Anne Marie turned the frame over and slipped the photograph out. Cockroach eggs tumbled into her palm.

Lucien le Marc, photographe. Fort-de-France, Mque.

Underneath in fading copperplate, written in pencil: "*A mon petit Hégésippe . . . celle qui t'aime toujours.*"

Michel said, "He'll never come back."

At the bottom, scrawled in a different hand, "*Je suis Hégésippe Bray.*"

Anne Marie slipped the photograph into her handbag, then turned to look at the unadorned walls. The musty odor of mildew. A colorless lizard scurried across the floor.

Michel was standing by the window.

"Where did he keep his gun, Michel?"

He shrugged. "I've only been here once." He rubbed his unshaven shin. "Over there, perhaps."

A pile of three cartons, the cardboard edges torn, that had once contained cans of vegetable oil, stood by one wall. Anne Marie rummaged through them. One contained folded newspapers. Another contained a couple of pairs of trousers and some tatty pajamas—inscribed in indelible ink, *Clinique N.D. de Lorette, Cayenne.* The box gave off a strong smell of mothballs. The third box was empty except for a packet of seeds. The packet had been opened, the torn top rolled back to prevent the seeds from spilling. Florida watermelon.

"He's a good gardener?" Anne Marie asked.

"He's an old man."

"You two are friends?"

Michel made a laughing sound. In the dingy light, his upper teeth seemed to move, pushing against his lip. "Bray doesn't talk with anybody, certainly not to an Indian. He used to go drinking." Michel made a gesture toward the other side of the valley. "Not now. He doesn't want to talk with anybody."

"How does he spend his time?"

"In the garden. Sometimes he sits outside." Michel gestured to the door. "Wave to him and he doesn't see you. He just sits there."

"His sight is going?"

The Indian shook his head and laughed. "I've seen him kill a pigeon or a blackbird at thirty meters. The eye of a mongoose."

26

Coconut

They stepped out into the fresh air. Michel slid the wooden door back into place.

"You don't like him?"

"Michel doesn't dislike anybody." He picked up the machete where it was propped against the wall. "That old man doesn't like to talk."

"Even with visitors?"

"Are you thirsty?" Without waiting for a reply, Michel walked away in his strange, stiff-legged gait, while the tip of the machete tapped against the side of his leg.

"He has visitors sometimes." Anne Marie caught up with him. "His half sister—and her son. You've seen them, Michel?"

"The fat old woman?"

"You've seen her?"

"Michel minds his own business."

"Did you see her the day Calais was killed? Did you see her on Sunday?"

They reached a small orchard at the back of the villa.

Michel took a ladder and set it against a tree. He climbed the ladder, then with one blow of the knife, he sliced the gnarled stem of a bunch of coconuts. The coconuts slithered downward through the branches, still attached together, and fell onto the grass.

He came down the ladder and, crouching on his heels, the frayed cuffs of his trousers rising away from his boots to reveal deformed ankles, he said, "Good." Michel grinned and sliced the top of a coconut with the ease of a man slicing a boiled egg at the breakfast table. A colorless liquid slipped over the rim.

Michel held the coconut out for Anne Marie. "Drink."

The juice was sweet and refreshing. She tipped her head backward, and holding the green coconut between her hands, she let the juice run into her mouth. A few drops ran down her chin.

Michel cut another coconut for himself. Then he took a bottle from his pocket. He cast away some of the coconut milk and poured liquid from the bottle into the coconut. "Better," he said with conviction and gave her a wolfish grin.

"You were here the day that Calais was murdered?"

He wiped his lips, drank and softly belched. "I live here." He nodded toward a wooden shack on the far side of the orchard. "I'm always here."

"You saw Bray that day?"

He took another swig. "Coconut milk's good for a man, particularly at my age."

"You saw Hégésippe Bray?"

"Good for a woman, too." He held out the bottle of rum and grinned. "Good for her mother's milk." Michel glanced toward her breasts and nodded encouragingly.

"Who came to see Hégésippe Bray on Sunday?"

"Are you from the police?"

"I am a judge."

"Michel doesn't poke his nose into other people's business."

"What did Bray do last Sunday?"

"Michel told everything to the white men."

"Everything?"

A neat stroke of the machete and he sliced the coconut into two halves. With a chip of hard fiber, he began scraping at the soft pulp. His eyes were hidden by the brim of the hat. "Michel saw nothing."

"You heard the sound of a gun?"

Silence.

"Michel, did you hear Hégésippe Bray's gun?"

"He killed a bird."

"When?"

"A blackbird."

"When?"

"He often shoots at the pigeons and the blackbirds. They eat his seeds."

"When?"

"I don't remember."

"Nothing else?"

"There were shots. But I didn't give up what I was doing just to go and look. I'm a busy man. Michel doesn't interfere into other people's business."

"What were you doing on Sunday?"

"You will get me the green pills, won't you?"

"Where were you on Sunday?"

"Working."

"All day?"

Michel nodded and the long hair moved on his shoulders.

"But it was Sunday."

"Monsieur Calais expects me to work."

"There were no visitors?"

The orchard was at the back of the villa, and they were out of the wind. Anne Marie caught the warm odor of the pigsty. Dusk became night; the breadfruit and mango trees stood silent.

"I saw no visitors." Michel stood up.

"Hégésippe Bray's not the only person to hate Calais." Anne Marie turned and walked out of the garden, her shoes distant, autonomous animals lost in the thick grass.

The Indian walked beside her, wiping his lips and his wide grin now parallel with the rim of the old hat. "Monsieur Calais's a bastard."

The moon was rising above the hill on the far side of the valley. A toad, alerted by Anne Marie's footfall, hopped nervously away. "Monsieur Calais deserved to die."

27

Madame Calais

Madame Calais was leaning forward, her hand on Anne Marie's shoulder. "Sorry to have kept you waiting."

Anne Marie must have dozed off.

"Marcia said you wish to speak with me."

Anne Marie came awake with a start and pushed herself out of the armchair. She got to her feet.

The two women shook hands. Madame Calais' hand was thin, and Anne Marie felt the angular bones of her knuckles.

"It was about your husband."

"Of course." Madame Calais was wearing a black dress and black shoes. A gold necklace lay on the skin of her neck.

"Madame Laveaud. I am the juge d'instruction."

"I was about to have tea. Or perhaps you would care for something stronger." With an outstretched arm, Madame Calais invited Anne Marie to follow her into the main part of the house. They went down the steps, and Anne Marie found herself in a long corridor. The smell of wax polish, the distant sound of frogs.

"I always have tea at this time. The heat of the day's over and it is time to relax. Sometimes, with my husband, I take. . . ." She corrected herself, "Sometimes we had cocktails but really I prefer tea. Darjeeling or lapsang. I have it sent specially from London. Fortnum and Mason's. Do you know that shop? Very good." She gave a little laugh. "When it comes to tea, I am afraid I am a bit of a snob. Aren't I, Marcia?"

The maid who was walking silently behind them, said, "Yes, madame."

They stepped out onto a balcony. Wooden balustrades protected it from the garden. There was a lamp and several low chairs about a white table.

"Please sit down."

A dog, probably a Labrador, was curled on the floor. He looked up at Anne Marie with melancholy eyes.

Madame Calais tapped the animal's broad head. "We call him Forty Percent."

Anne Marie sat down opposite her. "A strange name."

"All civil servants in Guadeloupe receive an additional forty percent weighting to their salaries."

"Life can be very expensive."

"The *métropolitains* working for the government have the expense of coming out to Guadeloupe, of equipping a new home. But for the local civil servants, the forty percent is an unnecessary expense. For the postman and the primary school teacher—what need do they have of an inflated salary?" She shrugged. "France is a big, bountiful bosom, full of milk. And France continues to pay. So now you've got an island of people who don't do anything. But they get fat salaries for sitting in their offices." She nudged the dog with her foot. "Like him—fat and lazy. Sleep all day and then expect to be fed. And only the very best will do." Madame Calais turned to Marcia who stood waiting, neat with her feet together and her hands behind her back. "A nice pot of tea, chérie. And perhaps there are some biscuits."

"Yes, madame." Marcia hurried away on her prim legs.

Madame Calais smoothed the folds of her black dress over her knees. Then, leaning forward, she whispered, "From Saint Lucia. They work better and they're honest. The people from Guadeloupe nowadays—they've all become thieves."

"Your husband disapproved of the immigrants."

She nodded. "The Dominicans—many are marijuana addicts. But the people from Saint Lucia—of course Raymond had nothing against them. Good workers. They don't ask for exorbitant rates, and like the Haitians, they're reliable."

There were bright lights at the far end of the garden, a hedge of oleander and a wire fence. Anne Marie could hear—beyond the relentless threnody of the frogs—the rhythmic bounce of a tennis ball as it hit a racket. Through the hedge, she saw a man and a woman, their white clothes standing out against the deep red surface of the illuminated court.

Madame Calais followed her glance. "My son, Armand." There was the dull thud of the tennis ball and then light, girlish laughter. "And his wife. Armand, I am quite sure, would love to meet you." The light from the lamp threw the older woman's face into shadow and gave her deep, dark eyes. "Please don't think I hate all civil servants. It's just that sometimes I have the impression it's the civil servants with their money who've spoiled this département. Guadeloupe, you know, used to be so lovely. So innocent."

She fell silent.

The scent of mahogany wafted from the garden. The irregular rhythm of tennis balls being struck.

"Nearly half past six." Madame Calais glanced at her gold watch. "I do love this time of day. For Raymond, it was sacrosanct. He'd always make an effort to get home by nightfall." A smile. "A time when we could be together and talk. For a moment, when I heard your car in the driveway. . . ." She shrugged and looked away.

"I'm sorry."

After some time, Marcia came back carrying a tray and a service of bone china.

"Raymond was so alive, so dynamic."

Marcia poured the tea from a willow pattern pot and handed a matching cup to Anne Marie.

"So hard to believe Raymond's never coming back. Dead and gone for good now. My husband was always doing something.

Even when he was away in Martinique or in Paris and I was here alone, I could feel his presence. It was something physical. We formed a happy couple. You know, when a man and a woman've been together for so many years, certain things. . . ." She raised her hands and let the sentence hang unfinished.

Marcia placed the pot on the low table and disappeared in silence.

"Afternoon tea," Madame Calais said, using the English words, "It was a rite. Me with my pot of tea and my saccharine tablets. An irony, isn't it, that we could own so much sugar and I can't allow myself a spoonful." She tapped her waist. "I have my figure—or what's left of it—to think about. Raymond said I was quite mad. Drank more punch than was perhaps good for him. But I always think a man's not a man unless he has . . . well, a big body. I don't say corpulent but. . . ." She hesitated. "At least substantial." She held her cup with the small finger pointing into the air. "A biscuit, mademoiselle?"

"I must watch my line, too."

"But you are absolutely lovely as you are. Lovely eyes. And such a nice smile. Like my daughter-in-law."

Anne Marie smiled and took a biscuit.

"Shortbread," Madame Calais said. "If I love afternoon tea, it is the English in me."

The biscuit was stale. "You're English?"

Madame Calais took a sip of tea. "Part French, part English, part everything. A lot of us are. It goes back to the Revolution."

"The French Revolution?"

"I grew up in Barbados. And I speak French because I had a French nanny. My family has close contacts with all the cousins and uncles who live in the various islands of the Caribbean. A lot of them returned to Guadeloupe after the French Revolution. When I was a child, in the days before there was all this flying, I used to come up to Guadeloupe with my sister. We used to stay with cousins who had a small coffee plantation near Basse-Terre. In the hills. In those days, the people were very simple and very good. I'm talking about before the war. People were so kind. There was none of this racial hostility. I'm afraid we imported that from the Americans—they are such racists, the Americans. The people here, they didn't have much, but they were satisfied with their lot in life. More tea?"

Anne Marie shook her head.

"The métropolitains here think that all the local whites are terrible, that we treat the blacks like dirt. It is not true, you know. Not now—things have changed. Thirty, forty years ago, perhaps. To be quite honest, I never really liked the Békés when I first came here. A very closed circle and I was shocked by the way they—my own relatives—treated their servants. In Barbados—and being part French—I'd always liked to think the French were a bit better than the English. The English have given tea to the world—and we're all a lot better for it. But the French have given their marvelous civilization. And human rights."

Anne Marie nodded.

"You have got to understand the Békés—and to do that, you must understand psychology." She lowered her voice to a conspiratorial whisper. "Treat the local people as equals—and they don't like it. They want you—that's the point—they want you to be white, and they want you to be in a position of authority. Because they don't want to make decisions for themselves, they're afraid. Now there's all this wonderful talk about equality—and really, the people of Guadeloupe don't want that at all. The people from France—not you, but the civil servants, the people who come for a couple of years to make a pile of money—they think they understand everything, and they criticize. They criticize the Békés, and they say we despise the blacks. It's just not true. We're all God's children, aren't we? It's not the color of our skin that's going to change anything—certainly not in His eyes. Try to understand. We have different traditions—and all this talk of equality is very dangerous."

Anne Marie finished her tea.

"The worst are the mulattos. They know everything. They think they're ready. They've studied and they've been educated—but of course, they're still African. Despite their nice clothes and the way they try to ape us."

"I find that I can't distinguish between skin colors."

"It was the mulattos who killed my husband."

"The mulattos killed Raymond Calais?"

"They're jealous, that's what they are, these mulatto revolutionaries." She stopped. "They killed him," Madame Calais repeated and then she started to cry. The skin of her face began to crumple, bright tears ballooned from the corners of her eyes. She put down the cup and saucer and took a handkerchief from where she had tucked it under her sleeve. The crying grew noisier.

Forty Percent raised his head.

28

Pol Pot

The Labrador followed her and sniffed at her feet.

Anne Marie looked out into the night. The air was cool.

"I'm sorry."

Anne Marie turned.

"I'm sorry—but as you see, after forty years together. . . ." Again, Madame Calais began to tremble. "Raymond was so alive."

"Why do you accuse the MANG?" Anne Marie asked gently. "No one has claimed responsibility for his murder."

There was pain in her eyes, and for the first time, Anne Marie noticed the scars of plastic surgery running behind her ear. "They're scared—scared they'll get caught."

"Normally MANG claims its involvement."

With the handkerchief she wiped at the damp tracks on her cheeks. "The MANG hated everything Raymond Calais stood for." Madame Calais attempted a smile. "You mustn't believe everything you hear about my husband. There are a lot of people who were jealous of him—and who wanted to harm him. They say cruel things and many lies. I know my husband and I know. . . ." She faltered. "I loved him for forty years, and I know what he was really like. A good man—a very good man."

Anne Marie's hand had started to itch. "Why would MANG want to kill your husband?"

The short lines about the mouth hardened. "Raymond loved France—that's why."

"I don't understand."

"The Calais family's been involved in cane sugar ever since the first plants were brought from India, more than three hundred years ago. Sugar was in Raymond's blood—but he realized it was now a thing of the past. Successive governments have seen to that—by increasing labor costs, by insisting upon social security for the cane cutters and all the crippling expenses—while at the same time favoring cheap sugar from the Ivory Coast and the other countries in Africa. Raymond felt he had to fight his battle; that's why he had to go into politics. Raymond had the courage of his convictions. He saw sugar was dying—this island's only real source of wealth—and he had to speak out. How is this département supposed to stay alive? Without sugar there can be no alternative. We need France. But the mulattos. . . ." She shrugged. "The independence people—what do they care about the future? They're all Marxists, aren't they? They seek power for themselves—they want to see Guadeloupe go the way of Cambodia—or Cuba—so that they can play at being Fidel Castro, smoking cigars and talking politics while the rest of the people slave and starve." She lifted the lid and peered into the teapot. "It was for this island, it was for these people, that Raymond went into politics. White, black, Indian—my husband saw the need to protect them all from the so-called educated classes. Believe me, mademoiselle. . . ."

"Madame," Anne Marie corrected her.

"Independence," Madame Calais snorted. "That's what they want, the Marxists—but independence from France will bring nothing but poverty." A bright smile. "You don't wear a ring. You look so young to be married."

Anne Marie held out her hand, "I've got an allergy—the ring only seems to make it worse." She added, "I've been married for nearly eight years."

"You must see a doctor—you must see Dr. Lebon. He's very

good." She passed a hand over the waves of her tinted hair. "Raymond had none of the viciousness of the—of the MANG people."

"Where did he get his money from?"

"I beg your pardon?"

"Did your husband enter politics for financial reasons?"

Madame Calais folded her arms before answering. "It cost him money. It didn't bring him any money."

"Your husband maintained he was not a wealthy man. Yet he owned racing horses."

"Madame le juge, the Calais family's been here for three hundred years—the Calais family's not poor."

"Sugar's a dying industry."

"My husband owned a lot of land."

"Some of which he sold off."

"Better than letting it lie unused." Madame Calais no longer smiled. "The soil is not always fertile."

"And the land that Hégésippe Bray has claimed?"

The two women looked at each other. Madame Calais smoothed the material of her dress. "I should prefer to talk about this at another time."

"You knew Hégésippe Bray before he was arrested and sent to the penal colony in Cayenne?"

"Of course." She raised her hands. "He used to work on the estate. He was very close to my father-in-law."

"You know why he was sent away?"

"We all loved Hégésippe Bray."

"Why did they send him to Cayenne?"

"He murdered his wife. It was very sad. A good man, a man of his word. A different generation."

"Why did he murder his wife?"

"She was a witch."

"You went to the trial?"

She shook her head. "I had just got married, and Raymond felt very protective toward me. He didn't want me upset."

"Hégésippe Bray's now in prison, accused of murder," Anne

Marie said, shutting from her mind the blue eyes and the tongue lolling from the hanged man's mouth. "The murder of your husband. I'm sure you'll understand why I'm here, why I have to ask these questions."

"Hégésippe Bray never killed Raymond."

"The gendarmerie at Sainte-Anne believe there's a strong case against him."

Madame Calais gave a brave smile and stood up. "With all this stupid crying, I must look a wreck." She hurried from the veranda, leaving Anne Marie and the lingering perfume of lavender water.

The dog had fallen asleep against Anne Marie's leg.

29

United States

Madame Calais had put on bright lipstick, and she was now accompanied by a man.

The man said, "Please remain seated." He shook hands with Anne Marie. He smelled of fresh soap and his face was still flushed with physical effort.

"Armand now runs the estate. My son studied management in the United States."

"Mother wanted me to go to England." He grinned. "But Florida is nearer, and the weather is nicer." He was good-looking. There was something familiar about the face, which surprised Anne Marie. He had the same, strong jaw that she had seen in the photographs of Raymond Calais—and he had his mother's bright eyes. But there was something else, something elusive that she recognized as being familiar, and she warmed to it. He had the sallow skin of the white man in the tropics. As he smiled, bright teeth peeked from the edge of his lips.

He sat down on the arm of his mother's chair.

"A few questions that I need to ask." Anne Marie smiled briefly. "Then I can be out of your way. Madame Calais, your husband had several men working for him—bodyguards of a sort, I believe."

Madame Calais laughed. "The only people who worked for my husband were the people here on the estate. The cutters, the laborers, and Marcia, our maid." She smiled ruefully. "Pointe-à-Pitre is not Chicago."

"He was often accompanied by several men. Large, powerful men."

"His life was in danger. Not bodyguards, mademoiselle, but friends who wanted to pay back all the favors he'd done them. They looked after him."

"Your husband was afraid of being attacked?"

"They got him in the end, didn't they? MANG hated my husband and wanted him out of the way. They'd tried to kill him before."

"But not in the same way."

"They killed my husband, and believe me, this won't be their last act of terrorism. They won't stop the killing—my God, how I wish France would wake up to her responsibilities and do something. These people will turn the poor département into a bloodbath."

Armand Calais spoke calmly. "MANG want power and won't stop until they've got it."

His mother patted his hand where it lay on her shoulder.

"Didn't Hégésippe Bray hold a grudge against Raymond Calais?"

Armand smiled and said, "Perhaps at the beginning when he returned from French Guyana. And understandably. There can be no doubt Papa'd taken some of Bray's land—but how was he to know Hégésippe Bray was still alive? Forty years is a long time."

"Especially in French Guyana."

"Papa never sent him there." Armand's eyes flashed. "As for the land, it was all a misunderstanding. Bray had no family to look after it, and during the war, land was at a premium."

"And his half sister, Madame Suez-Panama?"

"She was in France, and after the war, she never asked for the land."

"Until Hégésippe Bray's return from prison?"

Madame Calais said, "My husband agreed to hand it back—all of it."

"That's not what Bray thinks."

"That poor old man doesn't always understand. When he came back after all those years, Raymond and I were overjoyed to see him—even if he was only the shadow of his former self." Madame Calais shrugged. "I suppose we're all old now. Except Raymond—and he's dead."

"Bray came to see you?"

"Madame Suez-Panama and her son—he teaches at the university—came to see my husband, and immediately Raymond agreed to give the hut and the fields to the old man." She gestured in the general direction of the far side of the valley.

"Bray's entitled to more than that."

"He's going to get it all."

"How many hectares?"

"All the land that belongs to him by law. Eight, ten." She shrugged. "Our lawyer has been looking into the problem."

"It will be returned to Hégésippe Bray?"

"Of course. Hégésippe Bray knows that. He doesn't hate my husband—there's no reason."

"You've been very helpful." Anne Marie stood up. "I'm only surprised the gendarmerie didn't make these enquiries before deciding to bring Hégésippe Bray in."

Madame Calais smiled. "Civil servants. Forty percent and the sunshine."

Sleepily, the dog got to his feet and raised his head to look at Armand.

Anne Marie picked up her bag, and thanked Madame Calais for the tea.

The woman smiled. *Adan on dot soley!*"

Anne Marie frowned as she returned the smile.

"Until next time. It was so nice meeting you, mademoiselle."

"Until we meet under another sun," Armand Callais whispered as he accompanied Anne Marie out of the house. "Another day."

30
Machete

The wind tugged at her skirt.

"I dropped in on the estate on my way here," Anne Marie said, blinking, dazzled by the sudden brightness of the flood lamps. She shielded her eyes with her hand. "I met the old Indian with the long hair."

"Michel?" Armand Calais accompanied her across the gravel. "Another alcoholic."

"He works for you?"

"He lives on the estate."

"I'm afraid there may be something seriously wrong with his arteries."

Armand Calais laughed, and the bright garden lights were reflected on his even teeth. His face appeared frightening in that brief moment—there was something feral. "Michel's been complaining about his legs for years."

"He should see a doctor."

"Goodness knows how many times we've paid for him to go to the doctor. He just takes the money, goes to see some voodoo quack, and then spends all the rest on tafia."

"Get him insured."

"He doesn't want insurance."

"He works for you, doesn't he?"

"Never wanted to be a declared worker. For some reason Michel thinks it would be demeaning for him."

"That's against the law."

"Tell him that, madame le juge. Nothing we'd like more than to get rid of him. We don't need the garden—it's cheaper to buy the vegetables in the supermarket. As for the animals, they're more bother than they're worth." A gesture of impatience. "Michel just refuses to go. All because my father was too generous. Now Michel is there, quarrelling with everyone, and he's going to stay there until his last breath."

Armand Calais opened the car door for her.

"Thank you."

"If there are any other questions, don't hesitate to contact me. You're nothing like my idea of a juge d'instruction."

"Should I feel flattered?" Before he could answer, Anne Marie continued, "There's a question that I didn't really want to ask your mother." Anne Marie was embarrassed. "According to reliable sources, your father. . . ."

"Yes?"

"Monsieur Calais had the reputation of being very fond of the company of women."

He put his head back and laughed. "Who isn't?" This time, his mirth appeared genuine.

"The information's correct?"

"I certainly hope so."

"And your mother—she didn't object?"

"The West Indies, madame le juge."

"What about the West Indies?"

"You're in the Caribbean." The smile was now attractive. "Where men are men. White, black, mulatto—under the skin, we're all the same animal." He hesitated. "That reputation—Papa acquired it when he was still a young man."

"Your mother never objected?"

"Probably never knew."

Anne Marie said coldly, "You really believe that?"

"Perhaps she preferred not to know. Most women believe what suits them." Armand Calais shrugged. "He was a good father. And we all loved him."

"I see."

"Twenty, thirty years ago. When Papa was still relatively young and a bit thinner, with more hair on his head." He shook his head. "In more recent years, I think Papa had other interests that took the place of women."

"Men calm down with age?"

"I hope not."

"What other interests did your father have?"

"Politics—the future of Guadeloupe." He closed the car door. "The future of Sainte Marthe." His hand remained on the window frame. With the bright garden lamps behind him, Armand Calais' face was now in the shadow, and Anne Marie had the strange feeling of having met him somewhere before. A different place, a different time. "Now I have a question for you, madame le juge."

"Yes?"

"You spoke with Michel?"

She nodded.

"Michel didn't get irritable?"

"I don't think I did anything to offend him."

"He didn't find some reason to quarrel?"

She shook her head. "He was very polite."

"Michel doesn't like outsiders. Unless they're Indians like him."

"He even cut down a coconut for me."

"You must be careful." He turned slightly, and she saw the gleam in Armand Calais' eye. "Michel has a temper."

"Not the impression I got."

"A quick temper and a quick machete."

Anne Marie leaned forward and switched on the engine.

"Michel once took the machete to Hégésippe Bray, you know."

31
Shadow

"Michel!"

The breeze whistled through the coconut fronds and glowing night insects moved across the sky like planes with erratic lights.

"Michel!" Anne Marie left the headlamps on and stood by the car. The grass was damp, and the night dew fell on her instep. Clouds running in from the Atlantic hid the stars.

The rear lights of the Honda gave an eerie glow.

The shadow darted across the edge of her vision and Anne Marie shrieked. A fast moving shadow close to the ground. A shadow that disappeared into the darkness.

Instinctively she had put her hand to her throat, and another shadow came forward, zigzagging frantically, clinging to the ground.

Anne Marie screamed again and then recognized a hen as it darted into the flood of light from the headlamps. It moved noisily, flapping its wings, and when Anne Marie shouted, it flew off toward the oleander and the orange trees.

She took a flashlight from the car.

The breeze played in her hair. Her heart was thumping, her forehead damp with cold perspiration.

Anne Marie dropped her handbag and shrieked again as another chicken, fluttering, flapping and clucking, moved between her legs. It banged in headlong flight against the side of the car and disappeared into the night.

Anne Marie stood quite still and waited for her heartbeat to slow down.

"At night," she told herself, her voice still trembling, "chickens sleep."

Moving stealthily, the flashlight casting its circle of wan light, she went round the villa toward the orchard. She aimed the beam at Hégésippe Bray's hut.

The shutters were closed. The flaking paint on the door seemed undisturbed. She followed the outside veranda of the deserted villa. A toad jumped away.

She reached the orchard. There was the sound of banging.

An uneven sound: *bang, bang, bangbang.*

She held the flashlight down. The nape of her neck was chill.

The door of the chicken run was open; the wooden door banged in the wind. Anne Marie moved toward it, walking on the tips of her toes. She placed a hand on the doorjamb.

The warm smell of fowl came from the inside. She ran the light across the floor. Dry, dusty, a few pellets of chicken feed. Shadows danced with the movement of the flashlight.

A hen was perched on a transversal bar. Caught in the beam, the yellow eye blinked with disturbed gravity. The white head jerked.

"Ssshhhhh."

The hen rose up on its wings, fluttered, and then settled down. The head was held at an inquisitive angle.

Anne Marie saw the gun first.

Then she saw the laceless boots.

The battered trouser leg, besmirched with dirt, had risen up to reveal the thin, dark ankles and the protruding veins.

32

Mother and Son

There was a note for Anne Marie on the dining room table. She picked it up and read it.

"Monsieur Trusso has fixed your appointment. Dr. Lebon, 16.40."

Béatrice was now asleep. She lay on her back on the settee with a cotton sheet over her shoulders. Her head was to one side of the cushion. A crucifix at her neck hung lopsidedly on its chain and nestled against the swell of her breast. She stirred in her sleep. Anne Marie kissed her lightly on the forehead, turned off the light and went upstairs.

Fabrice was on the upper bunk. He had kicked aside the sheet, and his thin body was naked except for a pair of cotton briefs. His pajamas lay crumpled and discarded on the moquette floor, in the midst of debris—plastic soldiers, ray guns, cars tipped on their sides.

He was staring at the ceiling.

"Awake?"

"Where have you been?"

"You should be sleeping, Fabrice."

"It's hot."

"Turn on the fan."

"It's noisy and keeps me awake." He added, reproach in his voice, "Where've you been?"

"Working."

"I don't like it when you come home late."

"I'm sorry." She kissed him. His skin was hot.

"You smell of doctors."

"I had to get a very drunk man to the dispensary in Sainte-Anne."

"Why?"

"He'd drunk more rhum agricole than was good for him."

Fabrice still refused to look at her. "Why do you stay out late?"

"I have a job to do."

"In France you always came home. I'm lonely when you're not here."

"There is Béatrice. You like her, don't you?"

A tear had formed in the corner of his eye. It swelled, then raced down the side of his cheek. "I want to go back to France."

"No beach in Paris—no warm sea that you can go to whenever you want."

"I want to go home, Maman. I don't like Guadeloupe."

"You're exaggerating, Fabrice. You've got your cousins to play with—Jean Yves and Christophe. And the girls."

"I am not exaggerating."

"We went to the beach yesterday. Didn't you enjoy that?"

"Papa didn't come."

"Papa's looking for a job."

"It's not like before." He turned to look at her. "What does exaggerate mean, Maman?"

"And you like Mamie. Your grandmother plays with you."

"Too bossy. She won't let me put my toys on the floor. Instead she wants me to sit at the table and draw."

"If you leave everything on the floor, you get in her way."

"I don't like my cousins, and I don't like Mamie. They are all too bossy."

"You're exaggerating again."

"I don't like women."

"I'm a woman."

"But you're my mother," Fabrice said and he threw his arms about her neck. Within a few seconds, the thin, precious body was racked with sobs.

33
Place de la Victoire

Anne Marie watched her son until he disappeared from sight, hidden by the milling children, by the thick baobab tree and the bicycle shed.

She crossed the square.

It was not yet eight o'clock. Anne Marie walked slowly, savoring the freshness of the hour. Beneath the shade of the royal palm trees in Place de la Victoire, old women were setting up their wares of caramel peanuts, jars of chewing gum and doughnuts. Traveler's trees, like giant fans, swayed with the light breeze. Beyond the trees, the immobile white hull of a cruise ship rode at anchor.

"Madame le juge."

She turned.

School children, eating sandwiches, walked across the square. She could not see beyond the satchels perched high on their backs.

He raised his arm and called her again.

Anne Marie stopped, and Marcel Suez-Panama approached unsteadily. "You didn't even tell me." His shoulders were hunched. His eyes were red and lines ran along the eyelids. "Why?" He wore the same clothes as last time, but now they were wrinkled as if he had spent the night sleeping in them. The shirt was grubby and the expensive shoes were covered with dust.

"About Hégésippe Bray?"

"You could have told me—the least you could do after killing him."

"Your uncle hanged himself."

"Why?" Suez-Panama asked. "Why did you have to kill him?"

"I'm sorry for what happened, Monsieur Suez-Panama." Anne Marie gave a slight shrug. "Regrettably your uncle decided to end his life—and so he hanged himself."

"You believe that?" Suez-Panama made an angry movement of his hand. "My uncle hanged himself?"

"I've asked for an enquiry."

"Hanged himself—just like Dupont."

"Who's Dupont?"

Cars had formed a jam outside the Renaissance cinema where an army bus had stopped to let the school children alight. The impatient drivers honked.

Suez-Panama bit his lip and swayed unsteadily on his feet. "It suited you, didn't it, to kill him?"

"Nobody's been killed."

"Then why's my uncle dead?"

"Who's Dupont?" Anne Marie asked again.

"The American who hanged himself because it suited you."

"Suited who?"

"The French—the colonizers." Suez-Panama pointed in the direction of the rue Gambetta. "You think you can do as you please."

"Your uncle hanged himself. I can assure you," she said, trying to make her voice calm and full of conviction.

"Hégésippe Bray survived French Guyana and the forty years of prison." He shook his head. "Just so you could murder him in a cell. In his own land."

"I wasn't in Pointe-à-Pitre when it happened." She resented the lameness in her voice. "Your uncle left a note. A note saying he wanted to die."

"Hégésippe Bray, who couldn't read or write? Hégésippe Bray, who'd never been to school—he left a note?"

Anne Marie realized her mouth had fallen open. "How can you be sure?"

"You'll have to do better than that, madame le juge."

She shook her head. "But I have some of his writing." She was aware of a stammer in her voice. "Something Hégésippe Bray wrote on the back of a photograph."

"What photograph?"

"Of his wife—the woman from Martinique."

"No. A witch would never have allowed a photograph. It could've then be used against her. A evil spell cast against her."

"It is your uncle's writing—I can assure you." Again she spoke convincingly.

"The only thing Hégésippe Bray could write was his signature."

"He confessed to having killed Raymond Calais. In the note he said he wanted to die."

The morning had lost its freshness. Anne Marie put her hand to her throat.

A sense of failure. Failure and futility.

The pink tongue and the bulging eyes.

The memory of the prison cell came flooding back, and without thinking, she turned and glanced toward the prison on the far side of Place de la Victoire, with its low white walls and its green paintwork. Suddenly Pointe-à-Pitre seemed a hostile place—an alien place.

"I thought I could trust you," he said, and sarcastically added, "Madame le juge."

"I'm sorry." Anne Marie turned away. She walked fast in the direction of the Palais de Justice.

His voice called after her, "You killed him."

Heads turned in Place de la Victoire.

"A murderer. Just like all the others. You're a murderer with blood on your hands."

34
FR3

An abandoned spoon, bent and left upside down, glinted dully on the third step of the Palais de Justice. Anne Marie, slightly out of breath, went up the steps and past the procureur de la République. He was surrounded by three men. Two wore ties and neat tropical suits. The third—a tall, gaunt black man with sunken cheeks—had a pale, white raincoat.

Politicians, Anne Marie thought. Only politicians from France wore jackets in this heat.

The procureur and the three men stepped out into the street. The procureur nodded, a look of wisdom on his plump face. His hands were in his pockets, and a small, unlit cigar was stuck in the corner of his mouth.

The man in the raincoat bent over. "A spoon." He shrugged, gave a small laugh, and threw the spoon into the gutter.

The procureur laughed, too. Turning his head, he caught sight of Anne Marie. There was no sign of recognition, but the smile slowly died on the large face.

Anne Marie entered the bustling cloister of the Palais de Justice.

It was cool out of the sun. A crowd of people was breaking up, caught in the inertia of indecision. A television team was in the process of stowing away their equipment. A white man and two technicians. One of the technicians—he wore earphones and a soiled FR3 T-shirt—was unscrewing a microphone from a long metal pole.

"What's happened?"

The desk of the *greffier général* was surrounded by people who chatted excitedly and pushed against the desk, each person demanding the attention of the old man, nearly deaf and only a year away from retirement.

Anne Marie elbowed her way toward the television team. "What's going on?"

"Another bomb."

"Where?"

The reporter had sandy hair and iron-rimmed glasses. "At the airport."

"Anybody hurt?"

"A man's been killed."

"Who?"

"A soldier. According to the procureur, a bomb disposal expert."

"The bomb went off?"

"A second bomb. Booby trapped, and the poor bastard had climbed up onto the wing to defuse it."

The ground floor of the Palais de Justice was a large, cloistered courtyard and in the middle there was a pool of water that was made an improbable deep blue by the square tiles. A few rocks were scattered about the pool—dark, volcanic rock that in places emerged from the water's surface. Several sea turtles glided through the shallow water or basked on the outcrop of rocks, indifferent to the bustle around them and the inexorable course of French justice.

"The wing of a plane?" Anne Marie asked.

"The Miami 727. The bomb went off almost immediately and the man took all of the blast. Made mincemeat of him. The plane's virtually undamaged." He grinned. "Good news for Air France. Bad news for the soldier."

"And the other bomb?"

"It blew a small hole in the fuselage."

"Anybody else hurt?"

"At four o'clock in the morning? There was nobody about."

Anne Marie pushed the hair back from her forehead. Her skin was damp. "A professional disposal expert?"

"Ask the procureur, madame."

"Why?"

"He might give you a different answer."

"What did he tell you?"

"That the man'd been trained."

"And you don't believe him?"

The newsman nudged at the metal frames of his glasses. "Ever since the first spate of bombings, there's been a request for experts. But this is the first death—and the dead man had been in Guadeloupe since '78." He shrugged. "Not my idea of a specialist."

Anne Marie felt tired.

She sat down on the warm concrete of the wall that surrounded the pond. A couple of turtles flapped noisily across the rock and fell into the water.

"I reached the airport just before five. The procureur was already there. They'd put up a cordon—I've never seen so many blue vans in Guadeloupe. They wouldn't let us through—but I got to speak with the procureur. Said he wanted to keep it quiet and that he'd appreciate our cooperation." The man shook his head unhappily. "They blow up part of Air France's prestige fleet, and the procureur wants a media black out. Then we heard the second explosion. A dull thud."

"Who planted the bomb?"

"You work here?"

"Madame Laveaud, juge d'instruction."

He gave her a smile and held out his hand, "Michel Gurion."

"You look so different." She smiled as they shook hands. "I've seen you on television."

"It's the legs."

"Legs?"

"People get used to seeing the talking head when I read the news. They don't ever suppose that I've got legs." He looked down. "Two legs."

"What did he say?" Anne Marie's back was in the sun, and she could feel its heat on her neck.

"Who?"

She gestured to the equipment that was being packed away. "You interviewed the procureur, didn't you?"

Michel Gurion nodded.

"And who are those Frenchmen with him?"

"Renseignements Généraux, I imagine." Gurion shrugged. "The procureur didn't feel he had to introduce us."

"What did the procureur say?"

"The same thing he always says in front of television cameras: the Republic is strong, that Guadeloupe's a French island, a place where people are free, and where French citizens wish to remain French. He spoke about outsiders."

"*Agents provocateurs?*"

"That sort of thing." A grin. "No tradition of political violence in Guadeloupe. People here aren't violent. They know they can solve their problems in a democratic context. Within the system."

"Perhaps he hasn't noticed the graffiti on the walls."

"He said something about the encroaching threat of international socialism in the Caribbean Basin."

"At least he admits there's terrorism—and it's politically motivated." Anne Marie rubbed at the back of her hand.

The man coiling the television cable now lifted the drum onto his shoulder and carried it out of the Palais de Justice. He wore espadrilles, and the worn rope soles flapped against the ground. Anne Marie saw the television van outside—there was the blue FR3 insignia painted on the side door. The man unloaded the cable and threw it casually into the back of the van.

"He said reinforcements would be coming from France."

Anne Marie turned. "What reinforcements?"

"More police. And officers of the Cour de Sûreté de l'Etat."

"Which means the investigation will be taken out of his hands."

"Probably what the procureur wants. He wants to take his distance before it is too late."

Anne Marie scratched her hand, then dipped it into the warm, blue water of the pond.

Gurion frowned. "Something wrong with your hand, madame le juge?"

"I don't know."

"I had that."

"What?"

"An allergy, I suppose."

"And?"

"And," Gurion shrugged, "it went away."

Trousseau came down the broad flight of stairs. He would not have noticed Anne Marie, but she called to him and he stopped. He put a hand to his eyes, to shield them against the light. He was wearing the same inelegant trousers, but he had changed his shoes for a brown pair with thick leather soles. The sound of his feet echoed along the cloister. As he walked, one finger gently rubbed the thin line of his moustache. He was carrying the portable typewriter.

"Got my message, madame le juge?" They shook hands. "About the appointment with Dr. Lebon?"

"I can't go—but it was very kind of you. Very thoughtful to think about me like that, Monsieur Trousseau."

"Merely doing my job, madame le juge—and trying to do it properly." The dark eyes were ready to take offense. "I've lived in France, you know."

"Monsieur Trousseau, I know you've lived in France. I also believe your wife's from France. But I'm afraid I can't go to the doctor's this afternoon because my father-in-law's coming in on the afternoon flight. The family expects me to be there at the airport to greet him. My husband only told me this morning."

"Simply trying to be of use."

"You know I'm extremely grateful for your consideration—and perhaps you could phone Dr. Lebon to postpone the appointment."

"How's your hand today?"

"I thought it was getting better." Anne Marie rubbed at the skin.

"I know an old Carib at Trois-Rivières."

Again she dipped her hand in the warm water. "I'd rather see a doctor."

Trousseau shrugged. "But you're free at half past two for the funeral?"

Anne Marie asked sharply, "What funeral?"

"The family's been informed they can take the body. Hégésippe Bray's funeral is at Morne-à-l'Eau."

"And the autopsy?"

"The procureur didn't think it was necessary."

"He's dead?" Gurion asked. "Hégésippe Bray? The old convict from French Guyana?"

Anne Marie nodded without looking at him. She could feel the anger swelling in her stomach, forming knots.

"How did he die?"

Her voice was impassive. "Hanged himself."

"The procureur has called in reinforcements." Trousseau smiled, ran a finger along his moustache. "Not that I mind. Then we can get back to our normal work of prostitutes, shoplifters, and juveniles." The dark eyes sparkled. "Can't say I like helicopters."

"He hanged himself?" Gurion asked.

Anne Marie nodded stiffly.

"*Patron!*"

They turned.

The technician pushed his way through the crowd that still milled about the greffier's desk. He was panting slightly. The trodden-down backs of his espadrilles dragged against the ground. He was gesticulating, and when he reached Gurion, the man was out of breath.

"We're wanted down at the marina."

"I've got to get back to the studio," Gurion replied.

"A police launch's been blown up." The man nodded. "And the Calais yacht."

Anne Marie glanced at her watch. It was 8:22 A.M.

35
Sub judice

"I didn't know Calais had a boat."

"What?"

"I didn't know Raymond Calais had a boat."

"He didn't."

Anne Marie looked at Trousseau in surprise.

Trousseau had to pull hard on the steering to stop the car from going into the back of a municipal bus that had come to a halt at the edge of the marina. "Not Raymond Calais. The boat belongs to his brother. Jacques Calais."

Anne Marie was sweating.

There was a white and red barrier across the road; painted on one of the cement posts was the word CAPITAINERIE and an arrow. A man in uniform—a round face and a holster attached to his belt—approached the FR3 van.

Anne Marie saw Gurion talking. He gestured with his thumb toward the Peugeot and grinned at them. The rims of his glasses caught the bright sunlight.

The man in the kepi shook his head and approached the Peugeot and Trousseau. He saluted. "The marina's temporarily closed." The palm of his hand was a pale brown.

Anne Marie leaned across and showed him her card. He took it and studied it carefully. He pushed the kepi back and scratched his damp forehead. The lips moved as he read. He ran a finger along the red and blue diagonals. "I suppose so," he said, not addressing anybody in particular, his eyes still on the card. He returned to the pole and lifted it. The FR3 Renault went through, followed by Trousseau.

The man put the card through the window, and Anne Marie took it. He stepped back to salute. There was a small, red anchor on his kepi.

They parked near a police van.

The television team unpacked the equipment, their cameras, and their recording material. One technician carried a camera on his shoulder.

The wind was strong at sea level; it pulled at Anne Marie's skirt—a pretty, tailored skirt that she had bought on impulse in the rue de Siam while on a course in Brest. She brushed the beige material down and, turning, noticed a smile on Gurion's face. He looked away.

The tall masts rocked with the movement of the harbor waters. A regular tapping of wire against aluminum. The line of yachts and wooden jetties was deserted.

On the furthest jetty, a crowd had formed. Anne Marie could see the procureur.

The three men were with him and the gaunt West Indian had removed his raincoat and held it folded across his arm. Anne Marie pushed her way forward, with Trousseau just behind her.

"Over here."

There were a few children who had moved forward to the water's edge.

A couple of men in dungarees stood in an inflatable dinghy. One was shouting to the procureur. The other was looking at the yacht moored alongside.

No flames.

Smoke poured in black wisps from the cabin. It was a small yacht. Two outboard motors and a hull of scarred fiberglass. The roof of the cabin had caved in, and one side of the hull had been ripped away.

"Is the fire out?"

Pieces of wood floated in the water, knocking occasionally against the hull with muffled thuds.

"Make sure you extinguish the fire." The procureur had his hands in his pockets and the same unlit cigar in his mouth. His large face looked worried.

Anne Marie moved forward until she was standing beside him. She held out her hand and he took it absent-mindedly.

"Bonjour," he said, frowning.

"Anybody hurt?"

The procureur turned away without answering.

The three men looked at her, their eyes devoid of interest. The black man wore his dark hair parted and combed. The white suit was immaculate. He had a crimson tie and canvas shoes. There was the unmistakable glint of ambition in his eyes.

"Who's hurt?"

The man with the raincoat shook his head and turned away. He said something to the procureur, who nodded.

Anne Marie bit her lip.

There were a few shopkeepers from the nearby shopping mall—French women with manicures and heels that were too high for their tanned legs and for the wooden slats of the jetty. A few men—Anne Marie recognized a couple of Syrians who sold *prêt-à-porter*. Most of the crowd was made up of boat hands—Europeans with wiry arms and torsos, the occasional tattoo. One or two held a beer can.

She heard the whir of the television camera.

Gurion held out the microphone as he edged forward toward the procureur. The cameraman was close behind.

"Who let you in here?" The plump face showed no anger, but the procureur bit at the end of his cigar and spat dark shreds to the ground.

"A deliberate attempt to destroy a privately owned boat."

Gurion nodded toward the name written in gold letters along the warped hull, *La Belle Soeur.* "As well as another boat belonging to the gendarmerie—which would appear to have escaped relatively undamaged." Gurion extended the microphone. "In your opinion, monsieur le procureur, who would want to destroy these boats?"

The procureur looked at the microphone with diffidence. "As yet I'm afraid we have no information to work on."

"This attack occurs within hours of a similar attack at the International Airport Pointe-à-Pitre/Le Raizet. This would indicate, would it not, a recrudescence in violence?"

The procureur looked directly toward the camera. "There's never been political terrorism in Guadeloupe."

"There've been bombs, monsieur le procureur. Several months ago an attack was made on the gendarmerie at Sainte-Anne. Attempts have been made on several important citizens—not least Raymond Calais, who was found murdered a few days ago." Gurion paused and, before the procureur could answer, hurried on, "The number one suspect, an old man, an ex-convict who was helping with the enquiries—it would appear that he, too, is dead."

The procureur took a deep breath. His small eyes glanced at Anne Marie. "If there is terrorism—which has yet to be proved—it's most certainly the work of outsiders. Terrorism in Guadeloupe is an imported phenomenon. I know Guadeloupe." He smiled toward the camera. "I was born on this island and this is where I grew up. I know my compatriots. They don't resort to violence to solve their problems."

"Monsieur le procureur, the present situation is tense. Thirty percent of the population's out of work. Sugar factories are closing down. More and more people are being forced to emigrate to France. At the same time, the number of outside civil servants coming from the Métropole steadily increases."

The procureur held up his hand. With the same hand, he took the cigar from his mouth. He looked at Michel Gurion. He had forgotten about the camera, which hummed softly. "Of course there are problems—no country is perfect. However, here we're part of France where the laws of the Republic apply. Violence is no way to solve these problems."

"Can you be sure no Frenchman of Guadeloupe is involved in these acts?" Gurion's face betrayed no emotion but his eyes were bright. Beneath the glasses, his nose was hooked like a bird's.

"Violence is never a solution."

"If this," Gurion said, gesturing toward the damaged yacht, "if all this is the last of a series of terrorist attacks upon the political stability of Guadeloupe, then isn't it quite possible Raymond Calais was murdered for political motives?"

"I have no comment to make. The Raymond Calais affair is sub judice."

"How can it be sub judice, monsieur le procureur, when the principal suspect has committed suicide?"

Again the procureur looked at Anne Marie before turning back toward the camera. "These are things I cannot discuss. However, I can assure you the entire dossier is being prepared. Being prepared with all the rigor and all the efficiency that the people of Guadeloupe have grown to expect from the judiciary."

And without another word, without even a perfunctory smile, the procureur turned his back on the camera.

36

Laurel et Hardy

The boat seemed to slide along a cement wall.

"You shouldn't have done that."

The Italian flag fluttered limply. Two sleek hulls came into view. The catamaran cut through the green harbor water toward the far jetty.

Gurion shrugged.

"The procureur now thinks I betrayed him."

At the other table, the technician with the T-shirt laughed noisily and the other man nodded, while tapping his hand on the tabletop. His fingernails were encrusted with dirt.

Two cans of Kronenbourg beer, one had been tipped over and the liquid had formed a small yellow puddle that absorbed the scattered crumbs. There was a plate of croissants. Both men ate with their mouths open. They were talking about an oxyacetylene torch.

Gurion ignored them. "It doesn't matter, madame le juge."

"It's not your job that's in jeopardy."

Gurion raised an eyebrow.

"Your remarks about Hégésippe Bray—you think he didn't see you and me arrived together?"

"Hégésippe Bray's death's common knowledge."

"Of course it's not."

"You told me nothing—nothing more than what I overheard."

"The procureur now thinks I got you to ask your stupid questions."

Gurion looked at her and gave a slow smile. The eyes were intelligent and cold. "Are you Jewish?"

"I'm an outsider," Anne Marie replied, not hiding her irritation. "The procureur thinks I'm interfering in something I don't understand. Why he gave me this Bray dossier goodness only knows. He could've given it to Frémy—Frémy's West Indian. And he's a man."

"You are, aren't you?"

"A man?" Anne Marie sat back. "No such luck."

He pushed at the frame of his glasses. "You're Jewish."

"Catholic born and baptized." She lifted her handbag. "Or perhaps you would care to see the photograph of my first communion?"

Gurion drank more coffee from the shallow, Duralex cup. He was smiling, and his complacency irritated Anne Marie. "Why do you think I should be Jewish?"

One of the technicians laughed. Anne Marie did not know whether it was an obscene gesture he was making or whether he was still talking about the oxyacetylene torch.

"The world appears to rest on your shoulders," Gurion said. "You appear very tough, madame le juge. A bit fuzzy round the edges, perhaps, but you're one hard lady who won't allow anybody to fool around. You mean business—but underneath. . . ."

"Yes?"

"There's guilt. The belief it's your responsibility to save the world—even single-handed. Because if you don't save the world, no one else will." He looked at her keenly. "Madame Laveaud wants to save the world. Congratulations. And the French Empire, while she's about it."

Anne Marie finished her guava juice in silence.

"You've got to show you're as good as any man—as good or better. But you're so busy worrying, so busy being efficient and tough and responsible, that you don't have time to step back and get things into perspective."

"I'm not a television journalist, Monsieur Gurion. This may surprise you, but I have responsibilities—real responsibilities. I can't barge in and ask the procureur the first damn-fool question that comes into my scatterbrain, female head." She could feel herself getting angry. "For you it's easy. Like pissing, isn't it? You can stop at the first tree you come to. But as a woman, I've got to think of the long-term logistics."

Gurion grinned.

"While you get the bark wet, without giving it a second thought, perhaps you should think about the effects, all the possible consequences. Just for once." She pointed at him and she was aware that she was trembling. "Say what you like. It doesn't matter if you put the procureur's back up—you don't have to work with him."

Gurion laughed scornfully.

"You sit there in judgment of me, complacent and cocksure. Like a father talking to a wayward daughter. Like the arrogant man you are," Anne Marie said. Her face was now red. "Monsieur Gurion, you deliberately put me in an embarrassing situation. But please don't worry about how I feel. The bark of the tree is wet, and you've got your wonderful interview on tape." She pointed to where the equipment lay on the ground. "Now just zip up your fly, and leave me alone."

"The interview doesn't do me any good."

"You're damn right."

He smiled and the complacency had gone. "I enjoyed seeing the procureur squirm. But madame le juge, there's as much chance of that interview going out on television as you seeing the procureur in a striptease act."

She clicked her tongue.

"FR3 will show old folks' homes in Basse-Terre. That's what the local television is for—our France Régions 3. Or another documentary about mollusks on the coral reef. Or the new machinery from America for the sugar harvest. You expect them to talk about the real problems of Guadeloupe?"

"I don't watch television much."

"An intelligent woman. Anything that's political—anything that really touches upon the future of this island or questions the competence of all the good people in charge. . . ." He shook his head. "They're not going to show that. No chance." He nodded toward the two technicians. "They can clean that tape now. It'll never get onto the airwaves."

The technician in the T-shirt gave Anne Marie a wink.

"Then why embarrass me?"

"I've got my dignity. I'm a journalist with a job to do—and despite everything, I'd like to be able to do it properly. You're not the only person to feel you have a duty."

Anne Marie smiled. "So you're Jewish, too?"

"My hands are tied, my mouth gagged—but I like to pretend I'm doing my job. If only for my own self-respect. I don't blow up planes—but I'm angry, too. You don't have the monopoly on moral outrage, madame le juge. Seeing that fat man squirm—seeing his face unhappy because he's being confronted with the truth—that's my little revenge." Gurion shrugged. "Even if it's a complete waste of time."

The two technicians stood up. One said, "Patron."

Trousseau, who had gone off to look at the boats, now entered the terrace of the bar.

"I shouldn't have said those things, Monsieur Gurion."

He swallowed the rest of the coffee in one gulp. "Don't apologize." The crooked smile was genuine. "One hard lady, but underneath you're a softie."

Anne Marie smiled.

"Soft and decent." Again the crooked smile. "You're sure you're not Jewish?"

"Catholic born and baptized." This time her laughter was genuine. "My mother sent me to the best Catholic schools. But my father's from Oran in Algeria. He now owns a swimwear business in Sarlat. Isaac Bloch." She gave a shrug. "Now is that a Jewish name?"

37

Jacques Calais

"I never married."

The smile transformed Jacques Calais' face—tanned but blood-shot, with broken veins beneath the wrinkled skin.

Although the thin face and narrow features did not immediately recall the dead brother, there were traits that were common to both men. The same lines about the mouth, the same look of determination in the eyes.

Anne Marie was reminded of a kind, disappointed uncle.

"A mistake." He shrugged. "By the time I thought I was ready for marriage, the lady in question had found another man. And had children of her own. I sold a car to one of them only a few months ago. Nice boy." His smile died slowly. "To think he could've been a son of mine—him or someone like him."

They were sitting in his office. It was cool, and because the room had no window, it was rather dark. A metal lamp on the desk cast a small amount of light.

"Tell me about *La Belle Soeur*, Monsieur Calais."

"What do you need to know?"

"A strange name for your boat, isn't it?"

"A present to myself for my fifty-fifth birthday."

"An expensive present."

"I felt I deserved it." He laughed without amusement. "But of course, you're quite right. A complete waste of money."

"Have you seen the damage?"

An impatient gesture. "My insurer will see to that." Jacques Calais sat back in his swivel chair and crossed his legs. He wore dark trousers and a pair of broad American shoes. He clasped his hands together over the slight paunch beneath a leather belt. The buckle was of burnished brass and was embossed with the thick cross of the Chevrolet logo.

"You are married, madame?"

"Yes," Anne Marie replied.

"I shouldn't have listened to my family. Before I went to America, I should've just gone ahead and married her. But I thought it would be possible to wait." He sighed. "She was still very young— scarcely eighteen."

"You went to America?"

"To Detroit, madame le juge."

"You could have stayed on the estate."

"Sainte Marthe?" He shook his head. "Not after Father died. I wasn't going to be able to work with my brother. I tried it for six months and it didn't work out."

"Why did you go to America?"

"Raymond and I didn't see eye to eye. Father had left the land to him—and anyway, it meant more to him. He liked to see himself as a man of tradition. But he could never have been a farmer—a real farmer like Papa. Raymond never had that kind of dedication."

"Dedication?"

"Papa slaved for Sainte Marthe. It was his life—and in the end it was his death, too. He was getting old, and he refused to rest, despite the doctor's injunctions. Sainte Marthe's been in the family for centuries—and he loved it to the end. Of course, they were different times."

"When did your father die?"

"Late 1940—it was at the end of the harvest. He died in the fields. He was over near L'Étang Diable. Some people say he drank the water; others say he was deliberately poisoned. Nobody here wanted to believe he died because he was a worn-out old man who'd driven himself to death. They must believe in their devils and their evil spirits. Although he was a hard man in many ways, people loved my father. Because he was just. Black, white, Indian or mulatto—it made no difference to him. Hard—but scrupulously fair." Jacques Calais smiled at the recollection. "He pushed people, he made them work—but he also paid them a decent wage. Not like the other owners who'd never really accepted slavery was over."

Anne Marie looked at her hand.

"Father made us get up at five o'clock, and during the harvest, when there was no school, he'd put us out to work with the cutters. He didn't believe that because we were white we shouldn't know the meaning of hard work. The Békés—the others'll tell you the West Indians are all lazy, that they don't want to work. You ever been in the fields? Have you ever cut cane?"

Anne Marie shook her head.

"It's hell. With luck, you can work for about an hour, but then the sun comes up and there's absolutely no shade. The sun overhead and sweat pouring down your face and into your eyes, and you can't even see. And the handle of your machete grows slippery and it wants to jump from your hand." He unclasped his hands—large, powerful hands—and looked at the palms. "Still have the old scars."

The nails were clean, Anne Marie noticed, but the sides of the fingers had the ingrained traces of engine grease.

"The blades of the sugarcane cut your skin like glass. I hated it—the sun and the high cane all around. No breeze and the sweat and the insects that got in your eyes. Swish, swish." He made a slicing motion with his right arm as though it held a long knife. "For hours on end. No, I wasn't going back to that."

"But you worked with your brother?"

"For six months. Without any pleasure. Raymond gave me a horse, and he expected me to ride around the fields, giving orders. The men saw me as a slave master. And Raymond complained. All my fault if the cane wasn't getting cut fast enough. I don't think Raymond wanted me there. He wanted me out of the way."

"Why?"

"So that he could do what he pleased. And that suited me. Although I was very young, I could see the writing on the wall. Sugar was doomed. America was producing, Australia was producing—and they could afford to mechanize. That's why I went to America. The future lay in mechanization."

"When did you leave?"

"Early '41—before America came into the war."

"You were in Guadeloupe for Hégésippe Bray's trial?"

He looked at her carefully. "Yes."

"And what can you tell me about that?"

He shrugged. "Bray killed his wife. He cut her up and then he burnt her."

"That didn't strike you as strange?"

"Madame le juge," Jacques Calais sighed, "I was born here. I grew up here. Guadeloupe's my country—and the West Indian's my fellow countryman. But I realize we're worlds apart. Voodoo and black magic—they're things you or I will never understand. Why did Hégésippe Bray kill his wife?" He shook his head. "We were all sorry. My father liked Bray—and if it hadn't been for Papa, Hégésippe Bray would have been guillotined. Instead, he was sent to French Guyana. Unfortunately, he never came back."

"Until last year."

Jacques Calais nodded.

"You think he murdered your brother?"

A shrug. "Hégésippe Bray was not the only person who hated Raymond."

"Who else hated him?"

"That's your job to find out."

"And you can help me."

"I know very little about my brother's life—we tended to move in different circles."

"Did you like your brother?"

He smiled sadly. "You think I murdered Raymond?"

"You got on well with him?"

"Our interests were different. Raymond gave less and less attention to the estate. He got involved in politics—foolishly, in my opinion. We rarely met." He folded his hands. "But he was my brother and I loved him."

"How long were you in America?"

"I did the right thing." He gestured toward the engravings of vintage cars on the walls. Then at the model attached to an onyx ashtray on the desk. The little car was made of pewter. "I learned the automotive business. All aspects of it. Not just selling—also repair and maintenance. Father'd taught me there's nothing to be ashamed of in working with my hands. I came back after the war. In 1946. Hard times, but there was talk of making Guadeloupe into a département. Not much money around—apart from the civil servants, and they weren't interested in American cars. I discovered that she—that this woman—was now married. I was tempted to throw it all in, leave Guadeloupe and go to South America. To Venezuela—or perhaps Cuba. Cuba was beginning to do well—the Americans were investing at this time." His smile showed his teeth. "By comparison, Guadeloupe was a backwater—a forgotten, colonial backwater. I wanted to get away from my family."

"And from the woman who couldn't be bothered to wait for you?"

A shrug of acquiescence.

"But you stayed?"

"I stayed because there was a new move to import American machinery for the sugar. And because of de Gaulle—but of course, that was later, much later. . . ."

There was a light tap on the door and the secretary came in.

She had long hair dyed blonde and pulled back in a ponytail. The woman was wearing stockings. Pale breasts pushed against the restricting material of her bustier. A small face, bright lipstick, and unflattering, pendulous earrings.

"I need your signature, Monsieur Calais. Just had Puerto Rico on the line." She spoke in a high-pitched voice, giving Anne Marie a sideways glance. She bent over the desk beside Jacques Calais and placed an open folder in front of him. "About the two bulldozers for Guadex Spa."

"Ah." Calais took a pair of glasses and looked at the document. The girl stood beside him. She was young and she wore a ring. Anne Marie saw that the woman's hand gently brushed against the larger, tanned hand of Jacques Calais where it lay on the desk.

"San Juan wants you to ring back."

"Later." He signed, closed the folder, and handed it back to the secretary. He looked up at her. She was very close beside him. "Thank you, Colette."

Colette eyed Anne Marie. "Your friend is outside, madame. Seems to have grown bored with the harvesting machine brochures."

"Kindly tell my greffier I shan't be much longer." Anne Marie added, "Mademoiselle."

The girl nodded imperceptibly, turned on her heel and the click of her shoes followed her out of the office. She closed the door.

"An excellent secretary." Jacques Calais' eyes looked over the top of the half-frame glasses. "Colette's the best I've ever had."

38

de Gaulle

"You were talking about de Gaulle, Monsieur Calais."

Jacques Calais returned the glasses to their case. "De Gaulle?"

"You stayed on in Guadeloupe."

"That was later. It must've been in '58."

"When de Gaulle came to power?"

He nodded. "There was a new attitude toward us—toward all that remained of the French Empire. New schools, new hospitals, and at last, new roads." He smiled. "Before de Gaulle, we were jealous of the English islands—Barbados and Trinidad. De Gaulle changed all that. The result, I suppose, of what had happened in Indochina and Algeria. Most Békés don't like de Gaulle, you know. During the war, we were with Pétain and de Gaulle was a dirty word. But by 1958, there'd been too many wars, and de Gaulle didn't want to see a repeat of Algeria in the Caribbean. Winning our hearts and minds. About this time that we started getting all these people posted from Paris. Good for business—good for everyone."

"Except the sugar industry."

"Sugar was going to die."

"But your brother stayed on."

"What choice did Raymond have? He saw the need to invest in new machines. Fortunately, I was there to help him. I got the equipment from America, and through me, Raymond was able to make considerable savings. He's never really had money—he's always had to put it back into the land. And he's got expensive hobbies."

"The villa? The maid? The cars? His standard of living—where did he get the money from?"

"He's been known to gamble," Calais said simply. "The estate still pays its way—but to pay for the machinery, he had to sell land." He clicked his tongue. "There were other problems for him, too. Problems that all the planters have to face. Mechanize and you put people out of work. At least there were never any threats against Raymond, to my knowledge."

"Threats?"

"Like against the other planters. A dying breed. The factories have virtually all closed down, and any Béké with any sense has moved out of sugar. Those who stick to sugar are in trouble. You take Dominique Blanche—been up against it for the last ten years. A mulatto but all the workers say he's white because they're convinced he exploits them deliberately. He's got a Mercedes Benz— and that's about all. Most Békés send their children to France, but Blanche has to send his children to school here. He can scarcely afford a maid. He's had at least ten strikes in as many years. Once they even tried to kidnap his daughter. Took her and held her for an afternoon until the gendarmes arrived. Two Indians were thrown in jail—Indians are always the ring-leaders. They had to be let out."

"Why?"

"Because otherwise, madame le juge, there would've been an insurrection." He laughed. "Back in 1952, four laborers were shot dead during the riots in Le Moule. Guadeloupe's always been a powder keg. Barricades in the streets and cars set on fire? It's just not worth it. The Indians were set free."

"Where was this?"

"In Goyave. Things have calmed down a bit now with the possibility of work on the new bypass road. But soon that will be finished and then there'll be more problems. No alternative but to mechanize."

"Who hated your brother?"

"Raymond wasn't unpopular. Of course, it's always hard to tell with the locals—they can give you a bright smile, and at the same time, behind your back, they're cursing you and sticking pins in little effigies." He laughed.

"And Michel, the Indian?"

"I wouldn't worry about Michel if I were you. Half-mad—and completely harmless." Jacques Calais frowned and was silent for a moment, as if trying to remember something. "My brother was a difficult man. Difficult but there were things you couldn't help respecting about him. He was much closer to Maman than to Father. He could get angry and threaten to kill you—and I think he was capable of it, too—with that big face of his getting bigger and redder and angrier." Jacques Calais' own face seemed to soften with the recollection. "When we were kids we often fought. Two years older than me, and when you're little, that can make a lot of difference. Yet Raymond could be tremendously loyal—and he was also very protective." He hesitated, as if embarrassed. "In many ways, my brother was very innocent. Blustery, of course, but that was really just a way to hide things—just appearances. In his heart, he was an innocent. That, too, he inherited from Maman— a good heart. He was capable of tremendous loyalty."

"But he had enemies?"

"In Guadeloupe, there's always somebody who's jealous of you."

"Tell me why your boat was blown up, Monsieur Calais."

"Goodness knows."

"A lot of people know that the boat belongs to you."

He did not respond.

"Is there anybody you suspect?"

"It's only a boat. It is not a human life." His eyes remained on hers; then he said softly, "You have children, madame le juge?"

"A boy."

He breathed in and his nose was pinched. "A wife and children. And now I would be a grandfather. I'd have somebody to talk to, to share my life with. There'd have been a purpose to it all." He tapped the desk. "Instead, I thought it would be possible to wait. I thought things'd change, and that while I was waiting, I could go off and learn a skill. To earn money. Now I've got money—more money than Papa ever knew, money that I can spend whenever I want. So when I was fifty-five, I indulged in a little birthday present for myself. A boat, a nice boat." He added, "And nobody to share it with."

There was a workshop manual open on the desk before him.

"Raymond had less money than me. But he had a family—a wife and children." The eyes looked at Anne Marie and they glistened. "He didn't have a boat."

"Who blew your boat up?"

"I don't care." He glanced around the room before continuing, "What do I need with this office? With this job? With all the cars that are out there in the showrooms and in the garage? What good are they to me?" With the back of his hand, he rubbed his eye.

Anne Marie looked down at her hands.

"I should've married her, damn it. I was weak, and like a fool, I thought the best solution was to get away for a few years. I left her—and how was she to know that for every day since, every day of my life, I was going to think about her? I was going to love her just as much thirty-five years later as I did on the day we first met? She got married—and it was the right thing to do. All my fault— I was weak. I didn't have the courage to break with my family and marry a mulatto woman. Too afraid of what Maman would think. I knew she'd never forgive me for marrying a woman who wasn't white." Jacques Calais ran a hand across his chin. "I still love her—a grandmother, damn it, and I still love her."

39
Funeral

There had been a time in Paris when Jean Michel had taken her regularly to the cinema to see an endless diet of American films. He loved Westerns. Anne Marie had asked him why he refused to see anything French. Jean Michel merely shrugged. "There's always a funeral in a French film," he had said. They were waiting to buy tickets for *The Magnificent Seven* at the Cinéma Champollion in the rue des Écoles. "And it's always raining."

Anne Marie wished that it would rain now.

Trousseau had parked the Peugeot beneath the shade of a thick gum tree, but the sun was still overhead and moving slowly. It was very hot inside the car.

The walls of the cemetery were on the far side of the road; they were now covered with posters and red graffiti hostile to the French colonial presence—*FWANSÉ DEWO*. The gates were closed with padlock and chain.

"What time's this funeral at?" Anne Marie asked for the third time.

"Half past two." Trousseau did not look up from his religious book.

They should have eaten something more substantial than a sandwich and a bottle of Pepsi Cola. Anne Marie did not feel very well. She rubbed at the back of her hand.

Lafitte turned up at a quarter to three. He parked his car—a rack for cycles on the roof—and then got into the Peugeot. He shook hands and smiled warmly. He was carrying a large camera around his neck. There were cases for various lenses.

Anne Marie said, "Two cars on the sidewalk and a zoom lens. You don't think somebody might get the impression we're watching them?"

"They'll all have their heads down in sorrow and prayer."

Anne Marie was silent. She thought about her meeting with Suez-Panama that morning. She had done her best for the old man, she told herself; there was no need to feel guilty.

Anne Marie now sat, looking out of the window, staring at the movement of the traffic. From time to time, she turned her head toward the distant steeple of the church that rose up through the foliage of breadfruit trees and the tin roofs of Morne-à-l'Eau. A fall in the temperature by several degrees would have been welcome. There were a couple of clouds away to the north, but they promised no relief from the stifling heat. Anne Marie was sweating profusely. She was hungry. With the tips of her fingers, she scratched at the back of her left hand.

Lafitte laughed. He was chatting with Trousseau. Anne Marie was surprised to see them getting on. She had always believed that Trousseau shared her dislike for Lafitte.

"You believe in all that?" Lafitte asked.

Trousseau shrugged.

A bus went past and the hot fumes enveloped the car. Anne Marie looked at her watch for the third time in five minutes. Another half hour and if by then the procession had not turned up, she would ask Lafitte to take her to the airport. She wanted to be in time for the arrival of her father-in-law on the Paris flight.

She could now feel the perspiration running down her body. Her skirt was badly rumpled.

"Spoons? Why spoons?"

Trousseau put his head to one side. "It's another local belief. People think that it will bring them luck."

"Luck?"

"Put a spoon on the steps of the Palais de Justice, and the judge will come down favorably on your side."

Lafitte laughed. He had picked up the West Indian habit of putting his hand to his mouth.

"Or you can sacrifice a toad."

"Monsieur Trousseau, the handwriting."

The two men turned in surprise.

"The handwriting," Anne Marie repeated. "Monsieur Trousseau, I want you to get a copy of the note."

"The note, madame le juge?"

"The suicide note—the note Bray's supposed to have left."

"The procureur has it."

"Then get it from him."

"You think he'll give it to me?"

"I need to have the handwriting tested." She took the photograph from her handbag. "Get it, Monsieur Trousseau."

In the photo, the woman stared with sepia-tinted eyes. "*A mon petit Hégésippe . . . celle qui t'aime toujours.*" A Creole woman with an intelligent face, unafraid of the passage of time. At the bottom, scrawled in a different hand, "*Je suis Hégésippe Bray.*"

Anne Marie pointed to Hégésippe Bray's faded signature. "I want the writing checked against this."

Without conviction, Trousseau took the photograph and tucked it carefully into his pocket. He did not glance at the photograph of the woman in madras.

"Here they come at last."

Lafitte had raised the camera and placed the long, dark snout of the lens against the edge of the rear window. "Not many mourners." The hum of the camera's winding mechanism.

Anne Marie turned to look.

Her vision of the accompanying cortege was largely blocked by the hearse. It was an American car with a wide radiator of chrome that glistened in the afternoon light. A couple of men, both in blue uniform and peaked caps, were walking slowly in front of the car. They carried wreaths. Another man hurried forward to unlock the gates to the cemetery.

The traffic toward Pointe-à-Pitre was blocked.

"Probably been better if the poor bastard had never come back to Guadeloupe." Lafitte lowered his head to look through the viewfinder. "For all the good it did him."

The stupidity of Lafitte's remark caught on the edge of her raw nerves.

"Madame Suez-Panama," Lafitte announced. He continued to press the shutter. "And that's her son with her."

Marcel Suez-Panama walked with his arm supporting his mother. He had tidied himself up, shaved and put on a dark suit and a clean shirt. Both he and his mother held handkerchiefs to their faces. The old woman moved forward unsteadily, as if unsure of her black shoes and the raised heels. A large black hat with a broad brim and a black veil hid part of her face.

"That must be your Indian, madame le juge."

He had laced up his boots and tied the laces into large bow knots. He wore a shirt and a crumpled pair of dark trousers. Although he had brushed the long, greasy hair, Michel looked out of place. Without a machete, his hands seemed empty. He walked with his distinctive, stiff-legged gait. A smile hovered at his mouth. He raised his head to look at the trees.

Anne Marie took another glance at her watch. Another ten minutes and with luck, she could be just in time for the plane.

The air had started to cool.

"There's Armand Calais representing the Calais family." Lafitte indicated with the camera. "I'll take a few shots."

"Carreaux has got a nerve." Trousseau's voice sounded offended as he tapped Lafitte on the shoulder. "Get a good profile on our friend Philippe Carreaux."

The American car drew past. It was followed by a handful of mourners. At the back of the cortege, and only a couple of meters in front of the impatient, blocked traffic, a man was walking with his head bowed. Light-skinned and good looking. He held his hands loosely clasped in front of him.

"Paints graffiti on the walls and when he gets caught red-handed. . . ."

"Who is he?" Anne Marie asked.

Lafitte said, "They're afraid to put him in jail. Afraid there'll be another insurrection in Pointe-à-Pitre."

Trousseau shook his head. "When Philippe Carreaux becomes the first president of the independent Socialist Republic of Guadeloupe, believe me, madame le juge, I'll be on the first plane out of here."

Lafitte turned to look at her and gave Anne Marie one of his bland smiles, "Philippe Carreaux, university lecturer and president of the Mouvement d'action des nationalistes guadeloupéens," he said. "The MANG."

40
Panhard

"Sixty years of marriage, the old bastard."

"I like your grandfather."

"A vulture," Jean Michel called from the bathroom. "Only interest is money. Doesn't talk about anything else."

"He's still your grandfather."

The sound of the tap running. "He never bothered about us when we were children."

"Your father loves him enough to come back from Paris just for the diamond wedding anniversary."

"He always exploited Papa."

Her wedding ring lay in the empty cigar tin on the dressing table. She picked it up and tried to slide it along her finger. The itching had gone, but the skin was still swollen, and the ring would not slide over the numb flesh. Anne Marie placed the ring back in the cigar tin. "That's no reason for not visiting him. And anyway, your mother's expecting us to take her to the church."

Jean Michel turned off the tap. "You know why?"

"Why what?"

"Why he's ashamed of Papa—because Papa has dark skin."

"Your grandfather's always been very nice to me."

"A vulture—and as deaf as a post. That old man smiles and

nods—but he hasn't heard a word you've said. Ask him about his health, and he complains about the price of tomatoes."

"I don't blame him complaining about the price of tomatoes at twenty-eight francs the kilo."

It was Sunday morning.

Anne Marie felt relaxed. Her skin had been toned up by a chill shower. Her hand did not hurt—just a slight feeling of nausea in her stomach.

"Only a few more years on God's Earth—and all he cares about is the price of tomatoes."

Anne Marie stared at herself in the mirror. "Why did you marry me, Jean Michel?"

"Eh?"

She raised her voice. "What did you want to marry me for?"

"We've been into this before."

"Tell me."

"For your mind," he called from the bathroom.

"You didn't find me attractive?"

"What?"

"You didn't find me beautiful? Like the girl with the headscarf that looked like Pascale Petit?"

There was no reply. Only the sound of the shower being turned on and her husband's tuneless whistle.

In Paris, Jean Michel used to have an old Panhard coupé, and in the afternoons, the car could be seen cruising up and down the Boulevard St. Michel, along the rue de l'Odéon and as far as the rue Monsieur le Prince and the Luxembourg Gardens. The roof was always down, despite the chill spring weather of Paris, and the back seat was packed tight with grinning friends from Martinique and Guadeloupe, with bright teeth and short hair and American Army raincoats. Invariably sitting beside Jean Michel was a girl, with skin of alabaster and a scarf round her head like the actress Pascale Petit.

Anne Marie put a few finishing touches to her nails then studied herself in the mirror.

More white hairs. She ran one of her outstretched fingers along the line of her jaw and wondered whether these were the first signs of a double chin. Her eyes looked back at her. There was an expression of quiet resignation on her face.

Jean Michel made her jump. He was standing behind her, dripping wet and quite naked.

Anne Marie said, "I hope Béatrice's gone."

"She might learn something."

"You're making pools of water on the floor that the poor girl cleaned yesterday."

He smelled of toothpaste and the faint, sulphuric odor of shaving powder. He placed his chin on the top of her head, and they looked at each other in the mirror.

"Be sensible, Jean Michel. We're in a hurry and I've got to get Fabrice ready." In the same breath, Anne Marie asked, "Why did you marry me? You could've married the princess from the Cameroon. She had a better body than me—and now you'd be a tribal chief with lots of little children running between your legs."

He smiled. His body was warm against her back. "Perhaps I want something else running between my legs."

"Why did you marry me, Jean Michel?"

He stroked her hair. "My princess."

"You're sopping wet, you're ruining my hair, and you're ruining one of the few decent dresses that I own." Anne Marie grinned into the mirror. "What's your dear mother going to say when she sees the princess turning up in church dressed like a scarecrow?"

41

Reception

"Don't get your clothes dirty, Fabrice."

A trestle table and at least twenty chairs had been set up along the veranda and women were distributing plastic knives and forks and piles of paper plates. At the far end, another table was weighed down by bottles of wine, fruit juice and mineral waters.

Jean Michel said, "The champagne should be chilled." He turned to look at his wife. "How's your hand, *doudou?*"

"Getting better."

As they stepped through the low iron door onto the veranda, an uncle approached and the two men kissed.

"You know my wife?" Jean Michel asked.

He was tall and well-dressed. There were broken veins beneath the large nose. "Uncle Casimir," the man said, introducing himself. The features were thick. In his hand, he held a glass of whiskey. "We met at the time of your honeymoon."

Anne Marie smiled.

Jean Michel moved away toward the other guests.

"How are you enjoying Guadeloupe, madame?" Casimir took her by the arm and steered her toward the drinks table. "Something to drink after a thirsty morning in church?"

"A glass of water."

He opened a bottle of Perrier and poured it for Anne Marie.

He then raised his own glass—it had a motif of painted diamonds and hearts—and said, "*À votre santé.*" He finished the whiskey in one gulp. His eyes watered and he coughed. Then he said, "You went to the Saintes for your honeymoon?"

Anne Marie nodded.

"You've now got a job here?"

"At the Palais de Justice."

"Secretary?"

"Juge d'instruction."

His eyes widened. "Then I better be careful—but I can't imagine a more charming person to be arrested by."

"I can only arrest you if you've done something wrong."

His lips were wet. "We can soon remedy that." His hand had returned to her elbow. "It must be a very difficult job."

Anne Marie smiled. "Difficult?"

"There are still a lot of old fashioned ideas in Guadeloupe. And for many people in this département, a woman's role is to be a mother—to stay at home and look after the children."

She pointed to where Fabrice was playing with his cousins; already the seat of his trousers was pale with dust. "Our little boy."

Casimir ran his tongue over his lips. "You work among men—a good-looking young woman. People don't always accept that very readily. And you're white."

"Something I'm learning to live with."

Casimir wanted to say something, hesitated, then said, "Another drink?"

Anne Marie shook her head. She had not finished the Perrier.

Casimir stared at his own empty glass. Then he went back to the drinks table.

Anne Marie folded her arms.

When he came back, his glass was full of whiskey. "Has Jean Michel found a job?"

"Nothing definite—but several possibilities."

"A bright boy—he takes after his mother. I'm sure he'll find something. Just a question of knocking on every door.

Fortunately there's the family that can help, that can give its support."

"Jean Michel's been unemployed for more than a year."

Casimir was not listening. His watery eyes had moved from Anne Marie to a group of men who were approaching the table. "Come," Casimir said.

There were three men, all in their mid-fifties and extremely well-dressed. Lightweight suits, expensive shirts and keysrings that were weighed down with keys. With them came a pungent cloud of aftershave.

Anne Marie recognized two of the men.

"I must introduce you to the company. It's not every day that the family celebrates sixty years of marriage."

More cars were arriving in the garden. The priest had changed out of his robes and arrived in a Deux Chevaux, accompanied by an unsmiling nun. He was wearing dark trousers and a grey shirt.

Casimir had wandered off to pour himself another drink.

Anne Marie found herself in conversation with a distant uncle, a school teacher. From time to time, he pulled at the tight fabric of his trousers. In his hand, he held a gold lighter. "A lucky man, our Jean Michel, marrying such a beautiful girl."

He kissed her on the cheek.

42

Cole

Lunch was served, and Casimir thrust a glass of rum and fruit juice into Anne Marie's hand. She shook her head.

"You must drink, madame le juge—it is part of our cuisine, part of our traditions."

The children were herded up and set at their own table. They were fussed over by the aunts and by Louise, Jean Michel's youngest sister, who, at seventeen, was still at the lycée.

For the adults, large dishes of grated cucumber, carrot and avocado pears were set out along the trestle table. Bottles of good wine were opened. There was music—Julio Iglesias, Jim Reeves, and Nat King Cole—and the guests took their places. Pappy sat at one end of the table, and Anne Marie found herself between Casimir and Freddy's wife, Odile. Opposite her, the priest smiled absent-mindedly, his eyes on the bottle of rosé wine.

The nun had disappeared.

Jean Michel was on the other side of the table. He was alongside his mother who had now removed her large hat. By leaning back in her chair, Anne Marie could see down the row of backs, and she saw the woman that Jean Michel was talking to with such interest. Elegant shoulders and smooth, matte skin that contrasted with the white dress. Very pretty—a cousin who occasionally visited Mamie in the rue Alsace-Lorraine. The shoulder straps looked as if they could slip at any moment.

"You don't know when you're lucky."

Anne Marie turned.

Odile smiled. "You've got a husband who's lived in Europe. Jean Michel doesn't think that women exist merely to keep him warm in bed."

"That was when he lived in France." Anne Marie returned the smile. "He was cold and I had to keep him warm."

"Jean Michel's a good husband."

"Where is Freddy?"

It was Freddy who worked at the town hall in Pointe-à-Pitre and had helped them get their apartment in the Cité Mortenol. He was younger than Jean Michel by two years.

"Who knows?" Odile held a cigarette between her long fingers.

"I thought he drove you here."

Odile shook her head. "I brought Pappy and the children."

Beside Anne Marie, Casimir reached for the bottle of rosé.

"Freddy's gone for a cycle ride. There was a time when he hoped to become a professional cyclist." Odile raised her shoulders. "Says he's out cycling with the club but I suspect he has other things to do on Sundays—like all the men on this damned island." She paused, inhaled on her cigarette. "He says this whole reception is a farce."

Apart from Freddy, all Jean Michel's brothers and sisters were there. Louise sat at the small table. She was looking after the children. Fabrice sat beside her, drinking from a tumbler.

"A farce," Odile repeated as she inhaled. She was a good-looking woman, with fine features. An attractive birthmark, a black spot at the side of her nose, moved as she smiled.

Anne Marie said, "That's what my husband says, too."

"Jean Michel's always done what his mother tells him to do." She stubbed out the cigarette.

"Jean Michel doesn't like his grandfather very much."

"Nobody likes that old devil—Freddy's just a bit more honest.

He doesn't want to have anything to do with the old couple." She pointed to where Ondine and Gaston sat. The woman that Gaston had married when she was just nineteen was nodding off in front of a plate of food, a senile old woman. She sat at a table that resembled a baby's high chair. Gaston smiled and fiddled with a beige hearing aid.

"They're still his grandparents."

Odile laughed. "You know how old your father-in-law is?"

Anne Marie glanced at Pappy. He was eating, and he placed a large piece of blood sausage in his mouth. He had put on a red tie.

Anne Marie shook her head.

"Sixty-four."

"Well?"

"Sixty-four—and that couple has been married for sixty years."

"He must've been born out of wedlock."

"That's his mother. Your husband's grandmother."

"What?"

"Over there. The old woman."

Anne Marie turned, following the direction of Odile's gesture.

An old woman in slippers, with white hair against a leathery head, sat in an armchair by herself. A loose cotton dress with floral patterns came down to her ankles. As Anne Marie looked, the woman lifted her head and their eyes met. Eyes that were bright in the African face. The skin creased to form a warm smile.

A kind face.

Anne Marie turned away, embarrassed. "Jean Michel never mentioned anything to me."

"You never wondered why Pappy had such dark skin—when those two over there are almost as white as you?"

Anne Marie shrugged. "Never gave it a second thought."

"You didn't wonder why the priest never mentioned Pappy during the sermon? But mentioned all the other brothers and sisters?"

Anne Marie shook her head. Again she glanced at her father-in-law.

"The Catholic Church only recognizes her own marriages." A sour laugh. "If the old man'd had any sense, he'd have stayed with the black woman. As bright as a button—eighty-five if she's a day. Got all her faculties—which is more than can be said for the legitimate wife."

"Gaston and Ondine look happy enough."

Odile clicked her tongue angrily. "Money's the only thing they're interested in."

"Why didn't he tell me?"

"Jean Michel?"

"I thought Ondine was his grandmother. Every time I see her, I kiss her."

Casimir had dozed off and now he came awake with a start. The smoldering cigarette had fallen from his mouth onto his trousers.

"My husband should have told me the truth. Nothing to be ashamed of."

43
Seersucker

"I hear you're pregnant."

Anne Marie shook her head in amused surprise. "One child's more than enough."

"There are times when I wonder how I manage to survive with my two. Always at each other's throat. Five years' difference between Jean Yves and Christophe they're like cat and dog." Odile brought her mouth closer to Anne Marie's ear. "They've got two half-brothers."

"Jean Yves and Christophe?"

"Freddy and your husband—they've got two half-brothers. Pappy had an affair with a woman before he got married—and never recognized the boys. They sometimes come to the house in Alsace-Lorraine."

Anne Marie drank water from her glass and then started cutting the chicken that had been set on her plate. She did not feel hungry.

"They're all the same."

Anne Marie smiled. "Men?"

"If Freddy had several women, then perhaps I wouldn't mind so much. Then there'd be nothing special. But one woman . . . a woman who's taken my place. . . ." Odile fell silent.

The priest's eyes were almost closed, and his lips were greasy from the fat of the chicken. Clumsily, he got to his feet, mumbled an apology and walked on unsteady legs into the house.

"You know the woman, Odile?"

The sister-in-law shook her head. "Aren't there enough men without her having to take mine from me? Freddy's been disappearing on weekends for two years now. Doesn't tell me where he's going. Or he invents some lame excuse. Afterwards, in bed at night, he's too tired for me." She pushed the food away and lit another cigarette. "I'd leave him—believe me, Anne Marie, I'd leave him if only I could. Be rid of him—just to see how his mother would react. She hates me—she wanted all her children to marry white people. I'm not good enough for one of her boys." She inhaled a mouthful of smoke. "I'd leave him, but there's the children to think about."

A mosquito bit Anne Marie's leg.

"I don't earn enough." Smoke eddied up from her nostrils. "So I put up with him—and he knows it. There to make his meals and bring up his children and do the washing—and share his bed when his woman's not available or willing." Odile's eyes squinted in the rising smoke. "Which is not very often."

Anne Marie picked at the chicken in silence.

"West Indian men despise their own women—our skin reminds them of themselves." A laugh. "You're white. At least your husband can respect you."

"You really think it's a question of color?"

"I ought to go to France. There'd be freedom. There wouldn't be all these people watching me, knowing exactly what I do, laughing at me behind my back." Again Odile inhaled. "I want to live my life, and if I can't, then I'm quite willing to sacrifice myself for the sake of the children. But I'm not going to sacrifice myself for him." Her eyes were damp. "I'd earn more in Paris."

"You work in Pointe-à-Pitre, Odile?"

She nodded. "By the end of the day I'm washed out, but I've got all the housework to do—and the kids."

"You've got a nice car."

She laughed mockingly. "Freddy's got a nice car. You think he lets me use it? Today—but that's just to impress his mother."

"Where d'you work?"

Odile bit her lip. "I'm a secretary." She turned away, putting an end to the conversation.

Later, the plates were cleared away, and the women brought out a large bowl of fruit salad.

Tatie Lucette, Anne Marie's favorite sister-in-law, the children's favorite aunt, who by day was headmistress in a local school, took the aluminum ladle and dished out the fruit—pineapple, banana, soursop, and grapefruit in red wine and sprinkled with brown sugar.

Jean Michel came over. He bent down beside Anne Marie and told her that he was leaving.

"Where're you going?"

"Stay and take coffee."

"I don't want to stay, Jean Michel."

"It'd be rude for you to leave now. Fabrice's enjoying himself."

"Tell me where you're going."

"I'll be back later." Her husband gestured toward the Alfa Romeo where a couple of male relatives stood waiting. Anne Marie recognized the bald school teacher. "I think we've found someone to buy the car."

"You don't need to sell it, Jean Michel."

He took the keyring from his pocket and played with it impatiently.

Anne Marie whispered, "Jean Michel, I don't want to stay here." There was nervousness in her voice. "I want to go home. I don't know all these people—I don't belong here." She was holding his wrist.

"I'll be back in an hour." A brief smile. "Talk to the girls. You've made a very favorable impression on Tonton Casimir." He pulled his wrist away, bent over and kissed her on the cheek.

Anne Marie said nothing as she watched her husband step into the afternoon sun. He got into the car, laughing. The two men climbed into the back seat. Jean Michel backed the car, did a sharp turn, then sat, his arm through the window and the engine idling.

The cousin came running across the grass.

Her high heels were unsteady on the dry earth. The woman pulled a loose, seersucker jacket over her shoulders and the straps of her white dress. Jean Michel opened the door and she climbed in beside him, her smooth, brown calves glinting.

The car drove away in a cloud of dust and petrol fumes.

Later, as the afternoon cooled, the women made ice cream, using an ice bucket and an old American mixer that was filled with condensed milk.

Afternoon became evening, and the mosquitoes rose up from the mangrove in their endless search for blood.

44
Pro Patria

Light poured through the high, stained-glass windows. The church of Saint-Pierre-et-Saint-Paul was crowded. There were a lot of soldiers in damp uniform. Some wore kepis, others wore flat berets pulled down on the side. The air smelled of flowers and wet clothes. A middle-aged woman knelt beside Anne Marie. Eyes firmly closed behind dark glasses, a dress that had been drenched by the rain. Water trickled down the closed umbrellas and formed meandering rivulets on the slabs of stone.

The organ was overhead, in the gallery of steel girders.

The light from the windows bleached the image on the color television sets. A set had been placed on a shelf at each pillar. As the priest moved down the aisle, a score of electronic images moved in eerie unison.

The bishop gave the sermon. He was a local man with a dark skin, a receding hairline, and a gentle, almost effeminate manner. Anne Marie had once met him at a garden party at the residence of the *Sous-Préfet*. He now went from the far side of the altar, genuflected, and climbed the winding stairs that led to the cast-iron pulpit. He placed his hands on the edge of the pulpit. The congregation sat down. Those people standing in the aisles shuffled their feet and crossed their arms.

"A wife has lost her husband. A mother has lost her son. Many of you have lost a comrade and a friend." The bishop spoke into the microphone and the thin voice echoed round the church and off the high roof of steel. "The Church has lost a child."

Anne Marie's feet were damp.

The rain had worked its way through the leather. Her best pair. Distractedly, she scratched at her hand. She tried to concentrate on the sermon. At the front of the church, she recognized the Préfet in tropical uniform and black epaulettes, heavy with gold braid. His hair was as white as the uniform.

Beside the *Préfet*, their heads turned attentively toward the pulpit, sat the local dignitaries. The thin face of the mayor of Pointe-à-Pitre, mayors from the other towns, officials from the Chamber of Commerce. Anne Marie recognized a *député*. And in the row behind him, wearing a black suit, sat Jacques Calais, accompanied by his nephew, Armand.

The women wore black dresses.

The image moved on the television sets.

"He gave his life selflessly for his country, without any thought for himself."

A woman stood in the front pew; a black veil covered her head. Her shoulders were bowed.

"Today we mourn the loss of a young soldier. He has left this world to go from here to a new, brighter and happier world." The bishop raised his hands. "We are sad; we feel the emptiness of our loss. We miss the man—he was young, he was full of life, he was innocent. We miss our friend."

The microphone picked up the soft sobbing of the widow in black.

"We miss the soldier who placed duty above self-interest, devotion above egotism, love of others and of his country before love of himself."

45
Rain

Only the tortoises seemed to be enjoying the sudden change in the weather. They had clambered out of the water and up the sides of their artificial rock. They gazed with obsidian eyes at the circles of falling raindrops across the surface of the pond.

Anne Marie went up the stairs of the Palais de Justice.

Trousseau looked up and smiled.

The office was somber. He had closed the shutters and the lace curtains—dirty and needing to be replaced with the other set that was somewhere in one of the trunks in the rue Alsace-Lorraine— hung limply against the wood.

Trousseau sat behind the typewriter. His glance went from her face down to her shoes.

"My best shoes," she said, "and it starts to rain."

Trousseau ran his finger along the thin line of his moustache. "Getting married, madame le juge?"

"I must be at the funeral in twenty minutes." She looked at her watch. "In fifteen minutes." She paused to catch her breath. "I wanted to ask you to get hold of Lafitte. I'll be needing to speak with him."

"You've heard the news, madame le juge?"

"About Giscard's speech on the radio?"

He shook his head. "The local news." Trousseau stood up and brushed past her. He unfolded the newspaper that lay on her desk. He pointed to the headline on the front page. A LETTER FROM THE ASSASSINS.

"What is it?"

A dry laugh in his throat. "From the independence people."

"MANG?"

"MANG is a political party—they could never admit to committing acts of violence." He shook his head. "But it's probably the same people."

She put down her handbag and looked at the paper.

"You're wearing perfume, madame le juge."

"I always wear perfume," Anne Marie said. Aware of the rudeness in her voice, she added, "Van Cleef and Arpels. You like it?"

Trousseau returned to his typewriter without answering.

There was an article on the front page. The letter itself was reproduced on the middle pages: "An open letter to the widow of officer René Bruant." A photograph of the hole in the side of the plane; another photograph, badly reproduced in somber blacks and grays, of Madame Bruant. She wore dark sunglasses and was being supported by a young officer in uniform.

"It's going to be a grueling funeral for the poor woman," Anne Marie said, taking the center pages. She folded them carefully before putting them in her handbag.

Trousseau did not look up. "They're scared."

"Why?"

"They never intended to kill anyone." Trousseau counted on his long fingers. "It's Monday today—it's taken them nearly four days to claim responsibility."

"They still haven't claimed responsibility for killing Calais."

Trousseau rubbed his moustache again. "The mulattos hate the whites—but they also hate the blacks."

"They hate all of us?"

"All the whites—you, madame, and all the minions of the occupying colonialist regime." Trousseau nodded to where the newspaper was folded in her bag. His face creased into a large smile. "You've got to leave before the end of the year. Before the thirty-first of December—because if you don't, the armed forces of the People's Republic of Guadeloupe's going to put you all under the ground." He laughed. "My wife and I, we've already booked our flight."

Trousseau's laughter accompanied her down the stairs of the Palais de Justice.

46

Bally

Odile held out her umbrella. "I've got my car."

Anne Marie, grateful for the protection, moved under it. Like a shower of stones, the rain battered against the taut, black fabric. "Not a BMW, I'm afraid—but at least it's better than walking."

"Bally." Anne Marie had to walk fast to keep up with her sister-in-law. "My best shoes—and I've only worn them once."

Water bubbled along the gutter and eddied about the wheels of the cars; even the crest of the road was covered by a sheet of fast-moving rainwater.

Odile gave her the umbrella and unlocked the car—a Fiat with rust that formed orange acne along the once-white paintwork.

"The BMW's for Freddy's mother—not for his wife."

Anne Marie climbed in beside Odile. The surface of the road was visible through the holes in the floorboard.

"With this weather, it's probably best to take the ring road."

Odile was an aggressive driver. She sat upright behind the wheel, and the beauty spot on her nose moved as she spoke. "You'd better open the window, Anne Marie. The exhaust pipe's dropped off. Don't want you or me dying of carbon monoxide poisoning." A grim smile. "It would bring too much joy for Mamie."

They went past the hospital, up the curving slip road and onto the four-lane highway. It was not yet ten o'clock, but the traffic was heavy, composed mainly of lorries.

The wipers were not fast enough for the sheets of tropical rain that transformed everything into surrealist shapes.

"And it's not even the rainy season yet."

The window misted on the inside.

Anne Marie slipped off her shoe and looked at the sole.

"The boss said we could take the morning off—but I wanted to come."

Anne Marie turned. "Your boss?"

"Kacy." The beauty spot quivered.

They reached the turning for Le Raizet. Without slowing, Odile pulled into the exit lane and headed back into the city. The car went through several puddles. At the traffic lights, Odile turned right and bumped the car up onto an unsurfaced sidewalk that was fast being transformed into yellow mud. "We can walk the rest," she said as she got out. She added, "Freddy didn't get home until midnight last night."

"Neither did Jean Michel."

"You went home with Casimir?"

Anne Marie opened the umbrella, and together the two women hastened through the deserted market. Ginger roots, green limes and mangoes lay out on the stone benches, protected by thick plastic sheets. "He tried to kiss me."

"They're all interested in just one thing—until they marry you."

Cars were cluttered about the entrance to the cemetery. The black hearse was empty. Two men in uniform stood by the gates, beneath a shared umbrella. Their eyes scarcely moved as Anne Marie and Odile went up the narrow strip of road.

The path rose steeply between the neat rows of gravestones.

The cemetery was laid out on the edge of the hill. At one time, in accordance with Napoleonic law, it must have been beyond the limits of Pointe-à-Pitre. Now it looked onto the grey skyline of the drab city housing projects.

Low clouds rolled across the sky.

The family tombs, with their plastic, tawdry flowers and their factual epitaphs, were heavy marble boxes stuck on the slope of the hill.

On several headstones, there was an embedded photograph of the loved one who had been laid to eternal rest in the ground beneath. Men from the city, with collar and tie; buxom mothers and the serious faces of children. They stared out tirelessly at the living world and at the falling rain.

Odile nodded to several people who were already coming down the path. They were detaching themselves from the crowd that had formed around a fresh tombstone.

The rain hammered down on a sea of umbrellas, onto other, exposed mourners, onto the kepis and epaulettes and onto the damp gravel underfoot.

"There he is—look!"

"Who?" Anne Marie turned.

"Kacy." Anger and a kind of excitement in her voice. Odile moved her head to one side and raindrops splattered onto her cheeks.

Anne Marie followed her glance. She saw a small man without hat or umbrella. Dark eyebrows and hunched shoulders. He had the thick wavy hair of an Indian. His skin was dark—almost jet black. Rain ran down his face.

"A bastard, too."

"Why?"

"A little bit of power and they treat you even worse than the whites—and now there's talk of half of us getting the sack." Bitterness in her voice. "He can run around in a Jaguar—but lately he's been telling everyone he's got financial problems. So I'll probably lose my job before long." Odile turned sharply and almost caught Anne Marie's eye on the metal tip of the umbrella. "You work for the police, don't you?"

There was a bareheaded officer standing before the grave. His head was lowered in prayer.

A priest swung the incense holder while a little boy held an umbrella above his head.

"Ministry of Justice."

"Then perhaps I should tell you."

"Tell me what, Odile?"

The officer carried a large wreath in his hands. His uniform was turning dark with rainwater.

"About a phone call at the office."

"Well?"

A slight hesitation. "Kacy works in construction. He's got a fleet of bulldozers and lorries. Excavation work, leveling, putting down foundations. Has a reputation for bidding low offers—very low offers. Goodness knows how he does it. But on several occasions, it's landed him the best jobs." Odile shrugged. "What do I care? I get my salary, and I mind my own business." She ran a hand across her forehead. She looked tired.

Over the pounding of the rain against the umbrella, she went on. "A lot of Pointe-à-Pitre used to be underwater until it was filled in by us. And in Gosier, there's been a building boom in the past few years. We've been involved in the construction of four of the five new hotels there. And each time, the final cost's been way over Kacy's initial bid."

"Interesting."

"Nobody seems to mind. The hotels get built, we keep our jobs and Kacy has his Jaguar, a villa in the Grands Fonds. He's a supporter of Le Moule football team, and when they got into the national quarter finals a few years back, he could afford a weekend in Paris—just to see his team defeated." She paused. Her lips were quivering at the corner. The beauty spot trembled. "He's got a mistress. A little girl at the Chamber of Commerce who's supposed to be one of Giscard's favorites when he comes here on his Christmas visits."

Another wreath, the dark leaves glistening, was placed before the tombstone.

"You know about Raymond Calais?"

Abruptly Anne Marie turned to look at her sister-in law. She said, "He's dead."

"They were friends, or at least, Kacy and Calais used to work together."

"Why would Kacy work with Calais?"

"SODECA."

"What's that?"

"*Société d'économie mixte pour le développement de la Caraibe.*"

Anne Marie shook her head, not understanding.

"A consortium—part private, part state-owned—with responsibility for developing land and getting it ready for the builders to move in." Odile gestured toward the sprawling high-rise towers of Pointe-à-Pitre. "All that used to be inhabited by people living in shacks. SODECA bought them out, dried out the land, and then prepared it for the big building companies." Odile was watching her employer and there was repressed anger in her voice. "Raymond Calais phoned up. I was in the office and I took the call. Kacy was downstairs talking to the drivers, so I put the phone down and I went out to tell him he was wanted."

The widow was kneeling before the tomb. Beside her, the Préfet held an umbrella that protected her from the rain. Her head was bowed, her hands clasped together.

"'You're wanted on the telephone,' I said. 'Who is it?' he asked me and I told him."

The widow wore gloves.

"Kacy got angry. Went off the handle."

"With you?"

Odile shook her head. "He said, 'Calais? Haven't they murdered that white bastard yet?' And that was on Friday. The following Tuesday I heard about Calais' death on the radio."

A single bugle began to play the Last Post.

47
Fairy tales

"I want all possible data on Kacy."

"Kacy?"

"My informant tells me the accountants have been in. Monsieur Lafitte, see what information you can get out of them."

"What's the company called?"

Anne Marie rubbed the back of her hand. "*Travaux et Terrassements Antillais*. It's just possible there's a connection between Kacy and Calais' death. A possibility I should look into."

Lafitte was sitting on the far side of the desk, his hands clasped between his knees and his eyes on the floor. "Madame le juge, I thought you'd dropped the Calais affair."

"Whatever made you think that?"

He looked up. He had the dull eyes of a faithful dog. "Because of the other juges d'instruction."

She frowned. "Other judges?"

"I just thought. . . ."

Anne Marie interrupted him. "I'm still very much in charge of the Calais dossier, Monsieur Lafitte. And for the time being, I don't think anybody's seriously envisaging taking it out of my hands. Certainly not the procureur."

Lafitte studied the polished mahogany floor.

"No need to remind you the Code goes to considerable lengths

189

to ensure the freedom of action of the juge d'instruction. It's absolutely essential the investigating judge have complete freedom in preparing a dossier. That freedom is sacrosanct—and not even the procureur himself has any power over it without the written permission of the Ministry of Justice."

"It's just that I heard that. . . ."

"Sacrosanct, monsieur l'inspecteur, and anything you might have heard to the contrary is tantamount to fairy tales." She accorded him a tight smile.

The blinds had been drawn against the driving rain. The office was dingy, the lace curtains were dirty. Anne Marie's lamp cast its yellowish circle of light onto the desk. Trousseau was behind the Japy typewriter, pretending to take no notice of the conversation while he compared lists of figures. Occasionally he muttered under his breath and ran a finger along the line of his moustache.

"You understand?"

"Yes, madame le juge." For a second they looked at each other, then Lafitte turned his eyes downward to the mahogany floor again.

"You have any information on Hégésippe Bray?"

"Nothing from Basse-Terre." Lafitte gave a shrug. "We still haven't had an answer from Paris."

"Monsieur Lafitte, Bray's been dead now for over a week. I need this information."

"Paris doesn't answer."

"Well, phone them, for goodness sake."

"We're supposed to use the telex."

"Use the telex, use whatever you want, Monsieur Lafitte. Throw a bottle with a message into the sea—do what you have to. Put the taxpayers' money to some use. Anything, Monsieur Lafitte. I need the records on Hégésippe Bray—and eight days is already too long. I need them now."

"I understand, madame le juge."

"I can't begin to understand why Calais was killed if I don't know what happened in 1940."

"I'm doing my best."

"There's a connection between the return of Bray from South America and Raymond Calais' death—and I don't think it's got anything to do with the land. According to Calais' widow, Bray was going to get the land back, anyway. Perhaps they were hoping he'd die before it was necessary for them to return the land. I need to know what happened before Hégésippe Bray was sent to French Guyana."

"I'll do my best."

"I don't want you to do your best, Monsieur Lafitte. I want results."

A silence that hung awkwardly. "Yes, madame le juge."

Trousseau continued to mutter over his figures.

"And I haven't seen the photographs of the weapon."

"Photographs, madame?"

"The photographs of the gun."

"They were in the dossier."

"I haven't seen them. It was an old gun, I believe."

"A twelve bore. An Idéale."

"That's why I'd like to see the photographs. Bray's name was engraved on the butt, wasn't it?"

"Engraved on a silver plate that'd been screwed onto the end of the butt."

"That's precisely what I don't understand."

Lafitte shrugged. "Probably screwed on with a screwdriver."

"A pre-war gun, Monsieur Lafitte?"

"Yes, madame le juge."

"With Hégésippe Bray's name on it?"

Again he nodded.

"We can assume Bray bought it new—at a time when he could afford to have his name engraved on a piece of plated silver."

"Yes."

"Bray bought it before the war." Anne Marie spoke slowly. "He then spent forty years in French Guyana. I'm sure the penal authorities in Cayenne had no intention of allowing Bray keep his gun in prison."

Lafitte's face seemed to brighten. "You mean he must've left it here?"

The telephone rang shrilly, and Trousseau picked up the receiver.

"Find out, Monsieur Lafitte, where his gun was during all that time."

"Your husband, madame le juge." Trousseau held out the receiver.

Lafitte had got up to leave.

"One other thing, Monsieur Lafitte."

His shoulders slumped and for a fraction of a second, Anne Marie felt a stab of guilt. She pointed to the newspaper on her desk. "You've seen the open letter addressed to the widow of the bomb disposal man?"

Lafitte nodded unhappily.

"They mention the insurrection of 1967. They also mention—and I quote—the American freedom fighter, Jerry Dupont, who sacrificed his life in the cause of anti-imperialism. This same Jerry Dupont was mentioned to me by Suez-Panama." She looked at Lafitte. "There's a dossier on this Dupont somewhere. Perhaps with Renseignements Généraux. I'd like to see it. See if you can get hold of a copy, please."

"Yes, madame le juge." Hurriedly Lafitte shook her hand and left the office.

Anne Marie took the receiver from Trousseau.

"Jean Michel? You're up already?" She looked at her watch. "Not even eleven o'clock."

"I'm sorry about last night. You must understand…"

"Why are you phoning, Jean Michel?"

There was a pause and she heard his breath over the line.

"I can't pick up Fabrice after school. I've got to go out."

"Again, Jean Michel?"

"You remember *Le Domien*? The magazine in Basse-Terre? The editor's just phoned asking me to go down there this afternoon."

"I see."

"I won't be back until late."

"I'm getting used to that, Jean Michel."

"I'm going round to the rue Alsace-Lorraine now. Mamie will fetch Fabrice from school, and she'll give him his afternoon tea. I'll tell her he can watch television. When you've finished at the Palais de Justice, could you go round and pick him up?"

"You don't leave me much choice."

Silence.

"So I'll see you later, Anne Marie."

"Yes," she said flatly, and then the image of the woman, dressed in black and kneeling on the damp gravel while the Préfet held an umbrella, suddenly passed before her eyes. "Jean Michel."

"Yes?"

"Drive carefully."

48
Tear gas

"Who died in 1968?" Philippe Carreaux asked.

The university of Paris closed down, and it was one day in mid-May 1968 that Anne Marie was caught in the métro station Odéon. The riot police sealed the exits and then began to fire canister after canister of tear-gas into the closed station. The air turned into a thick grey blanket as women and children lay coughing on the cold stone platform, seeking fresh air.

The only escape was on the trains, but the trains refused to stop.

"How many people died in Paris?" Philippe Carreaux asked again.

"I don't know." Anne Marie shrugged. "Theoretically nobody."

"Here in Guadeloupe they killed more than a hundred during the riots of '67."

"Those are the statistics of the independence movement. Of people like you, Monsieur Carreaux." She tapped the newspaper that now lay open on top of the photocopying machine. "I've read the letter in the paper."

"A hundred—perhaps more."

"Your statistics."

"The French papers hushed it up. At best, a couple of

paragraphs in *Le Monde*." He gave an amused shrug. "Who in Paris or Marseilles wants to know about riots in the colonies? We're only natives, after all."

They were in the basement of the university library, next to the stacks. A smell of glue and ink, the hum of the photocopier. An untidy pile of *Bulletins Officiels*.

At the far end of the long table, a man—one of the library technicians, wearing blue overalls—was turning the handle of an enormous paper press. He took no notice of their conversation. He had sunken eyes and wore a peaked cyclist's hat that advertised Mumm champagne.

Rain fell against the single glass door; wind worried at the wet grass outside.

"Why were there riots?"

"Why are there ever riots?" Philippe Carreaux paused. "Because people realize they don't have freedom."

"What happened?"

Carreaux took a deep breath. "There was a cobbler. An old man who had a little business—an old man with skin as dark as the night who used to repair shoes outside one of the shops in the main street in Basse-Terre. Quick heels or stick-on soles— nothing very sophisticated. For some reason the shopkeeper wanted to be rid of him. The man'd been there for years, never harmed anybody. But the shopkeeper got the idea the cobbler's presence was bad for business. So he chased him away—and each time the old man came back bringing his box and his tools. One day the shopkeeper came out and he was more furious than ever. His racial supremacy had been questioned. I don't think he was French. Probably a Jew—all Jews care about is money. He kicked the old man in the rear and sent him flying. But still the man came back. And that's when the white man set the dogs onto him. A crowd gathered. My people are not violent—but we hate injustice. We've already seen too much in our history, and so the crowd started to throw stones at the shop. That's how the rioting started."

"The people of Guadeloupe may not like violence, yet some-one has killed an innocent army officer with a home made bomb."

"Innocent?" A wry smile behind the small goatee. "A member of the occupying forces." Philippe Carreaux's dull features appeared tired. "Madame, I am the first secretary of the Mouve-ment d'action des nationalistes guadeloupéens. I know absolutely nothing about the bombings at the airport. I'm tired—I'm very tired—of being interrogated by police officers concerning my whereabouts last Thursday. You're a reasonable person—indeed, madame le juge, you're a very attractive person."

"Thank you."

"So if you're hoping to trick me into some admission concern-ing the airport bombing, you're wasting your time and mine." Carreaux removed the newspaper and lifted the rubber flap lid of the photocopier. "I've got a lot of work to do. The new term starts in a couple of weeks."

"Tell me about the riots of '67."

"As for your accusation of violence," Carreaux went on, turn-ing back to face her and tapping the chest of his loose jacket, "it wasn't the Africans who introduced slavery to Guadeloupe—the worst violence of all."

"About the riots of '67, Monsieur Carreaux?"

His eyes were uncertain. Then he shrugged. "The rioting spread to Pointe-à-Pitre. The situation was already tense—the building profession had been on strike for some time—they wanted better pay, but the bosses had all the support of the regime. They said there was no money—and got the riot police to patrol the streets. Fighting broke out in the streets of Pointe-à-Pitre." Carreaux ran his tongue along his lips. "The French reaction was exactly what was to be expected. Gendarmes, riot police—they came pouring into Pointe-à-Pitre in armored cars and half-tracks. Terrifying—but that's what de Gaulle wanted. The black race had forgotten to be grateful. And then the shooting started. Not tear-gas, madame le juge, but bullets. Real bullets."

The university stood on the hilltop and through the glass door and the falling raindrops, Anne Marie could see the forest of rocking ship masts in the marina.

"A hundred killed—and that's a conservative estimate. In France, scarcely a word in the so-called democratic press."

"Please go on."

For a moment, his face softened. "I've seen you before, haven't I?"

"I don't think so."

"At the funeral."

Anne Marie asked, surprised, "You were at the funeral this morning?"

"At the funeral of Hégésippe Bray." His eyes scrutinized her face and then ran over her clothes. "You were with the police, weren't you? Taking photographs."

"You knew Bray?"

"Another victim." Carreaux smiled. "And of all the colonialists, you French have been the worst. Or the most cunning. The English—when they say they're going to leave, they leave. France turns round—after centuries of exploitation—France turns round and suddenly tells us we are all her children. Black-skinned—but still her children."

"How did you know about Hégésippe Bray's funeral? It wasn't mentioned on the radio."

"I am the first secretary of a legally formed political party whose primary aim is the improvement of the living conditions of my compatriots. I don't have to tune into the French radio station to know what's happening on my island. I prefer to hear the truth. And the truth I get elsewhere—not from Giscard's mouthpiece, which some people foolishly refer to as a radio."

Anne Marie tapped the newspaper. "Who was Jerry Dupont, Monsieur Carreaux?"

"A friend of the people of Guadeloupe."

"What did he do?"

"Nothing."

"But he died."

Philippe Carreaux nodded.

"In police custody, Monsieur Carreaux?"

"No."

"But he hanged himself?"

Philippe Carreaux leaned against the photocopier and folded his arms. "You really want to know the truth about Jerry Dupont?"

"That's why I've come to see you. In the normal course of things, I would rather stay in my office—particularly when it is raining."

"Rain's good for the vegetables."

"Only nobody grows vegetables any more in Guadeloupe." She shrugged. "Cheaper to buy them in the supermarkets."

"I see you're beginning to understand the absurdity of our colonial situation."

"Even an investigating judge has to go shopping."

"No one to help you?"

"My husband is West Indian. Like yours, Monsieur Carreaux, mine is a mixed marriage."

"Ah." He ran his tongue along his lip. "You have studied my file, I see. Yours or that of the Renseignements Généraux?"

"Just common knowledge."

"Does your file tell you about my mistresses?"

"You dislike the whites—but you have a white wife. A French wife."

"Your name is Laveaud?" Philippe Carreaux looked at her thoughtfully. "I believe I know Monsieur Laveaud . . . a student here once. He gave up his studies to go and live in France."

"And marry me."

"A very wise choice." Carreaux gestured toward the wooden stool. "Please be seated, madame le juge."

The man in the blue overalls looked at his watch, then took a packet of cigarettes from his pocket. He lit a Gitane. He sat down at the far end of the table and started reading a magazine.

Anne Marie rubbed her finger. The itching had returned.

"Jerry Dupont turned up here in 1971. I'm surprised he ever managed to get through customs. A hippy—and this was still at the time of Vietnam."

"An American?"

"He had an American passport—but he could speak French. The father was French, and Jerry'd grown up in Morocco, where his father worked for a big oil company. Later he went to the Lycée Français in New York. Jerry Dupont didn't look like an American—more like an Arab. I first met him by chance."

"Where?"

"Walking down the rue Frébault. Long hair down to his shoulders and a band round his forehead. Dirty clothes, cut-off jeans, and bare feet. Here in Guadeloupe, we don't like dirtiness—and walking barefoot is for us an insult. We no longer live in the jungle, and we ask for a minimum of respect. But Jerry Dupont didn't realize that—he didn't seek to offend. I can remember being very surprised when I discovered he was teaching at the university."

"Teaching what?"

"English. A degree from Tufts University. So he got a job on the small campus. In time we got to be friends. Intelligent—he understood the situation with surprising acuity. Also very gentle."

"Flower power."

"Precisely."

"How did he get arrested?"

"More riots—this time the cane cutters and the kids at the lycée. Windows got smashed and the administration—with the tacit support of the Communist party of Guadeloupe, their Uncle Tom lackeys—called in the riot police."

"And more people got killed, I suppose?"

He shook his head. "Then Dupont disappeared. Vanished."

"Where to?"

"Ten days later, he re-emerged. His face covered with bruises. A black eye and his hair had been shaved off, down to the scalp. Jerry was no longer a hippy—he looked more like a convict who'd been thrown to the sharks off Devil's Island. Another French specialty, as no doubt Hégésippe Bray could've told you."

"Where had Dupont been?"

"In police detention."

"Scarcely likely, Monsieur Carreaux." Anne Marie shook her head. "Police detention for more than a week? Without a formal accusation? That's not possible."

He laughed. "We're not talking about France. We're talking about a colony."

"The Republic doesn't make up the law as it goes along."

Philippe Carreaux lowered his voice. "Jerry came to see me. At that time I was sharing a flat in the university—a small, stuffy room that smelled of blocked drains—with several million cockroaches."

"Where did Dupont live?"

"In one of the new blocks of flats that were being built at that time. One of the new estates. I think it was Cité Mortenol."

"That's where I live."

"Where they've rehoused people who used to live in shacks?" He raised an eyebrow. "A working-class area for a juge d'instruction— for a white juge d'instruction."

"You don't think distinguishing between social classes is a form of racism?"

Carreaux laughed. "A Marxist juge d'instruction?"

Anne Marie went on. "What did Dupont tell you?"

"They'd kept his passport at the gendarmerie, and Jerry was terrified. He had a desperate need to talk to somebody willing to listen, and so I listened. I made some coffee and got him to sit down—but he was very agitated. His hands shook—he spilled half the coffee."

"Why was he so worried?"

"They wanted him to be an informer. The gendarmes had confiscated his personal belongings—including several grams of marijuana. Told him he could have everything back—provided he infiltrated the anti-colonialist movement among the students and staff at the university." The corners of Carreaux's mouth turned upward. "In those days, the university had the reputation of being a center of political dissent. Renseignements Généraux told Jerry Dupont, either he worked for them. . . ."

"Or?"

"He'd be facing charges for the possession of drugs. And be deported." He scratched his salt-and-pepper beard. "There was a drugs charge waiting for him in the US. The last thing Dupont wanted was deportation back to the United States."

"He had sympathy for the revolutionaries?"

"Not revolutionaries, madame le juge. Anti-colonialists. And yes, I think he did have sympathy for us."

"What did you advise him to do?"

The man in the blue overalls lit another cigarette. He raised the magazine he was reading—it was wrapped in brown paper— and placed it on the table.

"I tried to calm him down. The gendarmes had told him they wanted him to report back a few days later—the gendarmes acting under the orders of Renseignements Généraux."

"He calmed down?"

"Jerry Dupont told me he would never go—that he'd rather kill himself."

"But he went?"

"Because I accompanied him. I told him to act rationally. A new experience for me, seeing a white man getting this treatment from a colonial regime." He smiled softly at the memory. "I went to the gendarmerie, and I waited outside, thinking he'd be out in a few minutes—a quarter of an hour at most."

"And?"

"I spent more than five and a half hours waiting for him, just hanging around."

"Dupont was released?"

"I went home."

"Without waiting for him?"

"A lot later—around midnight, Jerry turned up at my place. I was in bed, and he banged on the door and woke me up. You can't imagine how glad I was to see him, the poor bastard."

"Hadn't caused you to lose any sleep."

"You're very cynical, but in fact I hadn't been sleeping—I'd been worrying. He came into the flat and I offered to make him a hot drink. Almost as much for myself as for him. Only this time Jerry needed something stronger—a lot stronger. I gave him rum, which he drank neat, one shot after another. As you can imagine, he got drunk very quickly."

"And you?"

"Stuck to a tisane. Soon he went off to the lavatory. By this time I was pretty tired. There was nothing physically wrong with Jerry; the police hadn't touched him—and at the time I was convinced it was an act."

"An act?"

"He was overreacting."

"So you kicked him out?"

"I let him drink. I thought he would calm down. I was relieved, you see. I'd been worried."

"Did he calm down?"

"Not exactly. He went to. . . ."

"Yes?"

"He went to piss, and when he didn't reappear from the lavatory, I went looking for him. Found him sitting on the lavatory seat, his trousers round his ankles and blood all over the tiled floor. He'd taken my razor, the stupid bastard, and had tried to slit his wrist."

Anne Marie said, "Messy."

"Less serious than it looked at first. People say I'm a hard man—and perhaps I am. But I abhor violence. I detest unnecessary suffering." He shrugged. "That night Jerry slept on my bed, and I slept on the floor."

"Good of you."

He looked at Anne Marie. "Not much else I could do for a fellow human being who'd fallen into the hands of the colonialists. The following morning I gave him a good breakfast. I got the impression he'd cheered up."

"And Jerry Dupont went back to teaching?"

"No."

As the technician turned the page of his magazine, Anne Marie recognized the soft colors of pornographic photography. The look on the man's face was of deep concentration. The tip of his tongue was visible between his lips.

"It was Whitsun and I had to visit my parents in Marie Galante. I invited Jerry to come with me. The trip would've done him a world of good. But he refused. Said Renseignements Généraux had forbidden him to leave Pointe-à-Pitre."

"When did you next see him?"

"I didn't, madame le juge."

49

Massif central

Carreaux's eyes were cold. "Jerry didn't come into the university the following week. Or ever again. We all assumed he'd been arrested. The atmosphere was tense. Riot police and armored cars patrolling the streets of the city. I'd once visited him in Cité Mortenol and so I went back looking for him. I went with a colleague—a man called Auguste. We knocked on Jerry's door, but there was no reply. The neighbors said they hadn't seen him for several days and so we left. What else could we do?"

"The police had arrested him?"

"The newspapers and the radio tried to hush everything up, but they couldn't stop people from talking. The neighbor—the same woman that Auguste and I had spoken with—had noticed a smell and it got worse as the days went past—it was the beginning of June when the temperatures are up in the thirties. Then she was plagued with flies. She spring-cleaned her house—but the flies wouldn't go away."

"She alerted the police?"

"Not something my compatriots like doing. But the smell got a lot worse—and finally she felt she must contact the police. When those gentlemen felt they could spare a moment from beating natives and firing at the cane workers on strike, they sent round a patrol. An officer tried to knock the door down."

"You were there?"

"No, madame le juge." Carreaux shook his head. "When the officer couldn't get through the front door, he went through the neighbor's apartment and climbed in over the balcony. "

"And?"

"Hanging from the ceiling. That's how he found Jerry Dupont." Philippe Carreaux smiled grimly. "Dead and in an advanced state of putrefaction."

"He wasn't murdered?"

"Of course he was murdered. Renseignements Généraux were as guilty as if they'd put the noose round Dupont's neck. The poor bastard—he'd managed to live twenty-three years of his life, and it was in Guadeloupe—in a strange country and at the hands of the forces of reaction——that he had to die. Like a tracked animal."

The technician put the magazine away, stood up and went to the glass door to stare out at the marina and the falling rain.

"What did you do, Monsieur Carreaux?"

"We held a meeting of the university staff. A lot of us were shocked, but of course, the university was controlled by the Communists who were playing the game of the colonialists. Time of political tension, they said—it wouldn't do any good to drag Jerry Dupont's death into the political arena. The real problem"—Philippe Carreaux snorted angrily—"was the cane cutters' wages. They're all the same, the Communists. They love to maintain they're patriots—but their well-disciplined hearts all belong to Moscow—and to the soul of Joseph Stalin."

"You let the matter drop?"

"Jerry Dupont had given Auguste an address in New York, and I wrote to his parents personally. They never replied."

Silence.

Carreaux said, "Auguste was from Bordeaux. He had his *agrégation*, and there was a good university career in front of him. Auguste was teaching in the West Indies instead of doing his military service. A Frenchman—but he had a certain amount of human decency. He was badly shaken by Dupont's death. He wrote a couple of letters—one to the Ministry of Education, another to the Ministry of Defense, who was his employer at the time. Felt he couldn't let Jerry Dupont die just like that, murdered and forgotten. Auguste despised the Communists even more than we patriots did. Then one day he was contacted. He was a Freemason, Auguste—all those secret signs and small aprons and grown men playing like silly children—and it was at a meeting he was given the message. By nobody less important, less influential that the Préfet's first secretary."

"What message?"

"To let the matter drop."

"Why?"

"There was more to Jerry Dupont's death than met the eye. Let the matter drop, he was told, or on returning to France, at the end of his service, instead of teaching at the University of Bordeaux, he would be finding himself teaching in some godforsaken lycée lost in the Massif Central."

50

Basse Terre

Modernization had not reached the third story of the Chamber of Commerce.

There was a floor of rubberized linoleum and the walls that had once been whitewashed were streaked with dirt and the passage of time. Anne Marie walked down the corridor and stopped a moment to stare out across the roofs of Basse-Terre. The small, colonial town nestled against the side of the Souffrière. A bright sun and a cloudless sky had transformed the Caribbean Sea into a Mediterranean blue.

ARCHIVES.

Anne Marie knocked and then pushed the door open. The hinges screeched unpleasantly.

A man stood directly in front of her. He appeared surprised. "Can I help you?" Several of his teeth were a grey metal.

"*La Coloniale.*"

"Yes?"

"Do you have the volumes for 1940?"

"Two volumes per year." He looked at Anne Marie carefully. Behind the glasses, the red edges of his eyelids were humid. "I suppose you're another of these students."

"Le juge Laveaud. I'm from the Ministry of Justice. I've just driven down from the university library in Pointe-à-Pitre. The chief librarian told me to contact Madame Cléopatre."

"Madame Cléopatre." An unpleasant laugh. "She's on maternity leave. Perhaps I can help you." His voice was not enthusiastic.

"I need *La Coloniale* for 1940."

He nodded, put down the pair of scissors he had been holding and approached the main bookcase. "Of course," he said. "What year?"

"1940—April and May."

Crouching down on his spindly legs—he was wearing shorts and a pair of battered sandals—the man ran a finger along the faded volumes. "1940, first semester." He muttered to himself. "Then here you are." He added, "They don't want to put in the conditioning because they want to do away with us."

"Us?"

"Microfilm—that's what they want. They say it's cheaper—but I don't see how it can be." He hauled the book up onto the wooden counter. "All that film—it must cost a lot of money. But they go quite wild over anything they think is modern." He shook his head, "Guadeloupe's not America, you know."

She took the book. "I want the volume for 1940—this is 1932."

The spindly man held the book in both hands, turned it and studied the gold script. "You're right, you know." He tut-tutted. "What year do you want?"

"1940."

"1940, you say? Bizarre."

"What?"

"I beg your pardon, madame."

She ducked under the hinge counter and crouched down beside the old man who was looking along the lower shelf. The dull eyes glanced at her with disapproval. His pink lips were wet. "Who are you?"

"1940, please."

"Precisely what I'm looking for." He sounded offended. "You're all the same. You come barging in here—you think you own the place—you and all the friends of Madame Cléopatre. She's not the Préfet, you know. She's not even God Almighty, whatever she may claim to the contrary. If she thinks she can boss me about, she's got another think coming." He added, "She's not going to force me into retirement."

The volumes of *La Coloniale* were out of order. The 1940 edition was wedged between the 1974 handbook to South Africa and a moth-eaten copy of the Caracas telephone directory.

"This is what I'm looking for."

The archivist said spitefully, "Then you've found it, haven't you?"

Anne Marie took the bound volume and sat down at a desk at the far end of the dusty reading room. For a while the man peered at her in angry silence, then he returned to his scissors, his spineless books, and the glue-pot.

"Madame Cléopatre," he muttered to himself.

51

La Coloniale

The pages of *La Coloniale* were coarse and had yellowed with time. The mites had been at work, giving their own punctuation to the dusty pages.

It did not take Anne Marie long to find the first reference to Hégésippe Bray. FOREMAN MURDERS WIFE AND DISAPPEARS.

The article was in the edition of Thursday, May 2. It took up one of the columns on the last page:

> The lifeless remains of a young woman, believed to be Eloise Deschamps, of the Sainte Marthe estate, Sainte-Anne, were found last Saturday by schoolchildren. Eloise Deschamps had been hacked to death and burned. The young woman, originally from Saint Pierre in Martinique, had worked for several years for Monsieur Calais, proprietor of the Sainte Marthe estate. She was the common law wife of the first foreman, Hégésippe Bray. Bray went missing at the beginning of last week, and it would appear that he frequently quarreled with his concubine, who was considerably younger than he. The military are actively seeking the runaway, and they believe that he may be in hiding in the Pointe-Noire area where, until recently, his sister was a primary school teacher.

Anne Marie turned the pages. Under the desk, she kicked off her shoes. They were still damp.

Most of the paper was now filled with events in Europe. There was a pervading sense of optimism concerning the outcome of the war. The paper spoke of the Shining Example of Democracy while denouncing the racial policies of the Germans. There were several references to Victor Schoelcher.

ARREST OF MURDERER OF SAINTE MARTHE

The article was on the front page of the paper, and it came a week after the first reference to Hégésippe Bray.

> *Hégésippe Bray, foreman at the Sainte Marthe estate for the past twenty years, was arrested Saturday, May 4, in the hamlet of Bouliqui, Sainte-Anne, where he had been hiding. He is now in the maison d'arrêt in Pointe-à-Pitre, accused of the murder of his wife.*
>
> *The body of Eloise Deschamps, a domestic in the employ of Monsieur Calais, was found on April 27. After a detailed examination by the Prof. Foucan at the Colonial Hospital, the officers of law were able to identify the mutilated remains as those of the young Eloise Deschamps. There was no offspring to the doomed union; a son had died at the age of two. The enquiries of the gendarmes have been much aided by other laborers of the Sainte Marthe estate who were in a position to inform the investigators of the frequent quarrels between Bray and his young companion. On several occasions, the woman was reported to have left the conjugal hearth. Indeed, it was generally believed that the girl had quit the Sainte Marthe estate for her native Martinique until she returned to Bray at the beginning of the month of April. Like the eye in the midst of the hurricane, the ill-starred couple found a brief respite in their altercations.*
>
> *The last person to see the young woman alive was Roland*

Remblin, cowherd on the Calais estate, who claims he saw her on April 23. He accompanied her to the house. Hégésippe Bray was waiting for her and according to Remblin, he held a whip in his hand, and he assailed the woman with a kind of language too coarse for the readers of these columns. Bray, a veteran of the Great War, has the reputation of a quick temper.

The date of the trial has been set for Monday, May 20.

Anne Marie leafed through the remaining pages. More advertisements and a single, isolated paragraph showing French troops along the Maginot line. There were two Senegalese, smiling in outsize uniforms, too loose at the neck and across the shoulders.

THE COLONIES HAVE NOT FORGOTTEN THE MOTHER COUNTRY

The volume ended with the end of May. There was no further reference to Hégésippe Bray. Anne Marie got up and, holding the pages open, walked barefoot to the counter. "I'd like a photocopy."

The man looked up. His glasses had slipped down his nose.

"Who exactly are you?"

"I work for the Ministry of Justice, and I would like a photocopy of these two articles, please. I am le juge Laveaud."

"You'll have to pay, you know."

"I will ask you for a receipt, of course."

He resembled a tired rat. What had once been intelligence in the brown eyes was now senile cunning. He took the volume and went over to the photocopying machine. "Which article?"

"The entire front page, please."

He nodded unhappily.

Anne Marie lifted the hatch and approached the shelves, looking for the second volume to 1940. Surprisingly, it was where it should have been—on the bottom shelf, next to the first semester for 1941. She took the book and went back to her desk. Her feet sought her shoes under the desk.

There was no reference to the trial in the first weeks of June. Instead, the paper spoke solely about the tragic events in France. The optimism had vanished from the faded pages. The word defeat made its first appearance; similarly, there was no mention of the faithful role of the colonies.

The report came at the end of June. The trial had taken place on Wednesday the 26th, and the article took up most of the back page, beneath an advertisement for a dental surgeon—with the latest equipment from Paris, Berlin and Rochester, New York, including electric drills.

Anne Marie ran a finger along the title.

MURDERER CONDEMNED TO PENAL COLONY FOR SEVEN YEARS.

"One franc fifty for the photocopy," the man said, aggrieved. Anne Marie nodded. "In a few minutes."

The one-time foreman on the Sainte Marthe estate, Hégésippe Bray, illegitimate son of Florentine Bray of Douville, Sainte-Anne, was condemned last Friday to seven years of forced labor in the penal colony of St.-Laurent-du-Maroni in the Guyanas. This judgment follows several weeks of frenetic labor on the part of the colonial gendarmerie and the admirable juge d'instruction, M. Timoléon, despite considerable administrative difficulties arising from the situation in Europe. The avocat général *was successful in obtaining the condemnation of Hégésippe Bray after two days of impassioned debate, thanks largely to the evidence of neighbors and fellow workers on the estate, several of whom were called to the stand. They testified to having heard and seen violent struggles between Bray and his young concubine.*

Bray's defense was bizarre, to say the least, and clearly put his lawyer, Maître Gillon, to some difficulty. Bray admitted to having killed his woman. The weapon, he said, was her magic potion! Despite frequent laughter from the public benches, obliging the president to call for silence more than once, Bray forcefully maintained that the woman was a she-devil inhabited by evil spirits who delighted in tormenting him. Speaking solely in vernacular, he went on to state that Eloise Deschamps frequently changed her appearance. At nights, he maintained, she would travel the countryside of the Grande-Terre in the form of a bird or a dog. Bray admitted that in her womanly state she frequently mocked him for his lack of amatory ardor. Furthermore, he believed that his companion had been pregnant at the time of death.

This last assertion, however, was soon conclusively dismissed by the science of Dr. Foucan, who was called to the stand.

According to Bray, after a particularly vehement altercation between Eloise Deschamps and himself, the young woman had left home. The woman led him to believe that she was carrying the unborn child of another man. She stayed away for several weeks, returning to Sainte Marthe in April. Although there was a reconciliation between Bray and her, Mlle. Deschamps continued to practice her black arts, Hégésippe Bray stated. One day, while she was working in the house of Monsieur Calais, Bray returned early to his own abode where he found two vials belonging to the woman. Each vial contained a sluggish liquid. Following the advice of a Voodoo doctor, Bray carefully decanted the liquid, exchanging the contents of the two bottles, each of which was marked with hieroglyphics beyond his understanding. The following Tuesday night, Hégésippe Bray was awoken from his sleep, and leaving the house, he found his companion lying in the grass. He said that she had been burned. After a few words of Voodoo prayer that Bray failed to comprehend, the poor woman breathed her last. Overcome by remorse and fear, Bray cut up the corpse and then hid it. Hindered from accomplishing this grisly task by the dawn, he carried the remains to L'Étang Diable where they were later found by schoolchildren.

Called to the witness stand, Prof. Foucan acknowledged that the cadaver had been subjected to burning. He said it had been sprinkled with paraffin. But as to the cause of death, he was equally adamant. Eloise Deschamps had been poisoned, probably with oleander.

The court was not inclined to believe Bray's tale of black magic and witchcraft. Indeed, Maître Gillon for the defense merely tried to show that the foreman was a man who had made the mistake of sharing his bed with a headstrong and beautiful woman much younger than himself and whose appetite for excitement clearly outstripped his own. His head had been turned by her beauty; then his anger and jealousy had been aroused by her willful behavior. In his simplicity, he had attributed her headstrong nature to a form of witchcraft.

The fees of Maître Gillon, who once again astounded the court with the range and depth of his eloquence, were most generously met by Monsieur Calais. Despite his advanced age and the difficulty he had in walking, Monsieur Calais stepped onto the stand and, in his firm, well-educated voice, spoke in eulogistic terms of the merits of Bray, who, the court was told, had been Monsieur Calais' right hand man for more than twenty years and who, in his youth, had fought valiantly at Verdun.

It was most certainly this testimony, given by a man loved by both friends and employees, which saved Bray from that most dreadful of chastisements, the guillotine. Throughout the trial, Bray remained calm, speaking only when told to and stating that it had never been his intention to harm the poor woman.

On hearing his sentence, Bray remained unmoved, but there was evident satisfaction among the many people who had come to follow the trial. The uxoricide Bray would appear to have been a harsh man and a demanding foreman, placing his master's interest before all else. Let us hope that his evident merits and loyalty will be put to good use during the seven years of sojourn at St.-Laurent and that it is as a reformed and wiser man that he will return to his native Guadeloupe.

"One franc fifty."

"Of course." Anne Marie reached for her handbag. "But I'll need another photocopy."

"Then you'll have to pay me first.

"I have no intention of not paying you."

Like the claw of a scavenging bird, his fingers took the ten-franc coin that Anne Marie held out. "Sometimes I think you people are worse than the locals. No manners. There are no manners anymore."

"Can you give me a copy of this page, please?"

"No respect anymore."

Anne Marie stood up and slipped her feet into the damp shoes.

"And," the man continued, "I can tell you, mademoiselle, that the volume would have been in its right place if that man friend of Madame Cléopatre hadn't taken it." He clicked his tongue. "They're all the same—and all of a sudden, everybody's wanting to read *La Coloniale*. And so they have to come here and pester me."

"Who wanted to read it?"

"No respect." He turned away. "Because they think that I'm an old man."

Anne Marie caught him by the arm. "Please tell me who wanted to read it."

He looked at her over the glasses.

"Who's been reading the old newspapers?"

"You think I don't know?" He was silent for a moment, then he reached out and touched the volume that was grimy with dust. "The Calais murder—you think I don't realize what you're all interested in?"

"Who?"

"He teaches at the university in Pointe-à-Pitre."

"University?"

"He forgot his keys. Always playing with them and then he left them behind." The wet lips trembled. "He telephoned from the university. A strange name—like the canals."

"Canals? You mean Suez-Panama?"

52

Shoe box

Fabrice was holding her hand as they came up the stairs in the Cité Mortenol.

"Maman, you're wearing new shoes."

New shoes and a matching Céline handbag. Impulse shopping in Basse-Terre, an expensive boutique in the Cours Nolivos. "I ruined my best pair in the rain this morning."

"Wish I had money."

"When you're grown up, you'll have as much money as you want."

It had ceased to rain in Pointe-à-Pitre, and the evening air was cool. The sun had gone down behind the penciled line of the mountains to the west.

"I thought Papa was coming to fetch me."

"Papa's looking for a new job."

"He's always looking for a job."

"It's not easy, Fabrice."

"You've got one."

"It's easier for me."

"Because you're white?"

Anne Marie laughed. "Because I'm a civil servant—and there's always work for a civil servant."

"I want to be a civil servant when I grow up—or help children cross the road outside school."

They were on the last flight of steps, and Fabrice was out of breath from the effort of keeping up with his mother. The satchel bumped against his back. "Are you cleverer than Papa?"

"Of course not." She added, "We're just different, Papa and I."

"The girls at school are cleverer than the boys—they're good at spelling and irregular verbs." He turned up his nose. "But I don't like girls—except Cécile."

"She's pretty?"

"Cécile is the cleverest girl in the class. She's white."

"The color of your skin doesn't affect your intelligence. A lot of white people are very stupid."

"Jews are clever."

"Who told you that?"

"Our mistress says Jews are very clever—but that they use their cleverness to cheat poor people. Hey, what's that?" He let go of her hand and ran up the last steps. The sound of his feet echoed against the stair wall.

"Don't make such a noise."

"Hey, look. It's a box—Maman, it's a box."

"Don't touch it—Fabrice, don't touch it."

He stood back, suddenly frightened and his eyes wide open.

It was too late.

Somebody had left the box in front of the apartment door.

Accidentally, Fabrice had knocked off the lid.

Anne Marie crouched down and gingerly she looked into the box. She looked at the dark, black object.

R.I.P.

A coffin. A small coffin made from black cardboard.

"What does it say, Maman? What does it say?"

FABRICE LAVEAUD, 1973–1980 Requiescat in pace.

Anne Marie stood up. With a trembling hand, she searched for the door key in her new handbag.

She felt sick.

53
Forensic

Land crabs scurried away before her like an army in retreat. One or two fell into the brackish water that had been cut off from the sea by the falling tide.

Beneath her breath, Anne Marie cursed the driver.

Mist was coming from the lagoon, and somewhere a dog was barking.

Anne Marie found the path. It was scarcely discernible—a thin, sandy track beneath the stunted grass. Mosquitoes danced before her eyes. Then through the bushes and the tilting coconut trees, she caught sight of the revolving light of a police van.

Trousseau was leaning against a tree trunk. The sun had at last peeped over the horizon and was lighting the sea with the first strips of red. Anne Marie could not make out Trousseau's face as they shook hands, but she recognized the glint of his teeth and saw that he was smiling.

"You should've got the Indian to drive you another couple of kilometers. There's a turning near the hotels. No need to walk, madame le juge." He had set the typewriter case on the humid sand, and the red crabs were hurtling their bodies against it in organized futility.

"I don't like being pulled out of my bed at five in the morning. What's going on, Monsieur Trousseau?"

He gestured. "You'd better ask them."

Anne Marie went toward the police van and caught her shoe in a hole. She looked down and saw the naked roots of the tree. More crabs.

An ugly place.

The coconut trees stood only a few meters from the edge of the sea. Rotting branches, rotting roots, tin cans and plastic flotsam from the sea.

She recognized neither of the two gendarmes, but she nodded as they came to attention to salute her. Then she saw the old Peugeot pickup. An ancient car in battleship grey, the driver's door open lopsidedly, and the gear stick stuck out from the steering column. Sitting in the passenger seat was a little boy.

His head was in his hands, and he was crying.

To the east the sun was getting warmer, and the trees were taking on long, giraffe-like shadows. The craters in the sand formed weird penumbra. A man in overalls leaned against the back of the pickup that sat low on its wheels. The tailgate was down and a square-handled shovel stood upright in the mountainous cargo of grey sand.

"Christ, it's taken them nearly an hour to get here."

A vehicle came bouncing down the sand track road. Like the police van, it had a revolving blue light. The wail of the siren was strident in the morning air.

A body lay on the ground.

Anne Marie approached the body as the ambulance came to a halt and the driver jumped out. The assistant followed him. Both were dressed in white, and they hurried over to where the man lay on the chill sand. "They told us to go to Morne-à-l'Eau," the driver said defensively. "Not our fault if we're late. Only ten minutes ago the radio told us it was Gosier."

The wail of the siren died as the driver knelt down and felt for the pulse of the man.

Anne Marie crouched down beside him. "Well?"

"Still alive."

In his state of unconsciousness, Michel Gurion had taken on the appearance of a younger man. Despite the paleness, despite the fact that one of the lenses of his rimmed glasses had been smashed, the television journalist seemed both healthier and younger than when Anne Marie had last seen him at the marina.

The chest rose and fell almost imperceptibly. A look of contentment on the face; there was also several days' growth of beard.

Anne Marie touched his forehead. It was cold. She stood up. "How the hell did Gurion get here?"

She turned round to face the other man, but the man ignored her. He was looking at his watch. Young and good looking, he was dressed in a two-piece white linen suit that looked as fresh and well-pressed as if he had just come from a dinner party. Particles of sand stuck to the soles of his shoes but the polished leather was immaculate. He wore a blue shirt, a red and blue striped tie.

"Are you going to tell me how Gurion got here?"

The stretcher was lowered and the body carefully shifted onto it, then ferried to the waiting ambulance.

The man said to the ambulance driver, "I'll have to report your being late."

The second ambulance man did not reply but climbed into the back of the vehicle. The doors were slammed shut. The blue light still flashed against the whitening sky. The siren came alive as the ambulance pulled away, bumping slightly on the ridges of the track.

"I'd like to know how Gurion got here."

The man turned, and it was only then that Anne Marie recognized him: one of the men who had been with the procureur outside the Palais de Justice and then later at the marina. She recognized the ambitious eyes.

His smile was unexpected and appeared sincere. "Azaïs." He

held out his hand. "Jacques Azaïs, Renseignements Généraux." He wore gold cuff links.

They shook hands. "I don't see why I had to be brought here."

"You're the juge d'instruction, I believe," Azaïs said.

"Madame Laveaud." Anne Marie nodded. "I got a phone call twenty minutes ago—and the police chauffeur picked me up. Azaïs, I've got better. . . ."

"Call me Jacques—everybody does." The *Négropolitain*—a West Indian who lived in France—gave her a broad smile. He had the physique—and the accent—of a rugby player from the Southwest. His nose must have been broken a couple of times. He had the hair of a *métis*, combed into a part.

"I was taken from my bed."

Azaïs raised an eyebrow.

"And Monsieur Trousseau—my greffier—I'm sure he's got better things to do at this time of the morning. Like sleep."

The sun had risen, throwing its sparkling reflection across the windless surface of the green Atlantic.

Azaïs looked at his watch. "Nearly seven o'clock."

"I didn't come all the way from Pointe-à-Pitre for you to tell me the time." She tapped the shabby Kelton at her wrist—Jean Michel had promised her a Swiss watch with his first pay slip in Guadeloupe.

He shrugged.

"I have a family to look after, Azaïs."

"Jacques."

"A son who must be dressed and fed before being taken to school."

"You've had breakfast, madame le juge?"

"And you could have the courtesy of telling me how Gurion got here."

"Gurion?" he asked, as if slightly surprised by her request. He placed a hand on her arm and guided her toward the Peugeot pick-up. The man in overalls had climbed in behind the steering wheel. "Kidnapped."

The little boy still wept. He was about the same age as Fabrice, and she gave him a smile.

"Who'd want to kidnap Gurion?"

A military-type trunk stood on the sand. It was like the trunks that she and Jean Michel had used to bring their possessions from France, but a bit larger. The combination lock hung from one of the hinges. The metal flap of the hinge had broken off.

"He must have broken his way out."

Anne Marie asked incredulously. "Gurion was in that?"

"They took him on Sunday—and nobody seemed to notice his absence. Not FR3—not even his wife."

"I didn't know he was married."

Azaïs looked at her quizzically.

"How long was he in that thing?" She touched the trunk with the tip of her moccasin.

"Most of the night."

"He could've died."

"A lucky man. He managed to break the hinge—and then the old man saw him and alerted the police. Perhaps the combination lock will be able to tell us something." He turned and called to the two gendarmes.

One gendarme was smoking. He threw the cigarette onto the sand.

Azaïs pointed at the trunk. "Put gloves on and make sure you handle it carefully. Get it to *Médico-Légal*. You got your camera?" He made no attempt to be polite.

They shook their heads.

"Can't be moved until we've got a few photographs." Azaïs swore under his breath. "Call up *Médico-Légal*. Heaven knows why you didn't do it before."

"Waiting for your orders, monsieur."

"Time you learned to make decisions for yourselves."

They nodded unhappily.

"And keep me informed."

They saluted and returned to the van.

"Idiots," Azaïs whispered. "No better than the blacks—no initiative, no common sense." He raised his voice and shouted at the retreating men. "What are you going to do with the old man?"

The two gendarmes turned sheep-like faces and shrugged.

"You put handcuffs on him," Azaïs said coldly, "and you arrest him." He turned away and said over his shoulder, "I'll be back after I've had my breakfast."

54
Hotel

"Why arrest the old man?"

Azaïs was raising a glass of pineapple juice to his lips and he smiled as Anne Marie sat down opposite him. "You managed to make your phone call, madame le juge?"

"I'll try again in five minutes."

"While you wait, enjoy your breakfast." Azaïs smiled brightly. "I love breakfast, don't you?"

"When I'm with my family."

Anne Marie was tired. Jean Michel had laughed off the coffin and had snored softly beside her all night. She had been unable to get to sleep and just as she finally began to doze off, she was woken by the phone. Now she felt sick, and her hand hurt. The skin was marked with red weals that burned at the flesh between her fingers. "Are you married, Monsieur Azaïs?"

"I was."

"You have children?"

"A boy of ten—he lives in France."

Anne Marie bit her lip. "Perhaps with a more thoughtful attitude toward your own family, a separation wouldn't be necessary."

"My son lives with my parents in Bayonne." Azaïs gave her a friendly smile. "My wife died in a road accident."

She looked down at the cup of coffee.

"Hit on the way to the pre-natal clinic."

"Monsieur Azaïs, I have a job to do and I try to do it well. I am sorry to hear your wife died, but my problem is I don't enjoy being woken during the night and then being taken by an unhelpful driver to the scene of a crime that is no concern of mine. Particularly when there's already on location a juge d'instruction better qualified than me."

"You believe that I am a juge d'instruction?"

"Renseignements Généraux don't wear bespoke tropical suits."

"Madame, I'm no more qualified than you."

"Gurion's your problem, not mine. You're responsible to the Cour de Sûreté de l'Etat."

They were sitting only a few meters from the hotel beach. His eyes caught the sunlight reflected off the surface of the sea. "You believe it was a political kidnapping?"

"Of course," Anne Marie replied.

"And Calais?"

"The Calais murder's not the same thing."

She turned to look at Trousseau.

Trousseau had not wanted to come to the hotel—unlike Anne Marie, he had known that it was little more than a couple of hundred meters from the forlorn beach and its lunar landscape—but she had managed to persuade him, and he was now sitting at the same table. He did not seem to be following their conversation.

The typewriter case was on the seat beside him, and Trousseau sat upright, his hands crossed on the blue tablecloth. He glanced at Anne Marie, but the dark, intelligent eyes said nothing. He ran his finger along the narrow line of his moustache.

Azaïs said, "Very good breakfast."

"Next time, I'd like to be invited well in advance." Anne Marie drank the bitter coffee.

"You mustn't blame me, madame le juge," Azaïs said. "I didn't kidnap Gurion."

"You had me brought here."

"Really, madame, now that you're here, you might as well enjoy the food."

"I worry about my son." She paused before adding, "A threat has been made against his life—a Voodoo threat. A coffin left on the doorstep."

Azaïs put his head back and laughed. In that moment, Anne Marie felt that she could happily have sunk her nails into his Uncle Tom neck. "Voodoo, madame le juge—but that's for these people. You really give credence to the vestiges of animist cults from Africa?"

"I don't want anything to happen to my son."

"You don't believe. . . ."

"You still haven't told me what the old man has been arrested for."

Azaïs did not reply. He pushed his glass of fruit juice aside and started slicing a watermelon. "We're not getting on very well, are we?"

Anne Marie gave him a cold smile. "Why are you having the old man arrested?"

"Who?"

"The old man with the Peugeot truck and the little boy."

"High time the local police and the gendarmerie did something about those thieves."

Trousseau was looking at the tourists who took their food from the buffet tables. Tourists in beachwear, white legs and blue veins.

"You saw the holes in the sand—you saw what a state the beach is in. There's just no more sand. These people come down at night, and they steal all the sand. And in this benighted country, nobody cares. All the gendarmes care about is their overseas bonus—and not getting their throats cut with a machete." He shrugged. "The people here are destroying their island, pillaging it—and if they go on taking the sand with impunity, there'll be no more beaches."

Trousseau turned. "The beaches are no worse than after a hurricane." He looked at neither Anne Marie nor Azaïs.

"They take the sand for cement. They steal it in the night—and then make a fat profit." Azaïs took a second slice of watermelon. "The man's going to jail—and he thought he was doing his duty. He was down on the beach at half past three with his son. Too dark to see much—but they heard a noise. Most people, I imagine, would've run off—an evil spirit, a zombie." He glanced at Trousseau, then gave Anne Marie a lopsided smile. "This old fellow had a flashlight, and he went to have a look. He found the trunk just as Gurion was breaking his way out. Instead of running away, he helped Gurion."

"He deserves better treatment for saving a man's life."

"He ought to have moved his truck before sending the boy to alert the gendarmerie." Again a patronizing smile. "We'll let him off with a caution. Not that it'll do much good. Until the mayors and the police decide to get together, people will go on destroying the beaches. More coffee?"

She shook her head and stood up. "Excuse me, I'll be back in a few minutes." Anne Marie pushed her way through the crowd at the buffet tables and went to the hotel desk. The telephone operator had returned. Anne Marie gave her the number and was sent to the wall telephone.

Anne Marie picked up the receiver and heard the distant ringing. She let the telephone ring seventeen times.

Rubbing her hand, she returned to the table. "Nobody's at home," she said. "If you don't mind, I'd like to get back to Pointe-à-Pitre."

"I'll drive you in." Trousseau picked up the case.

"There is one other thing, Monsieur Azaïs," Anne Marie said.

He smiled blandly. "Yes?"

"The police didn't know Gurion was missing—and there was no reason for the local gendarmes to contact you." She ran her hand through her hair. "What brought you here so early in the morning?"

Azaïs did not reply.

"Bright, awake, well-shaved, well-dressed and cheerful?"

He shrugged.

"You knew, didn't you?"

"Knew?"

"You were expecting Gurion to turn up. And that was why I was woken up. Isn't that the reason?"

Azaïs said nothing. He poured himself a cup of coffee. He added sugar and then said, "There are a lot of things we know at Renseignements."

"Really, Monsieur Azaïs?"

His voice had lost its bonhomie. "Things that may be able to help you."

"Really?"

"You're still in charge of the Calais dossier, after all. Nominally, at least."

Anne Marie controlled her voice. "What kind of things that could help me?"

"The fact that Marcel Suez-Panama is Hégésippe Bray's son."

55
School

The courtyard was empty and the asphalt baking beneath the harsh sunlight. The only shade was under a kapok tree. From the open classrooms came the reassuring sound of children at work.

The school offices were on the ground floor in an edifice facing the main building.

"Is my son here?"

The girl turned in surprise to face Anne Marie. She had been painting her nails. In one hand she held the thin brush. Behind her, the open doorway gave onto a small courtyard. "I can't help you."

At the far end of the courtyard, there was a low wall. Beyond it, the port where a navy mine-sweeper was moored alongside the main jetty.

"I must know where my son is. I've phoned home—but nobody is answering."

"Madame, I haven't got the class registers yet."

"Get them."

The girl raised her shoulders, screwed the brush back into the bottle of varnish.

"And please hurry up."

She stood up. She was dressed in a white blouse and trousers.

She was pretty, of mixed blood. "I'll get the *surveillant*." She stepped out into the sunshine of the playground.

Anne Marie scratched her hand and tried to control the beat of her heart. She regretted having drunk the coffee at the hotel. Acidity now rose in her throat. She approached the desk.

There was an open register. She looked down the names that had been written with a ballpoint pen. There was no Laveaud.

In one of the classrooms, the children were singing, *Nous n'irons plus au bois*.

"Can I help you, madame?"

Anne Marie had never seen the *surveillant général* before and had assumed he was an older man. His eyes went from Anne Marie to the register. He was younger than Anne Marie and was wearing wire-framed sunglasses that he now pushed up onto his forehead.

"My son—Fabrice Laveaud in CE2."

"Yes?" Hurriedly he shook her hand.

"I need to know if he's in school today."

The surveillant pulled a chair for Anne Marie to sit down. His smile was friendly. He had an olive complexion. "I'm afraid it won't be before nine o'clock that I'll get all the registers in."

The surveillant moved round to the far side of the desk. Behind him, through the open doors, the ship was flying a flag that was not French. Men in dungarees moved along the deck. "But of course, I can phone." He picked up the receiver of a large telephone. "What class did you say, Madame Laveaud?"

"*Cours élémentaire deux.*"

He nodded and dialed a number.

Anne Marie heard the click.

"Monsieur Galli? The surveillant général's office here. It's about the pupil Laveaud." He nodded and lifted his eyes to look at Anne Marie.

She heard the voice on the far end of the line.

"I see."

The surveillant put the telephone down.

"Well?"

"I am sorry, madame," the surveillant général said softly. "Your son's not come into school today."

56
Mother in law

She could almost ignore the bright sunlight, the sweat that ran from her temples, that coursed down her back. She could almost ignore the painful itching and the bitter taste of coffee and acid in her mouth.

Anne Marie stepped into the road and would probably have been run over if the young soldier driving a coach—*Transport d'enfants* stenciled on the sides—had not braked sharply. He looked at Anne Marie in amazement from behind the high windscreen and shook his head, tapping his temple with a finger.

Anne Marie did not even look at him. She hurried across Place de la Victoire. The shade from the sandbox trees was of no help.

Beads of sweat trickled down her face. A couple of women cleaners, dwarfed beneath their straw hats, watched her. They wore rubber boots and leaned on their brooms. One said something, and the other threw back her head to laugh. She covered her mouth with a plump hand.

"Fabrice," Anne Marie murmured under her breath, and the traffic seemed to draw apart as she crossed over the road and walked along the rue Alsace-Lorraine. She reached number 31, rang the bell, pushed open the heavy iron door. It moved reluctantly, scraping the bolt across the floor. Anne Marie went up the stairs. Sweating but a cold chill in her back. She called out, "Mamie."

The sound of her shoes echoed hollowly against the empty walls.

There were still breakfast things on the table. A coffee pot and the remains of toasted bread. Flies danced along the edge of the open jam jar.

"Mamie!"

Her mother-in-law held a woman's magazine and was wearing reading glasses.

"I can't find Fabrice."

Mamie had put her bare feet up on the edge of a stool. There was a look of surprise on her face.

"I can't find Fabrice. He should be at school. I've just been there, and I've seen the surveillant. Fabrice's not at school. I had to get up early this morning. I phoned home. There's nobody there—not even Béatrice. I don't know where Fabrice is." She took hold of Mamie's hand. "He should be at school. I'd've taken him myself, but I had to go to Gosier. He should be at school—I don't understand. Mamie, I don't understand."

"Fabrice's with his papa."

Anne Marie stood with her mouth open.

"Don't you ever listen to what your husband says? Fabrice's gone with his papa. He told you—last Wednesday he couldn't take the boy to the beach with you. So today he decided to let Fabrice take the day off from school. They've gone to the beach."

"He didn't tell me anything. He didn't tell me...." Anne Marie stopped.

It did not matter.

"My Fabrice," she said. She put her arms around Mamie's neck and cried with relief.

57

St.-Laurent-du-Maroni

"Family name?"

"Suez-Panama."

"First name?"

"Marcel Hégésippe."

"Place of birth?"

"Le Havre, Seine-Inférieure—now Seine-Maritime."

"Date of birth?"

"June 16, 1940."

"I don't believe you."

"Why do you say that?"

"Your father's name?"

"Suez-Panama, Amédée Marcel, born July 14, 1916, at Chazeau, Les Abymes."

"Profession?"

"Whose profession? Mine—or my father's?"

"Your father."

"Papa didn't work."

Trousseau sat behind the office Japy, rapidly typing the replies.

"Papa was a cripple."

"Your mother?"

"Suez-Panama, Mionette, née Pendépisse."

"Date of birth?"

"January 6, 1909, Sainte Marthe estate, Sainte-Anne."

"Your father was Hégésippe Bray."

"What?"

"Your real father was Hégésippe Bray."

"May I have a glass of water?"

Anne Marie went to the small sink. She let the water run over her hands before filling the glass and handing it to Suez-Panama. He drank thirstily.

"Was Hégésippe Bray your father?"

"I don't know what you're talking about."

"Kindly answer the question. Was Bray your father?"

Suez-Panama did not reply.

She opened the folder—the green folder that Azaïs had given to Trousseau. She read aloud, "*Madame Suez-Panama approached the services of* État Civil *at the préfecture of the* Département de la Seine–Maritime, *formerly Seine-Inférieure, in the month of September, 1946. She requested that a new birth certificate should be made out in the name of Suez-Panama, Marcel, born June 16, 1940.*"

"That's right."

Anne Marie looked up. "This was not a particularly strange request. As a result of the war, the Allied invasion and the heavy bombing in most of Normandy, many of the administrative archives were destroyed. Not only in Normandy, either." She returned to the dossier.

"*In accordance with the Article 902 of the Code Civil, a new certificate was made out and a fiscal duty of four francs was paid by the demander.*"

She folded her arms. "Monsieur Suez-Panama, you were not born in Le Havre, but in Guadeloupe."

"That's absurd."

"The truth. Truth that can even now be corroborated by several people. Including your adoptive mother."

"Be careful what you say."

"Madame Suez-Panama was headmistress at the primary school in Pointe-Noire—a good job—a civil servant with a house and enough money to have a maid. She lived within the school free of rent. Doesn't it seem strange she should give up all this in the middle of the year to go and live in France? In a France that was at war. . . ? Her departure was all the more surprising as it was quite unexpected."

"She wanted to be with Papa. He'd been called back into the navy."

"With the navy, he would have been away at sea. No need to have his wife follow him halfway across the world."

He shrugged. "Maman always wanted to get away from Pointe-Noire—to get away from Guadeloupe."

"She returned at the end of the war."

"You don't know how envious people can be here. They were envious of Maman because she had a good job, because she was a teacher. They cast spells. She would find sacrifices—blood sacrifices. Or crabs hung up outside her door."

"A coincidence Madame Suez-Panama left not more than two weeks before the discovery of the charred remains of Eloise Deschamps—and left when she—your mother—was well into her seventh month of pregnancy ?"

"You're accusing my mother of murder?"

"The timing's very strange."

"A coincidence."

"A coincidence you have no real birth certificate? Isn't it strange your father should have had only one child?"

"My father was a sick man."

"Your father was Hégésippe Bray."

"No."

"You've always suspected it—the way your mother spoke about her half brother. I don't suppose she told you everything—she had her own guilt to hide—but children have a way of finding these things out."

"What you say is quite false."

"You suspected something, and in the end, you decided to look up the archives of *La Coloniale* in Basse-Terre."

"You know that, too?"

"Never underestimate a woman, Monsieur Suez-Panama."

"I was never very close to Papa."

"He wasn't your real father."

"Maman worshipped Hégésippe. He was everything to her. Husband and father."

"But she took his son away to France."

He shrugged.

"Why did Madame Suez-Panama take you away?"

He hesitated before replying. "Because she must have thought my real mother was a witch."

"*La Coloniale* states Eloise Deschamps disappeared before her death. And Hégésippe Bray thought she was pregnant. She must have given the baby—you—to Madame Suez-Panama."

After a long silence, the man raised his shoulders. "Perhaps."

58
Point-Blank

"So she took you to France. And Hégésippe Bray never knew his son."

Trousseau paused in his typing.

"Hégésippe deserved better than that," Suez-Panama said.

There was satisfaction in Anne Marie's voice. "You felt responsible for him?"

"I wanted him back from French Guyana."

"When he returned, you felt he deserved better than a hut on the edge of the Sainte Marthe estate?"

"Calais said he would give the land back."

"But he'd taken it. For all the years that Hégésippe Bray—your father—was in French Guyana."

Suez-Panama said nothing.

"You wanted to punish Calais."

"What do you mean?"

"When you met Calais down by the rain pond, it was your chance."

"No."

"Hégésippe Bray had lent you his gun. Perhaps you didn't intend to kill Calais. But you did—at point-blank range."

His eyes had begun to water.

"Calais had taken your father's land—and by pulling the

trigger, you could expiate all the guilt. Your guilt and the guilt you felt for your mother—for your adoptive mother."

He pushed a tear from the corner of his eye.

"Never even occurred to you Bray would be arrested. You cleaned the gun and you hid it. You naturally assumed that the independence movement—the local terrorists—would be identified as the murderers. MANG had already made one attempt on Calais' life—and perhaps you didn't even know about the threats Bray had made against Calais. So when the gendarmes arrested your real father you were scared."

Suez-Panama shook his head.

"Faced with the prospect of spending the rest of his life in prison, he killed himself. Hanging himself by the neck until his eyes bulged and his tongue stuck out."

There was the last echo of the typewriter and then a long, painful silence.

The curtains—still dirty, still needing to be changed—shifted with the slight breeze. Trousseau ran a finger along his moustache. Patiently he folded his hands and waited.

Anne Marie got up and went to the sink. She let the cold water run over the back of her hand.

"That's why you shouted at me in the Place de la Victoire. You need to believe the police murdered Bray. You mentioned Jerry Dupont—you wanted your father's death to have been manipulated by the police. Because," she turned off the tap, "the real murderer's you. You didn't have the courage to step forward. When it really mattered, when you could really have saved your father, you were scared." She smiled. "Perhaps Hégésippe Bray knew that. Perhaps he hanged himself to save you. Who knows, perhaps he thought you were worth it?"

"He deserved to die."

"Hégésippe Bray?"

"Raymond Calais." The young man spoke quietly. A tear dried on his cheek. "A rich Béké who'd always had what he wanted—and who didn't care about anybody else. He sent Hégésippe to St.-Laurent-du-Maroni." The eyes shone. "Calais got what he deserved. And if I had to, I would do it all again. Just to see the fear in his eyes before I pulled the trigger."

59
Worry

Trousseau came back into the office.

"Did you get the note from the procureur?"

"Note, madame le juge?"

"I asked you to get Bray's suicide note—in order to compare the handwriting."

"I've phoned twice." He sounded offended. He returned to his seat behind the typewriter. "I spoke with his secretary."

"But you haven't got the note?"

Trousseau imperceptibly shook his head.

"Which implies, doesn't it, the procureur doesn't want me to have it?"

"You still don't believe that Hégésippe Bray committed suicide?"

Anne Marie stood up, smoothed her skirt and walked over to the window.

In the port, the mine sweeper was preparing to weigh anchor. The sun caught the grey paint, making it strangely attractive. The rear propeller began churning the water and the hull swung away from the land.

"Madame le juge." Trousseau was standing close beside her. There was a worried, embarrassed smile on his face. "I think you ought to go home. You're not well and you need a rest. Go home, and see a doctor about your hand."

"Not a witch doctor, Monsieur Trousseau?"

"You've been overworking."

"Do you believe Suez-Panama? You think I ought to sign a warrant for his arrest?"

"These are all things we can talk about at another time." Trousseau took hold of her wrist and stopped the movement of one hand against the other. "You're tired and you haven't been sleeping. And rubbing your hand like that can't do any good."

"Suez-Panama's reaction doesn't make sense."

"For my sake, madame le juge." He hesitated. "Please don't be stubborn. Go home and rest. If you wish, I'll phone Dr. Lebon."

"Suez-Panama admits to killing Calais."

Trousseau went over to Anne Marie's desk and started tidying up. "Take your handbag, madame."

"A twelve bore, Monsieur Trousseau. What sort of range does it have?"

He looked up. "Depends on what you're aiming at."

"A bird."

"Sixty, even seventy, meters. Ask Chinois—he's the specialist in ballistics."

"Suez-Panama's telling the truth?"

"Madame le juge, if he says he killed Raymond Calais, I don't see why you shouldn't believe him. The sooner we get this Calais killing out of the way, the happier I'll be. It's making you unhappy—it seems to have grown out of all reasonable proportion. You've been taking it too personally—and you've made yourself enemies."

"I'm not convinced he's Hégésippe Bray's son at all."

Trousseau switched off the desk lamp and turned to face her. "Yet that's precisely what you've just accused him of."

"I wanted to see how he would react."

"Please don't do that—you mustn't rub your hand like that."

"It hurts."

"See a doctor. Put on a poultice of clay, put on ice—but for goodness' sake, don't rub. It makes it worse."

"There are other things I've got to do." She turned her back to the window. "Phone Lafitte, would you. Tell him I must see him."

"I'm sure it can wait."

"Phone l'inspecteur Lafitte. And kindly don't tell me my job, Monsieur Trousseau."

"If you wish, I can drive you home." He ran a finger along the line of moustache. "Or get somebody to take you."

"Nobody at home—and they probably won't be back before this evening."

Trousseau slipped his hand through her arm. "Come." In his other hand, he held her handbag. "You really must get some rest."

Anne Marie did not move. "Because if he really was Hégésippe Bray's son, there wouldn't have been any reason for the Deschamps woman to go into hiding. No reason for her to go over to Pointe-Noire and see a woman that she didn't get on with anyway. Unless. . . ."

"Unless what, madame le juge?"

"Unless she was pregnant with another man's child."

60

SODECA

The bicycle was still there.

"Have you got the photographs of the murder weapon, Monsieur Lafitte?"

"I'm sorry." The smile did not disappear from the symmetrical features. "I forgot."

"On my desk by this afternoon, please."

"Yes, madame le juge."

"I want them by five o'clock at the very latest."

It was mid-afternoon, and both bicycle and parking meter were now in the shade.

"Is Monsieur Trousseau coming?"

Anne Marie replied, "He's with Suez-Panama."

Lafitte looked at her carefully before speaking. "You think Suez-Panama murdered Calais, madame le juge?"

"This morning Marcel Suez-Panama admitted to murdering Raymond Calais."

"Unlikely," Lafitte said, then he closed his mouth as the girl placed the drinks on the low table. Her hair had become more unkempt beneath the starched white crescent. Lafitte handed her a fifty-franc note.

"What's unlikely, Monsieur Lafitte?"

"There are enough potential culprits without your having to bother with Suez-Panama."

"I've reason to believe Suez-Panama's Bray's natural son."

Lafitte seemed unimpressed. He poured juice from the can into his glass. "Basse-Terre's being deliberately cagey. A case of the right hand not telling the left hand what it's up to. Basse-Terre's where the préfecture is, and they've adopted a policy of keeping Pointe-à-Pitre in the dark."

"Over what?"

The girl returned, bringing the change on a plastic saucer that she placed besides the drinks. Then she walked back to her stool and continued to stare out into the street.

There were no other customers in the pâtisserie.

"You mustn't do that."

"Do what?"

"Your hand's swollen, madame le juge. Rubbing it won't make it any better."

"In the dark over what, Monsieur Lafitte?"

"For more than a month, there's been a juge d'instruction in Basse-Terre. Working away in secret. And nobody—other than the procureur—knowing about his presence." A grin. "Slinging all Pichon's work out of the window."

"Pichon?"

"Renseignements Généraux. It was Pichon who dealt with the Pointe-à-Pitre scandal. Raymond Calais accused the mayor of connivance. According to Calais—the article appeared in a paper a few days after the attempt made on Calais' life—there was an illicit agreement between the mayor of Pointe-à-Pitre and a contracting company run by one of the city councilors. Calais claimed to have proof of corruption—and maintained that was why he was shot at."

"Pichon did all the investigation?"

Lafitte nodded. "As far as Pichon was concerned, there was no connection between Raymond Calais' allegations and his being shot at. The mayor was clean." Lafitte put down his glass. "Pichon is left-wing—and he's fairly sympathetic toward the Communist mayor of Pointe-à-Pitre." He was sitting with his legs apart and his elbows resting on his knees. "Pichon doesn't like the Békés, that's certain."

Anne Marie tipped the ice in her glass onto the back of her left hand. She held it against the skin till her hand turned numb. "What made Pichon so sure the mayor was innocent?"

"Witnesses."

"Witnesses to what?"

"When the decision had to be made to employ a contracting firm, the councilor in question got up, stated his connection, and left the chamber. It was all quite legal and proper."

"Raymond Calais must've known that."

"Of course."

"Raymond Calais was risking his reputation, surely, by making accusations that could be disproved so easily?"

"Calais' motivation was not political, madame le juge—at least, that's what Pichon thinks."

She dropped the rest of the ice into the saucer. "Why make a scandal?"

"A warning."

"A warning to who?"

Lafitte's smile was irritating. "A warning to anybody who chose to listen."

"Please don't talk in riddles."

"Calais was showing he wasn't afraid to sling mud. Some people thought it was just an ill-advised attack on the mayor—but that wasn't the point." He stopped. "Are you all right, madame? You look pale."

"The point, Monsieur Lafitte?"

"To frighten people."

"That's why they shot Raymond Calais?"

Lafitte shook his head. "Pichon's convinced it was one of Calais' own men who shot him."

"Why?"

"Raymond Calais had his own little gang—some of them were armed. Pichon believes they were paid on a part-time basis."

"Madame Calais told me they were merely friends who looked after Raymond Calais. It was their way of repaying the favors Calais had done for them."

"Riffraff—unemployed layabouts Calais picked up around the docks. He used them for sticking up posters—or for pulling down the posters put up by the mayor and the Communists."

"Where did Raymond Calais get the money to pay them?"

Lafitte finished his drink. "He didn't."

"Didn't what, Monsieur Lafitte?"

"He didn't pay his private army—or rather, he ceased to pay them. Because he was running out of funds." Lafitte corrected himself: "Because he had run out of funds."

"Calais had money. He was rich—he owned land."

Lafitte clicked his tongue. "Sainte Marthe would've collapsed years ago unless he'd continued to pump money in. And that's probably why Raymond Calais married his wife in the first place. This is all Pichon's theory, you understand. Calais needed her money to pay for Sainte Marthe—as well as for his horses and all the other hobbies. You sure you feel well, madame le juge?"

"Where did Calais get his money from?"

When he spoke, Lafitte's voice was softer. "Does SODECA mean anything to you?" His breath smelled of fruit juice.

"I've heard of it."

"*Société d'économie mixte pour le développement de la Caraibe.* Part privately, part publicly owned. And Raymond Calais—as a conseiller général elected to one of the cantons of Pointe-à-Pitre—was automatically on the board of directors."

"Go on."

"By making allegations of corruption in the town hall, Calais was showing he was willing and ready to pull the chain on another scandal." A grin darted across his face. "But this time a real one. At the SODECA."

"What scandal?"

"That's precisely what Basse-Terre's being so cagey about." Lafitte gestured with his hand. "If I wasn't a friend of Pichon's, I'd never have got this information." He laughed. "As your greffier likes to say, Pichon's not bad for a local."

"Tell me about the scandal."

"Sensitive information—and potentially very dangerous. I'd be grateful if. . . ." He took a deep breath. "You don't know the juge d'instruction Méry?"

"No."

"Always wearing a raincoat."

"Tall and thin looking?"

"I don't know," Lafitte said. "I've never met him."

"How do you know he wears a raincoat?"

"There's a major inquiry going on. For at least a month now. Several detectives from the *Brigade des Finances*. . . ."

"Including a certain Azaïs?"

Lafitte nodded. "Possible."

"Azaïs told me he was with Renseignements Généraux."

"I'll check with Pichon." For a moment he stared at the empty glasses on the table. "Fifty-three million francs have gone missing."

"Missing where?"

"In the SODECA accounts." Lafitte drove his fingers through the short, upright hair. Drops of perspiration had formed at his temples, giving him more than ever the appearance of a Flemish cyclist. "Somebody's been embezzling. Fifty-three million francs is a lot of money. And it's all vanished."

"Hence Méry's being here in Guadeloupe?"

Lafitte nodded. "Méry has been making use of Pichon's services."

"And why does Pichon tell you?"

He shrugged. "Perhaps he's afraid of a cover-up."

Anne Marie waited a moment in thoughtful silence. She looked at her hand. The numbness was going away and the need to itch was returning. "Where does Raymond Calais come into all this?"

"Fifty-three million francs isn't a sum that disappears overnight.

Someone's been embezzling—and he's been doing it for a long time. Long enough for Raymond Calais to have found out—and to make use of the knowledge. As I said, SODECA is jointly owned. Fifty percent is private; the other fifty percent is controlled by the département."

"What does SODECA do?"

"It is involved in virtually all building operations undertaken by the municipal authorities. In Basse-Terre as in Pointe-à-Pitre or the Saintes. Every town authority has to work with SODECA."

Anne Marie did not hide her irritation. "But what exactly does SODECA do?"

"Suppose the city of Pointe-à-Pitre wants to re-house people who are at the moment living in insalubrious shacks within the city limits—no plumbing, no drainage—and all the dangers of leprosy and tuberculosis. Pointe-à-Pitre calls in the SODECA— and SODECA does the entire job. It buys up the land, temporarily re-housing the local people elsewhere. It has the power of compulsory purchase. It subsequently calls in various private companies for the preparation of the land. As you know, most of Pointe-à-Pitre is swamp and needs reclaiming."

"Go on."

"SODECA needs the cooperation of certain construction companies. So it puts out to tender. All the new housing projects you see in Pointe-à-Pitre—they were put up by SODECA, who then sold them back to the city. But with a hole of fifty-three million francs in its budget, the SODECA would fall apart." Lafitte shook his head. "Disastrous. A lot of companies working for the SODECA—companies that SODECA owes money to—would collapse with it. They'd just go bankrupt. Plus, of course, the political scandal would be equally dangerous. And the unemployment— most unrest here starts in the building trade. That's why Pichon's afraid of a hush up."

"Bankrupt?"

"A lot of illustrious heads could fall." Lafitte smiled. "There's a total blackout. Even including you and me, there can't be more than a dozen people who know about the fifty-three million francs. I doubt if the mayor of Pointe-à-Pitre knows—and yet he's on the SODECA board of directors."

"How did the situation first come to light?"

"The irony is that Raymond Calais must have been threatening to spill the beans for at least several years. The accountants were called in as a matter of routine—and it's the accountants who've discovered what has been going on."

"Who are these accountants?"

"Cabinet Foch—a highly respected firm from Paris. Been in Basse-Terre since May."

"A reputable company can't remain silent over an affair like this—its reputation would be put in jeopardy."

"There'll be pressure on the Cabinet Foch to keep quiet at least until next year. Next May and the presidential elections. A scandal like this is going to put the local administration in a bad light. And the administration in Guadeloupe's the responsibility of Giscard d'Estaing. Politically speaking, silence is necessary until the elections are over."

"Does Pichon have any idea who's doing the embezzling?"

Lafitte laughed and the suddenness of the laughter after the hoarse whisper took Anne Marie by surprise. "They're all in it— all the rich Békés and mulattos who control this island. Even the president of the Chamber of Commerce." Again the hand through the short hair. "Can you imagine that? The president of the Chamber of Commerce—Giscard's right-hand man in Guadeloupe and on television every other evening—being thrown into jail? Or dear old Jacques Calais—respected managing director of General Motors Guadeloupe?"

His excitement was infectious.

"You think that Raymond Calais's murder was a revenge killing?" Anne Marie asked.

"Revenge among the Békés."

"And Suez-Panama?"

"An idiot."

61

New York

"You sound very sure," Lafitte said.

"Suez-Panama's confessed to the killing."

"A university man—not the sort of person to go around using a twelve bore gun." He cocked his head, "The idiot's probably trying to cover up for somebody in his stupid, quixotic way."

"He has good reason to hate Calais."

"Everybody hated Raymond Calais—including his own brother."

"You think Jacques Calais killed his brother?"

"It's obvious. Raymond Calais had been blackmailing his brother for years."

"How do you know that?"

"Not me, madame le juge." He tapped his chest. "Pichon. Pichon's got contacts everywhere—even among the Békés. They're not all corrupt businessmen—or so Pichon maintains." Again the unexpected laugh. "There are even Communists among them."

"What could Raymond Calais blackmail his brother over?"

"It was you who asked me to get the information on Kacy, madame le juge."

"Well?"

"Kacy owns Travaux et Terrassements Antillais—and poor bastard, he's got the Foch accountant in now. TTA's a big concern—but certainly not quite as big and certainly not quite as efficient as Kacy would like to make out. One hundred and fifty employees—administration, lorry drivers, bulldozer men. Big—but it's not the only company of its type." Lafitte grinned. "Strangely, though, TTA's always been able to offer more competitive tenders when an operation's been put up for bidding by the SODECA. More than once TTA's had to go back on the initial estimate. And then ask the SODECA for a higher price. What's amazing is that nobody seems to have minded. Which has let Kacy build up a virtual monopoly on the SODECA jobs."

"Connivance over the tenders." The back of her hand was red, and the throbbing pain was returning. "That doesn't explain how Raymond Calais was involved. More important, it doesn't explain why he was killed."

"Raymond Calais isn't involved, madame le juge. He never was—not directly. With his political aspirations, he felt he couldn't have his finger directly in the pie—even though the pie was so big and juicy. Virtually everybody else was in on it. But Raymond Calais kept his finger clean. He used a spoon."

"How?"

"Raymond Calais used his brother." Lafitte glanced over his shoulder. "Jacques Calais imports vehicles from General Motors."

Anne Marie waited.

"Not just cars—but also heavy machinery. Agricultural machinery used for sugar harvesting, and also all the stuff used by the building trade. Tractors, tip-ups, and rollers. The sort of thing Kacy needs for his company. Big, industrial machines that cost a lot of money."

"Well?"

"Just think for a moment, madame le juge." Lafitte sat back.

"I don't understand."

He edged forward again on the low armchair. "Kacy couldn't hand out money just like that. Earth-moving machinery—it's not the sort of thing you pay for in cash. You need financial help."

"You go to the bank."

"Precisely."

"Desist from using this patronizing tone, Monsieur Lafitte. Please. This is not a university class, and I'm not your pupil."

He made an apologetic gesture and knocked over an empty can of juice. "I'm sorry," he said, dabbing at the drops running across the tabletop, "I allow myself to get carried away."

"I am a juge d'instruction—not a cycling companion."

It was as if she had struck him in the face. His features became grey and drawn. "Yes, of course."

"There's nothing illegal in asking for a loan from the bank."

"I beg your pardon, madame le juge?"

"No crime in borrowing money from the bank to buy heavy machinery."

"Provided you do in fact buy machinery."

"I imagine Kacy needed the equipment."

"But he didn't need all the equipment that he got from Jacques Calais—the equipment that he got on paper, at least."

"There was false accounting?"

Lafitte nodded.

Anne Marie started rubbing at the back of her hand. "Kacy got false receipts from Jacques Calais for equipment that was never sold to him. With these he got loans from the bank. Is that it?"

"A bulldozer costs a lot of money. Kacy managed to get a lot of money from the banks for something that existed only on paper." Lafitte stopped. "You mustn't do that to your hand."

"What bank, Monsieur Lafitte?"

"The Lower Hudson Securities Bank of New York."

"There's a branch in Guadeloupe?"

Lafitte nodded.

"Any bank director before lending a substantial sum of money would make enquiries. Enquiries about the borrower's assets."

"Normally, yes."

"Are you implying the director of the Lower Hudson Securities Bank of New York was involved in this scam?"

Lafitte raised his shoulders in a gesture of acquiescence. "There are two elements that perhaps you are unaware of, madame le juge."

Anne Marie smiled wearily. "A lot more than two, I can assure you."

Lafitte leaned forward over the table until his symmetrical, earnest face was less than twenty centimeters from hers. "The director of the Lower Hudson Securities Bank of New York is Monsieur Charraud. Until last year, he was the president of the Chamber of Commerce. A man of considerable power, who by his position, was a de facto member of the governing board of the SODECA."

"And the other bit of information?"

"He's the brother-in-law of your boss, the procureur."

In the street, an old man was unlocking the padlock that held his bicycle to the parking meter.

62

Lies

Anne Marie ignored the proffered hand. "You lied to me."

Michel continued to grin.

"Who's your friend?"

"An Indian." The false teeth in the upper jaw shifted as he proudly added, "Like me."

"What's he doing here?"

"We're talking."

The other Indian stood up, leaning his weight against the concrete post. He was smaller than Michel and a lot neater. His hair was short beneath a pith helmet, and he wore khaki shorts and rubber boots that came up to the knees of his spindly legs.

"Edouard Ragassamy." He held out his hand and Anne Marie took it hurriedly.

She turned back to Michel. "I must speak with you."

The smile grew wider.

"Alone."

They left Ragassamy, who produced the stub of a cigarette from his shirt pocket and began to smoke peacefully.

Anne Marie walked round the empty villa. Michel was close behind her, smelling of dry sweat, goats, and rum. It was late afternoon, the air was cooling and from the nearby field came the gentle odor of newly mown grass.

"You lied." She turned to look at Michel. "On the Sunday afternoon—the day that Calais died—there were visitors." Over her shoulder she glanced at Ragassamy. Smoke was rising from under the pith helmet as he stared out across the valley, across the double row of coconut palms, the white track, the pond where Raymond Calais' body was found—and in the distance, the route nationale and the cars that moved along it like silent toys.

"Michel doesn't interfere into other people's business," Michel said.

"Because of you, another man died. Hégésippe Bray died because you didn't tell me the truth."

"He was going to die."

"His sister—the woman from Morne-à-l'Eau. She was here, wasn't she?"

Michel said nothing. He smiled and the long dirty hair danced with the wind.

"She came with her son. They came to visit Hégésippe Bray that afternoon, didn't they?"

"Perhaps."

"I can have you put in prison—and perhaps you'll die there. No more women—no more black women or Indian women."

Slowly, very slowly, the smile disappeared. There were short black hairs that protruded from his nostrils; the hairs quivered as Michel exhaled. "It's nothing to do with me."

"The sister and her son—were they here?"

He nodded.

"Good." Anne Marie started to walk again. "At least we've got that settled."

He fell into step behind her, with the tongues of his boots flapping against the muddied leather.

There was a breadfruit sapling that was protected by a fence of iron mesh. Anne Marie placed the back of her left hand against the jagged ends of hard wire. She could scarcely feel them as they pushed against the skin. "He could shoot a pigeon or a mongoose at thirty meters?"

"Who?" The grin had returned.

A grackle chirped overhead in a guava tree.

"Hégésippe Bray was a good shot, wasn't he?"

"Would you like a coconut?" He nodded toward her chest. "Good for you."

"At thirty meters?"

"Yes."

"Bring me the gun."

"What gun?"

Anne Marie held out her hand. "Hurry up, Michel."

"What gun?"

He stood in front of her. The wind whispered through the leaves of the guava tree and the young breadfruit. A pig snorted, and there was the hollow thump of hooves on the concrete floor of the sty.

"You stole Hégésippe Bray's gun."

"He left it."

"Where?"

"Over there." Michel gestured toward the hut.

"He left it—or you took it?"

"The gendarmes took him away. He left it with me."

Again the chirping of the grackle.

"How is your hand, madame?" Michel's face broke into an ingratiating grin.

"Fetch the gun."

The Indian shrugged and the smile died. Then he turned away and made off toward the wooden shack. The seat of his trousers was baggy, and when Michel returned he was carrying a rifle.

The muzzle was raised. It pointed toward Anne Marie's chest.

"Pests."

"What?"

"There are rats, madame. Calais never gave me anything—but he was the first to complain when the rats ate his lettuce. Or when the mongooses ate the eggs in the chicken run." The barrel of the rifle was like a third eye. "Calais said I stole the eggs."

"Give me the gun."

Apart from the first specks of dust along the thin barrel, it was in good condition. It could only be a few months old.

"Give me that gun."

Michel hesitated.

Anne Marie took hold of the barrel and the Indian let go. He did not resist.

"You should never have taken it."

"The old man didn't need it."

She opened the breech. It was not loaded. "A twenty-two long rifle."

"Good for the rats." Michel shrugged.

63

Couscous

It had been a long time since Anne Marie had done any real cooking for Jean Michel and Fabrice. Nothing more demanding than an omelet, an opened can of Paris mushrooms, and a salad.

She took a basket and walked the length of the open refrigerators. Vapor rose in wispy clouds.

Jean Michel would be back before 7 P.M., and tomorrow being Wednesday, they would be in no hurry to go to bed. Anne Marie smiled contentedly. For once they could all sit down together, turn off the television, and eat. She would make couscous.

She started looking for a packet of frozen lamb.

Despite the chill air of the supermarket, Anne Marie had started to sweat.

Butter, oil, Mediterranean spices.

She studied the shelves, looking for something that would go well with the meal. Bordeaux, Chablis, Côtes du Rhone. There was everything. She smiled when she saw the display, ten bottles deep, of Algerian wine.

Anne Marie no longer missed Algeria. But sometimes she thought about Maman, who had died before the long, painful journey to France, Sarlat, and a new life.

She placed a bottle of Bordeaux in the wire trolley.

There was salami—hanging in wrinkled old sausages from a

shelf near the refrigerator. It smelled good—a smell of Europe. Again Anne Marie ran a hand along her forehead. She was feverish. A germ she must have picked up somewhere—or perhaps a cold caused by the wet shoes at the funeral.

The rice crackled beneath the soles of her Mephisto moccasins.

Two men were transferring bags of rice from a wooden trolley onto the lower shelves. One of the bags had slipped from their grasp and burst open. Rice was scattered across the red tiles. The jute bag lay like a dead child.

"I'm looking for couscous."

The men were wearing overalls over naked chests. One man looked up and studied Anne Marie carefully before replying, "Over there." The gesture was vague.

Couscous with lamb and a spiced sauce. Followed by banana flambé.

She found the couscous between the sugar and the bags of imported flour.

"Like a good housewife, doing her shopping?"

She was crouching, and she had been too busy comparing prices to have noticed the man. She looked up in surprise and saw him smiling benignly.

He was wearing white tennis shorts that were too tight; the cotton shirt swelled above the leather belt. He was smoking a cigar.

"Like you, monsieur le procureur."

"My good wife's away in Florida, and so I've got to look after myself." He raised his shoulders and the thick lips broke into a smile. "We should pool our resources, madame le juge."

Anne Marie stood up and they shook hands.

"Very pleased to see you," the procureur said. "Been a bit worried about you, I must admit." He took the cigar from his mouth. "Not so much that I can't sleep, but lately I've been getting the feeling you're not happy with your work, madame le juge."

His trolley was full of bathroom articles. Nivea cream, talcum powder, shampoo, razor blades. And incongruously, several packs of Corsaire beer.

"Perhaps this isn't the best place to discuss my professional or personal problems."

He grinned and placed the cigar back in his mouth. Moving to Anne Marie's side, the procureur took her by the arm. "Come, finish your shopping, and then we can go for a drink."

The neon lighting of the supermarket flattened his face.

"I've got to get home, I'm afraid. It's very kind of you, of course. It's just that the family's waiting for me."

The procureur raised an eyebrow. "You do the cooking?"

For a moment, the round face seemed to swim before Anne Marie's eyes. "Sometimes."

"I see you're a very capable woman."

"Many, many women just as capable as me. . . ." She smiled, and crouching down, took a packet of couscous.

"An excellent cook, I'm sure. You must invite me around one evening."

"It'd be a pleasure. You can meet my husband."

They moved forward together.

Anne Marie felt hot. Sweat on the back of her neck. At the same time, the smell of the procureur's cigar caught in her nostrils. Like an angry sea, her stomach began to lurch.

"I'd be delighted to see him again, madame le juge. Has he found a job yet?"

She shook her head.

"A shame. An intelligent man. I met him a couple of times when I did evening classes at the Vizioz Institute. In those days, the university was next to the Palais de Justice." The procureur added, "Should've stuck to law, like you."

"My husband likes writing."

"Trouble is there's no work here."

"Jean Michel's thinking of doing a novel."

The cigar smoke was making her eyes water. Anne Marie pushed toward the row of cash registers, hoping that the procureur would go off to finish his shopping alone.

He remained resolutely at her side, his damp hand on her forearm.

"A novel—that's an interesting idea."

"The mineral water." She tried to keep the note of desperation out of her voice. "I forgot the mineral water—do excuse me." She turned, wrenched her arm from his grip, and, in an inelegant, fast walk, moved back to the far end of the supermarket. She held the back of her hand to her lips. The skin throbbed sullenly and now her eyes were watering freely.

The smell of the floor polish that a girl with a microphone was trying to promote made Anne Marie feel giddy.

She stared at the bottles in their plastic crates. Evian, Vichy, and a couple of bottles of the local Matouba water. Her heart thumped angrily. She moved slowly, trying to kill time. She waited. One minute. Two minutes.

Peeping down between the aisle of dairy products and the steaming refrigerators, her watering eyes sought the procureur but the plump man in the tennis clothes had disappeared.

The feeling of sickness, the tinge of cigar smoke on her nostrils slowly ebbed away. Anne Marie had begun to tremble.

Another two minutes before she moved toward the crêpes imported from Finistère. She picked up a packet. She also took a tin of Quality Street.

Waiting.

She wanted to go home. The presence of the procureur—even when dressed normally and not in the bulging, obscene tennis wear, even without the foul cigar—made her feel uncomfortable. Uncomfortable and vulnerable.

She made her way back to where she had left the trolley at the checkout register. She had overloaded her arms with articles to buy and her arms now ached from the weight of the mineral water.

At the checkout, she looked along the lines of customers. The procureur had gone, thank God.

The goods tumbled from her arms into the trolley. Anne Marie took her place in the queue. In front of her, a little boy played with a plastic car while his mother scolded him in resentful Creole.

Anne Marie waited. She wanted to get home. She wanted to

make the meal for her family, but perhaps, she told herself, it would be better if she simply went to bed. Lemon juice, brown sugar, and a shot of rhum agricole. The best thing to do was to sweat the fever off.

"Four hundred and sixty-three francs, madame."

She signed the check and gave it to the girl, whose green eyes were bloodshot from the flickering overhead light. The girl wore a pen stuck in the bun of her hair. "Identity card, please." She took the pen from her hair and scribbled something on the back of the check.

"Bonsoir."

The automatic doors slid open, and Anne Marie stepped out into the parking lot. After the chill of the supermarket, the warm air hit her like hot, wet flannel. She could feel the humidity working its way back into her clothes as she pushed the trolley over to the Honda.

The smell of roasting chicken came from a Renault where a woman was doing brisk business.

"You still believe he's innocent?"

Anne Marie spun round.

"Hégésippe Bray's innocent?"

His face was hidden because of the brightness of the overhead neon, PRISUNIC in bright red lighting. The tip of the cigar glowed against the black circle of his face.

Anne Marie swallowed. "Hégésippe Bray?" Although her hand was trembling, she managed to take the keys from her bag and unlock the car door.

"He killed Calais, madame le juge. Trust me."

"The evidence is far from conclusive."

He approached her, the hairs on his short arms touching her skin. "You must let me help you." He removed the shopping bags from the trolley and placed them onto the back seat of the Honda. "You need a man for this sort of thing."

She unclenched her teeth, afraid that she would vomit. "You're most kind."

"Sure you wouldn't care for a drink?" He gestured toward Gosier. "Sit on the veranda by the sea, sip a planter's punch, and relax. Enjoy the evening breeze, watch the cargo ships sailing out into the night." The bright end of the cigar flickered again as he caught his breath. "In this wretched job, we're so busy we often forget the good things in life." He took her by the arm.

"I've got to be getting on." Nausea was washing at the back of her throat. "My family is waiting for me, monsieur le procureur. You must let me go. Another time, perhaps."

"Of course," he said, his voice strangely soft. "Got to get back to your waiting husband." The grip on her arm remained firm. "Back to your waiting husband. The good and faithful wife."

"Au revoir, monsieur le procureur."

Although she moved forward, the man did not relinquish his grip on her arm.

"Please excuse me."

"Anne Marie, if you help me, then perhaps I can help your husband."

She could feel the weight of the procureur's rotund belly pushing against her. "You must agree to be helpful." His breath was bitter.

"I must go."

He was hurting her now.

"You really are a very pretty young woman." The cigar was only a few centimeters from her face. She could feel the heat on her cheek.

"Attractive and very intelligent. But I don't think you want to use your intelligence. You have so much to gain, Anne Marie— you don't mind if I use your first name? I can help you, you see. When there's so much at stake."

"You're hurting me." Anne Marie wrenched her arm free, and the procureur let her go. She could feel herself trembling as she climbed into the car.

"I can help your husband," the procureur said as he courteously closed the car door for her. "At this difficult time for you both."

Anne Marie almost stalled the Honda in her haste to leave the parking lot.

266

64
Van Cleef

The lights were off, and there was no movement in the house other than the gentle tapping of the curtain against the window.

She was out of breath after climbing the six flights of stairs. Anne Marie lowered the plastic bags to the floor, leaned against the door, and waited for her heaving chest and thumping heart to regain their normal rhythm. Then she kicked off her moccasins.

Anne Marie went into the kitchen. When she opened the refrigerator, it cast a golden wedge of light across the beige tiles of the floor. She took the ice tray from the freezer. Its aluminum stuck to her fingers. Going to the sink, she ran water against the tray until the cubes began to work themselves free and tumble noisily into the sink. It was then that Anne Marie turned the lights on.

She drank three glasses of iced water. She made no attempt to wipe away the water that dribbled round the edges of the glass, down her chin and onto her blouse.

She rubbed a block of ice against the back of her hand, and soon the swollen, ugly skin was numb.

The flat was tidy and empty. Béatrice had gone home to Le Moule. 7:15 P.M. and still her husband and her son were not back.

She turned on the television and while she put the shopping away—a cockroach lurking behind a can of asparagus—she listened to the evening news.

Gurion, the FR3 journalist, had been discovered on a beach near Gosier. Drugged, abducted, and then left in a metal trunk. He was now recuperating in a private clinic outside Pointe-à-Pitre. There was no anxiety concerning his health, but he would be resting for several weeks, possibly returning to mainland France.

Surprisingly, the cold water made Anne Marie feel better, and she wondered whether she was suffering from dehydration. She undressed slowly and went upstairs to take a shower. She felt a lot less tired and as she wrapped the towel around her body she decided the couscous would be for another time. She needed to relax.

At 8:10 P.M. she took her shower. The chill water revived her. She no longer felt sick, and her hand had miraculously ceased to itch.

Afterward, stepping out of the bathtub, she looked at her body as she rubbed herself dry. She ran her finger along the livid scar under her belly. Perhaps it was time to give Fabrice a little brother. Yet lately her husband had not seemed very interested in that sort of thing. Anyway, they could not think about having another child until Jean Michel landed a decent job.

She smiled at her reflection in the mirror. She had forgotten the nauseating stench of cigar and now dabbed a drop of Van Cleef and Arpels onto her wrist.

Anne Marie went downstairs and collapsed onto the settee in front of the television.

The American film with Steve McQueen and Yul Brynner that Jean Michel enjoyed so much. Anne Marie had seen it a couple of times before. It now failed to hold her attention. Frequently her glance went to the clock on the bookcase, next to the photograph of Fabrice.

They were still not back at nine o'clock.

There was an old packet of Royale Menthol cigarettes. She took a stale cigarette and started chewing at the mentholated filter.

At 9:15 P.M., she heated a *croque monsieur,* and then at 9:30 P.M.

precisely, the phone started to ring. She picked up the receiver before the second ring. "That you, Jean Michel?"

"Madame Laveaud."

"Yes?"

"Jacques Azaïs here. I'm calling you from the rue Gambetta. I think you'd better come down here to the police station immediately."

65

Commissariat

There was a bench by the door. It stood against the wall beneath the high metal blinds. A boy sat there. He had glistening dark skin and a bruise beneath his eye. A large woman also sat on the bench; from a cut on her cheek, blood dripped quietly onto the concrete floor. Between the boy and the woman sat a policeman who stared at his shoes. His kepi was balanced on his knee, and he was handcuffed to the boy.

Anne Marie went to the reception counter.

"Monsieur Azaïs, please."

The duty officer lowered his cup of coffee. "Who are you?"

She showed her identity card.

"I'll accompany you." He gave her a belated smile and left his coffee on the wooden counter.

Anne Marie followed the officer up the steps. The Commissariat was an old building and she came here as rarely as possible. Policemen—even the most intelligent—seemed to suffer from an inferiority complex before a woman from the Ministry of Justice.

"At the end of the corridor, madame." The duty officer saluted, turned, and went down the stairs.

At the top of the stairs on the third floor, there was a recruiting poster. A white policeman in crisp uniform was smiling and over his face somebody had scrawled in thin letters the single word, MERDE.

The corridor was empty and shadowless. Anne Marie had the impression of having been here before, at the same time, of doing the same thing.

There was no sign on the door. She entered without knocking.

"Ah, Madame Laveaud."

The room was gloomy. "Where's Azaïs?"

"He'll be back soon."

"Why does he want to see me? It's nearly eleven o'clock."

Dr. Bouton said, "Please sit down, madame le juge."

"My husband'll be waiting for me." They shook hands perfunctorily. "Why does Azaïs want to see me?" She kept the anxiety out of her voice. "He insisted it was important. I was about to go to bed."

The doctor shrugged. "Azaïs should be along any minute. He went out only an instant ago." The light from the desk lamp bounced off the frame of his glasses.

Anne Marie sat down and looked round the dingy office. A large desk was caught in the pool of light from the lamp. A pile of open books, an ashtray full of cigarette stubs.

And a photograph.

Dr. Bouton sat down in the armchair opposite her. His narrow face was in the shadows. There were filing cabinets beyond the penumbra of the desk lamp. "He wanted a place out of the way."

Overhead, a fan was rotating. A whispered, regular hum. She could feel the breeze of the artificial ventilation.

"He?"

"Azaïs' real office is in Basse-Terre, of course."

"Of course," Anne Marie repeated. She leaned forward and took the photograph from the desk. "Where did Azaïs get this?"

Dr. Bouton shrugged. He was smiling at her from behind the glasses. The thin hands were clasped together on his lap; the small fingers formed a steeple to the church of his knuckles.

"And why are you here, Dr. Bouton?"

"Waiting, madame le juge. Just like you."

The woman stared at her from out of the past—from the past

when Hégésippe Bray was still alive and still a young man. *Lucien le Marc, photographe, Fort-de-France.*

"You know who this is?" Anne Marie handed him the photograph, and he took it, turning it to get more light.

"Should I?"

"I'd like to know how this photograph got here. It should be in my dossier."

"Perhaps Monsieur Azaïs's studying the dossier."

"The dossier's in my office, *docteur*—where I keep all my files under lock and key."

Dr. Bouton nudged his glasses upward onto the long forehead. "Let me have a look at your hand." He frowned and took her left hand in his. "You really ought to do something about this before it spreads."

"It's going to spread?"

"You don't want it going up your arms, do you, madame le juge?" He ran his fingers along the deformed, red flesh. "Urticaria."

"You're a doctor of medicine?"

"What do you think?" He was now standing up, holding his body to one side in order to get a maximum of light. "What does your general practitioner say?"

"I haven't seen a doctor."

"You must look after your health."

She shrugged. It was cool in the office, but sweat was forming along her forehead. "Haven't really got the time."

He placed his hand on her forehead. "Too much time on your job—and not enough on yourself." His hand was cool. Close to her, he smelled of peppermint. "Fever."

"I'll take some aspirin when I get home."

"You ought to go to bed for a couple of days."

"I've work to do."

"Work can wait."

"Hégésippe Bray couldn't wait. He hanged himself—and it was my fault."

The thin man chided her, clicking his tongue. "Do you sometimes feel nauseated?"

She shrugged.

He slipped his watch from his wrist and took her pulse. His eyes were on the dial. "Bray was an old man and he was going to die. Familiar smells turn your stomach?"

"Sometimes."

"Loss of appetite?"

"I scarcely have time to eat."

"A nice healthy slow pulse. You used to be an athlete?"

"No."

Dr. Bouton moved away and went round to the far side of the desk. A smile softened the austere features. He picked up the phone.

Anne Marie let her head drop onto the leather backrest of the chair. Sleep—she needed to sleep. Her eyes burned. Steve McQueen's dubbed voice. She thought of coolness. She thought of Europe.

Dr. Bouton said, "You need antihistamine for that."

"Where's Azaïs? I want to go home."

His eyes turned away from Anne Marie, and he spoke into the mouthpiece, "Which chemist is on night duty?"

The voice scratched.

"Put me through please."

For no apparent reason, tears had begun to form at the corners of Anne Marie's eyes. "I want to go home." The pain seemed to be drifting away, losing itself. She was tired.

"Bring it up, then." Dr. Bouton then gave a series of names—trade names for drugs that Anne Marie had never heard of. "Good," he said, and hung up.

Go home—not to the Cité Mortenol but to Sarlat-la-Canéda and the Quartier des Peches. Papa, her sister, Nassérine the maid. Among people who cared for her. Anything to get away from the heat and the humidity of Pointe-à-Pitre.

"You will have to see a specialist, you realize."

She tried to open her eyes—she had closed them and now the eyelids were stuck together. Sleep between cool sheets, with Jean Michel beside her and Fabrice next door, while through the night the gentle rumble of trains pulling into the station. More tears of self-pity trickled through the closed lids.

"At least the ointment should relieve the itching. Some pills and some suppositories. And above all, rest, madame le juge."

She tried to open her eyes, but the desk lamp burned her pupils. She could feel herself falling into sleep.

"A week's rest—and you must try to forget about your work. It's making you ill."

She wanted to reply. She wanted to tell him that she must continue—not for her sake but for the sake of the old man.

"Hégésippe Bray is dead and you can't save him. Be reasonable, madame le juge."

Another tear. It ran into the hollow of her ear.

"After all, you've already had a child. A boy, I believe." Dr. Bouton was smiling. "It's not as if this was your first pregnancy."

66
97-1

"A rifle. It's in the boot of my car—if someone wants to go and fetch it."

At the bottom of the stairs, Azaïs turned, and Anne Marie thought he was going toward the reception desk.

"I need to get home, Monsieur Azaïs. My husband's waiting for me."

"You needn't worry about your husband."

The woman with the cut cheek—the wound now caked with dry blood—watched Azaïs' movement. The policeman sitting beside her continued to stare at his shoes.

"Careful, madame le juge." Dr. Bouton held her arm gently but firmly.

Azaïs turned left and they went down the stairs and through a couple of swing doors. The smell of detergent was stronger than the smell of Dr. Bouton's peppermints. Azaïs turned on the light. A short corridor, sawdust on the floor. The sound of scurrying legs—perhaps mice or perhaps cockroaches—moving at the approach of humans.

"It wasn't Bray's gun that killed Raymond Calais. He had his own twenty-two bore—a rifle he bought recently." She spoke toward Azaïs' back.

He did not turn. He took a key from his pocket and unlocked the padlock on a door of packing-case wood.

"The Indian stole it." Her voice was unnaturally high. "Which proves that Hégésippe Bray was innocent."

"I wonder if you can identify this for me?" Azaïs turned on a wall switch and stepped back to let Anne Marie enter. The neon tube began to flicker until it gave off a cold, insistent light that illuminated a small, dusty room. "You didn't recognize it on the beach at Gosier."

Of course she could identify it. And even if she could not, the top coat of blue paint had been peeled away from the side of the metal trunk and there stood revealed the neat letters that Anne Marie herself had stenciled:

Monsieur et Madame Laveaud, Jean Michel,
Rue Alsace-Lorraine, 31,
97110 Pointe-à-Pitre,
Guadeloupe—Antilles françaises.

The hinges had been broken.

For a second, Anne Marie wondered whether the Chantilly lace curtains were inside the trunk.

67

Casuarina

Anne Marie knew where Jean Michel had taken Fabrice.

The headlights sliced a yellow wedge along the road. The wind rushing through the window cut out the sounds of night. No moon and the surface of the Grand Cul-de-Sac Marin was dark as if flattened beneath a sheet of oil.

She saw the reflection of headlamps in the driving mirror and slowed down to a steady 90 kph.

Rain clouds rolled across the sea. Isolated drops fell onto the windscreen, and she saw the lights of Pointe-à-Pitre go out on the far side of the bay as the city was engulfed in a squall.

Then the downpour.

Heavy drops exploded against the windscreen and the wipers could not compete.

With virtually no visibility, she had no choice but to stop. Outside Petit Bourg she pulled the Honda onto the forecourt of a Texaco station. She switched on the warning lights and listened to the thunderous beating of tropical rain on the car's roof.

Sweat ran down her back. Bile and the chalky taste of pills lay on her stomach. Dr. Bouton had smilingly assured her that these pills would have no deleterious effect upon the fetus. The taste rose up in her throat, and she was afraid she was going to vomit.

It rained for over half an hour.

Not a car went past. Just the station, the shadowy petrol-pumps, and the spiky leaves of the casuarina trees lit up by the regular blinking of the Honda's lights.

At a quarter past midnight, the rain ceased as suddenly as it had started.

Anne Marie took her hand from where it lay on her belly and turned on the headlamps. The road was awash with swirling floodwater. The sky had cleared; on the far side of the bay, Pointe-à-Pitre and the airport lights twinkled serenely. At sea, a banana ship rolled beneath the red beacons on its masts.

Anne Marie opened the window, and the cool air chased away the mist from the screen and the rear window. In the mirror, not more than sixty meters away, on the same side of the road, she saw another car turn on its lights.

Anne Marie pulled out onto the wet tarmac, taking the direction for Trois-Rivières. She drove slowly between the eddies of swirling rainwater.

In the mirror, the car followed.

She drove through Petit Bourg and Goyave. The towns appeared bedraggled—waiting for a new day and the sun that would dry everything. That would heal everything.

The other car was still in her mirror.

Just after the first road sign for Trois-Rivières, Anne Marie came up behind the somber silhouette of a large cart. She raised her foot on the accelerator. The road was too narrow for her to overtake.

The cart was being pulled by a team of oxen. In her yellow beams, she could make out the legs of the animals beyond the wooden frame. The chassis was weighed down with a load of cane. The driver—a man in white clothes, a pith helmet, and his head held at a strange angle—sat on the high board, a whip in his hand. She could not see his face. He was very tall.

Anne Marie slowed down to walking speed.

In the mirror, the following car had disappeared.

When she reached the long, straight stretch of road beneath the royal palms, she changed into second gear, gathered power, and carefully pulled out onto the crown of the road. She did not want to frighten the oxen.

It occurred to her as strange that cart and oxen should be on the road so late at night. Strange also the load of cane, when the sugar harvest was already long over.

There were no lights on the rear of the cart.

As the Honda came abreast of the driver—Anne Marie was traveling at twenty kilometers per hour—she turned her head to look at him.

The man was smiling and he raised his hand to wave. He was tall, taller than any man she had ever seen before.

Beneath the helmet, he had white hair. High, Carib cheekbones. His blue eyes were bright—very bright—as if lit up from within. There were no teeth but as he opened his smiling mouth—he was calling to her—Anne Marie saw the pink triangle of his tongue.

Then she saw the deep scars that marked Hégésippe Bray's misshapen, broken neck.

68

Moon

"Fabrice!"

Anne Marie kissed her son, putting her arms about his narrow shoulders and hugging him.

"Eight years and. . . ." He scratched his head with the handle of the spade. "Eight years and. . . ."

"Have you eaten?"

"Eight years and two months—eight years, two months, and ten days."

The white beach was scattered with dry sponge. Fabrice's naked back was hot beneath her hand. "You should put on a T-shirt." She looked around for a beach mat, a towel, and some clothes. There was nothing.

"That's right, Maman. Eight years and two months and ten days."

"What on earth are you talking about, doudou?"

"If you had to walk to the moon. You remember, don't you? That's how long it would take." He folded his arms with satisfaction.

Anne Marie kissed his forehead, which tasted of salt; grains of sand glistened in the hairs of his eyebrows.

"Papa helped me—we used the calculator in the hotel. But that's without sleeping."

"Where's Papa?"

"If you walked all the way—and you didn't stop to sleep." He added, "Which is cheating, really—because you have to sleep. Four hundred thousand kilometers."

It was hot on the beach and there was no shade. A girl in a pink bikini was smoking while she read. She sat beneath a large parasol. Young, firm thighs shone with suntan oil.

"Where's Papa, doudou?"

Fabrice shrugged. "Over there."

"Where?"

"You're blind, Maman." Fabrice sighed. He pointed out to sea, out beyond the bay, between the two promontories where the sail of a single windsurfer emerged and then vanished beneath the swell. It appeared again. The sail heeled over into the wind and the white board skimmed across the water.

"Papa said you would be coming. Maman, did you come on the plane?"

"I came over on the ferry."

"I bet you were sick." He looked up at her and wrinkled his nose in amusement.

"A little."

"Want to make a tunnel with me?" He put his hands on his hips. A pile of plastic cyclists lay between his brown feet. "I'm doing the Tour de la Guadeloupe, and you can play if you want."

"I haven't eaten breakfast yet."

"Can we go to the hotel and have some ice cream? Papa lets me eat ice cream. He says I can."

She took his hand. "We'll see, doudou."

"And yesterday, in the plane, the pilot let me sit beside him in the cabin." He stopped and tilted his head to look at her. He held her hand to his hot cheek. "Maman, your hand is better."

69

Fontainebleau

Nothing had changed at the Hotel Fontainebleau. Not the table and the chairs, not the flowerpots standing like sentinels to protect the hotel from the advancing beach. The Byrhh ashtrays were the same.

The open terrace was as she remembered it. Even the serving girl had not changed or aged. She did not recognize Anne Marie, but Anne Marie recognized the woman's kind face. It was like rediscovering an old friend and for a few moments, Anne Marie sat watching her, remembering the way she walked, the sound of her shoes on the tiles, her gentle voice, the lilting accent of the Saintes.

A young woman, only a few years out of adolescence, with a gold ring on her finger. With Jean Michel, she had flown down to the Saintes and had stayed at the Fontainebleau in a bright, clean room that looked out over the vast bay, the precipitous sugar-loaf mountain and the green covered hills that reminded her of her Mediterranean. Marvelous breakfasts with fresh fruit brought from the mainland—bananas, grapefruit, and green oranges. During the long, sun-washed hours of the day she went snorkeling. Fish she had never seen before—striped, indolent fish that moved slowly through the clear water and the white coral.

Jean Michel soon got bored. He complained about the lack of food. There was little else other than fish, caught by the local fisherman in their bright boats, red and a vivid blue. And there was nothing to do. He did not enjoy lying on the beach. "Anyway," he said, "I'm already brown enough."

Anne Marie was appreciative of the cool winds that blew. And she felt healthy. Not since leaving Algeria in 1958 had she felt so well, so fit. Nor had she been so attractive as during the honeymoon.

They spent most evenings in Terre de Haut.

A television was placed on the sill of the town hall, and when evening fell, the set was turned on and the villagers—the children sitting cross-legged and the adults on the cement benches—watched the programs with innocent pleasure. Frantically they applauded the French team in Jeux Sans Frontières just as they applauded the arrival of Yul Brynner and his mercenaries in the dubbed Western.

Anne Marie was reminded of Algeria. People walking backward and forward along the main street, the girls hand in hand, the men quietly smoking. The children were often barefoot, and the women wore fashion-able high heels.

Anne Marie fell in love with the Saintes, with the flowers, with the lemon trees, the café bâtard and the wild cinnamon. They formed, these forgotten islands, a terrestrial paradise, a corner of another, long-forgotten France, old-fashioned and peaceful, existing on the far side of the globe. A part of the old Empire that knew nothing about insurrection, anti-colonialism and the murder of innocents.

Anne Marie drank her coffee, and the recollection of past happiness caused her eyes to water.

Fabrice stood up. His narrow swimming trunks had slipped down to reveal much of his backside.

"Come and finish your ice."

The little boy ran to the steps that led to the beach. "Here comes Papa."

Despite her anger and fatigue, Anne Marie could feel the same excitement that she had known when they had first met.

"I was expecting you, Anne Marie."

"So Fabrice tells me."

Jean Michel smiled and he kissed her cheek. His face was cold from the sea. He sat down and they looked at each other. He seemed pleased with himself.

"You wanted to escape?"

"I don't think there's much future for me in Guadeloupe."

"There are gendarmes in the Saintes, too," Anne Marie said.

"And juges d'instruction."

"Did you really have to bring Fabrice with you?"

"He's my son as well, you know."

Fabrice turned to his mother then to his father. He scrutinized the two faces carefully.

"Soon you'll be leaving your son, Jean Michel."

"Perhaps you will start looking after him properly."

"What does that mean?"

"Instead of leaving him with my mother—so that you can play at Perry Mason and earn your fat colonial salary."

"Who's going to pay for the food and rent if I don't work?"

"Anne Marie, you know you don't care about the boy."

She raised a finger in accusation. "You love the child—but you leave him when you feel like wandering off with your pretty young cousin. And with your childish, voodoo curses, you terrify me until I can't sleep." She closed one eye and squinted. "Your curses and your voodoo coffins."

Fabrice asked, "What curses?"

"Go and play."

"What curses, Maman?"

"Go and play when I tell you to." Anne Marie slapped his leg. "Learn to obey your mother." The blow was harder than she had intended and the red wheals appeared immediately on his young skin. "Go to the beach. Your father and I must talk."

"You shouldn't hit him."

Fabrice's eyes quickly filled with tears. He made no sound. He dropped the spoon back into the bowl of ice cream, slipped from the chair, and walked across the terrace. As he moved past her, she brushed his soft hair in an act of contrition.

At another table, a man coughed.

"You shouldn't hit him," Jean Michel repeated.

"Perhaps you should set him an example. I have all the responsibility." She spoke through clenched teeth. "Don't make me angry, Jean Michel—not more angry than I already am."

"The coffin was nothing to do with me."

"Then who put it there?"

He looked down at the tile floor of the open terrace.

"Who did it? For God's sake, tell me."

"My brother."

"Freddy?"

He nodded without looking at her.

"Why?"

"I need a cigarette." Jean Michel turned in his seat—he was wearing a damp T-shirt that stuck to his torso—and called the serving girl. "A packet of Gitanes, mademoiselle. Without filters."

"What on earth would make Freddy want to do a thing like that? Didn't he realize the effect? For heaven's sake, he's the child's uncle. Does he hate Fabrice? Tell me, Jean Michel. Why?"

"Of course he loves Fabrice."

"Why terrify me?"

"I didn't know you believed in voodoo."

The girl brought a packet of cigarettes and a book of matches.

"Why did Freddy do that? Why the threat?"

"Perhaps he doesn't like you."

"Of course he does. Freddy's always been nice to me. Always so willing to help. You know I like Odile—I went to the funeral with her. I like Freddy. He helped us with the flat."

"It's what you represent that he hates."

"That entitles him to scare me to death?"

Jean Michel tried to smile. "Freddy only confessed yesterday—and I nearly struck him."

"You should have killed him."

"He's my brother."

"I'm your wife."

Jean Michel shrugged.

"What did he do it for?"

"He wants you to let the matter drop."

"The matter?" She lowered her voice. "You mean the killing of Raymond Calais? What on earth for? What does he care about Raymond Calais?"

Jean Michel opened the packet of Gitanes and took a cigarette. "Do you want some more coffee?"

"Why does your brother want me to drop the enquiries?"

"As long as there is a doubt about Calais' death, people's attention will be attracted toward the movement for independence— and toward the idea of an independent Guadeloupe."

"That's foolish."

"Calais's death, foolish or not, was publicity for the MANG."

"You belong?"

No answer.

"You belong, don't you? You look for a job with *Le Domien*, but all along you're with the MANG."

He shook his head slowly. "There never was any job with the *Le Domien* in Basse-Terre."

She smiled coldly. "I know."

"You know?"

"On Monday, I was in Basse-Terre. I could have gone along to the offices of the *Le Domien*. I could have made enquiries. You were supposed to be having your famous interview. But I didn't go—because I knew you wouldn't be there. So I bought a pair of shoes and a handbag instead."

"How did you know?"

"I'm a woman—I know when you're lying. You're like a little boy, Jean Michel, and I didn't need to know why you were lying. You've always lied to me. Just as you lied to me in Paris all those years ago about the girl with the headscarf. Just as you lied to me about the princess from the Cameroon."

He lit a cigarette and smoked in silence.

Jean Michel used to have an old Panhard coupé. In the afternoons, the

roof was always down, despite the chill spring weather of Paris, and the
back seat was packed tight with grinning friends from the islands. Invari-
ably sitting beside Jean Michel was a girl, with a skin of alabaster and a
scarf round her head like the actress Pascale Petit.

Anne Marie drank her coffee.

Later the girl brought a fresh pot and another plate of croissants.

"Guadeloupe's a police state. That's what you can't understand, Anne Marie. Nazi Germany or Brezhnev's Russia or Iran—
the same thing, only more subtle, more sophisticated. Controlled
by a colonial power that owns the radio and television and the
only newspaper." He added, "It was Freddy's idea."

"You're beginning to bore me."

"The only debate left open to us is violence. Violence and frus-
trated graffiti on the walls." He stubbed out the cigarette. "What
alternative do we have?"

"You've never grown up, Jean Michel."

"Can't you see what France has done to Guadeloupe? Or perhaps you don't care?"

"France is a democracy. There's no need for bombs and bullets."

"You call this a democracy?" He shook his head in disbelief.
"Giscard and his local flunkies make quite sure we remain well-
behaved. They give us cars and supermarkets. They give us a civil
service. But do they give us our dignity?"

Anne Marie said nothing.

"We're not slaves anymore, and we ask for more than just the
flimsy tinsel of the big French consumer society. We want dignity—and our right to self-determination."

"With bombs?"

"What else when we're not allowed to speak freely?"

Anne Marie turned away and looked through the trees. Fabrice
was back on the beach and somehow he had persuaded the girl in
the bikini—she did look a bit like Pascale Petit—to play with him.
He was laughing, pleased to have an adult taking notice of him.

"If I had wanted to watch TV," Jean Michel had remarked when Anne Marie suggested they sat down among the children in front of the public television, "I could have stayed in Paris." He spent a lot of time phoning his mother from the hotel.

Toward the end of the second week, they decided to cut their stay short. They took the boat back to Trois-Rivières.

For the last five days of their honeymoon, they had stayed with Jean Michel's mother in the rue Alsace-Lorraine.

It had rained almost every day.

"You impose French laws," Jean Michel was saying.

"Me?"

"You, the French, you impose laws that have nothing to do with us, you ruin our economy with your bloated salaries." He laughed. "And like everyone else, you're manipulated by the Békés." He lit another cigarette, and his wife saw that his hand trembled. "Guadeloupe needs France—and Giscard needs the Békés. And now with the elections coming up next year, Giscard's got to be sure that the overseas départements—including Guadeloupe—vote for him. So France keeps the money pumping in, and everybody's happy."

"You had better hope he's defeated next May."

"Bread and circuses for the simple-minded West Indians—that'll keep them quiet." Jean Michel clicked his tongue. "You don't care about Guadeloupe, do you?"

"Jean Michel, I don't care about you—it's as simple as that. But I care about my son—and I care about his future."

"A future with France?" He laughed again and smoke escaped from his nostrils. "You forget that he's black like his father."

"The color of my child's skin is not an issue."

"Unemployment—that's all he can hope for—like all the young people of Guadeloupe. Unemployment while the Békés and the whites like you grow rich."

"You're lecturing me on the evils of colonialism, Jean Michel?" Anne Marie sighed noisily. "Unlike you, I was thrown out of my native land."

70

Pistolero

A humming bird perched upside down on the lip of the yellow letterbox.

Anne Marie felt calm.

Not the lull in a storm but the end of the storm. Now the sun emerged into a clear, cloudless sky. No more decisions to be made. They had all been made for her.

Jean Michel came back and sat down on the far side of the table. "There's a flight to Pointe-à-Pitre in forty minutes. I've phoned for a taxi to take you to the airport."

She nodded her thanks. "I wasn't aware there are taxis in the Saintes."

"You're sure you want to go?"

"Fabrice is coming with me."

Jean Michel shook his head. "The child stays with me."

"It's a good idea for Fabrice to see his father flirting with another woman? You must take me for a fool."

"I take you for what you are, Anne Marie."

"Your wife?"

"What other woman? I don't know what you're talking about."

She laughed. "And the white girl in the bikini? Or is that just an optical illusion?"

"You always were a fool. A clever, well-educated fool."

"Thank you."

"You're leaving me, aren't you? To go back to Pointe-à-Pitre and denounce me to your friends at Renseignements Généraux.

"They know."

"You're a free woman, Anne Marie."

"Our marriage is dead, Jean Michel. As far as I am concerned, you no longer exist."

"Our marriage's dead because that's what you've always wanted."

"A bomb that killed an army officer is no laughing matter. At best you can hope for ten years—or perhaps you think that independence is going to come and that you and Freddy are going to be liberated as heroes of the great nationalist cause?"

"I came here to be with Fabrice. There's no girl in a bikini."

"Fabrice comes back to Pointe-à-Pitre with me."

"No, Anne Marie."

"Where can you go? You can't get out of the Saintes—unless you want to try your luck sailing to Dominica on your surfboard."

"I'm not leaving."

It was all distant, all very matter of fact. She was an outsider, an onlooker. All this was happening to someone else. Jean Michel was somebody she had once known. A long time ago, in a different place, at a time of innocence. Now innocence was dead, and Anne Marie no longer cared. "You think the Cour de Sûreté de l'Etat is going to forget about everything?" Even her voice was distant.

"You'll help me. I'm the boy's father."

"I don't intend to risk Fabrice's future just for you. You made your choice, Jean Michel, a long time ago. Now you must live by it. Were you thinking of Fabrice when you planted the bomb? Or when you kidnapped Gurion?"

He stood up and moved toward her. "I need you."

"Remember the Western, Jean Michel?"

"What Western?"

"We saw it once in Paris—and another time, during our honey

moon? Remember one of the mercenaries? I think it was Charles Bronson. The little Mexican boys adored him, and they told the Americans their own parents were peons and cowards."

Jean Michel was frowning.

"Remember how Bronson got angry with the little boys?"

"*The Magnificent Seven?*"

"The hired gunfighter told the children to go back to their fathers. Anybody can be a pistolero and pull the trigger. But the man who works from morning till night to feed his wife and his family—that man's a real hero." She laughed coldly. "You always loved those American films. But you weren't listening."

"You're the intellectual, Anne Marie. I enjoy the action."

"You never listen. Instead you spend your life listening to the little boy in your head. Mamie's little boy."

"I need you now."

"Time you grew up."

"More than ever. I need you now, Anne Marie." There was pain in his eyes. He placed his hand on hers.

She removed her hand. She noticed that her skin had already begun to dry and was forming a hard, flaky surface. "I'm not your mother. God didn't put me on this earth just so that I could tidy up the mess you make."

"Help me."

"I'm not one of your black women. I'm not going to sacrifice myself or my child for you, Jean Michel. I'm a Jew, remember—as you're always reminding me. A North African Jew—and I have my son to think about. And I have my own life before me."

He placed his hand on her knee. "What am I going to do?"

"I haven't the faintest idea."

Outside, the taxi slid to a standstill beyond the grill gate of the hotel. The driver honked twice.

His voice broke. "They will send me to France. Perhaps I will go to prison—and I won't see my son."

She picked up her handbag and stood up. "You never thought of that before?" She moved toward the sunshine.

He caught her arm. "Help me." He was pleading.

"Hope for one thing, Jean Michel. Hope that over there in the France you profess to hate—just hope Giscard d'Estaing is defeated." Her voice was flat. "I wouldn't bet on it—but it's your only chance. Hope Mitterand and the Socialists get elected. Because then—and only then—can you hope for a presidential amnesty." She pulled her arm free and went down the steps.

The almond eyes of the taxi driver looked at her legs with interest.

"Stay. Stay with me—just for today." Jean Michel came down the steps and leaned past her as if to stop her from opening the gates. "You, me, Fabrice—we can spend the day together. Like before—like when we were on our honeymoon. You remember. We should never have returned to Guadeloupe—we were happy in France. We'll go swimming together—be with the boy. And eat in the hotel. And this evening, we'll go into town. We'll watch television. Do you remember? We'll sit outside the town hall, and with the children, we'll watch television in the open air."

"If I wanted to watch television, I could have stayed in Pointe-à-Pitre." She pulled the iron gate open just as the taxi driver gave another, insolent honk.

71

Return

"Good to see you," Anne Marie said. "I wasn't sure you'd be able to get to the airport."

"I'm not like the others, you know." Trousseau frowned, irritated. "I do my best to be reliable."

"And unlike the blacks, you know how to work."

He nodded, placated. "The car's outside."

It was late morning—past 11:30 A.M. and there was a lot of movement through the airport. Overhead, the fans moved through their lethargic circles. Trousseau directed Anne Marie toward the exit from the terminal building.

The car had pulled up onto the sidewalk, near a bush where the allamanda flowers formed bright yellow eyes. Anne Marie recognized the Simca. The driver smiled, and Trousseau put down the typewriter case he was carrying to help her into the back seat.

"You said you were coming with your son, madame le juge." Trousseau got in beside her.

"Fabrice wanted to get the boat back. I'll pick him up tomorrow." She added in a whisper, "Did you tell the driver?"

The car bumped down from the sidewalk and out of the airport. The tires whispered along the tarmac, soft beneath the midday sun.

On the roundabout, the driver accelerated, and Anne Marie was thrown against Trousseau's bony shoulder.

"Tell him what?"

"I don't want everyone to know I was in the Saintes."

"Madame le juge, on the phone you told me not to tell anyone. If you believe I'm not reliable, perhaps you'd care to employ a different greffier. . . ."

"I'll get the gendarmerie at Trois-Rivières to send the Honda back."

They came to the road junction where a large hoarding advertised Air France flights to Disneyland. Mickey Mouse smiled at the passing cars. His face was deformed by black daubing. The meaning of the words escaped Anne Marie. She noticed that the graffiti had been sprayed on recently:

Bwé = Dipon = exécution d'état.

Trousseau laughed and Anne Marie imagined that his mirth was triggered by the sight of a man urinating against one of the poles supporting the hoarding.

"They get everything wrong!" He laughed again and she turned to look at him.

"Who?"

"You saw the graffiti, madame le juge?"

She shrugged.

"Bray and Jerry Dupont executed by the state."

"Well?"

"All on the central computer." Trousseau nodded. "It never occurred to me to look."

"You know who killed Dupont?"

"No." Trousseau placed his finger along his moustache. His dark eyes twinkled as he held the black typewriter case to his chest. "I don't know who killed him—but I found out who he was."

"On the central computer?"

"Jerry Dupont wasn't on it."

"Then who was he?"

The car stopped for traffic lights at the intersection with Nationale 1.

"Madame le juge, Jerry Dupont didn't exist."

"No riddles. I'm not in the mood, Monsieur Trousseau, and you're not Lafitte."

The lights changed and the car moved forward. Anne Marie was pushed back against the seat.

"It's here." He opened the case and took out a folder. "Pichon's report—just for you."

"Perhaps you could explain."

"Pichon's good, and for the last nine years, he's been sitting on his little secret."

"If it's a secret, why's he telling you and me?"

"Sick of seeing Renseignements Généraux being used by the politicians."

Anne Marie looked through the window as they drove into town. WELCOME TO POINT-A-PITRE. No sidewalk, but a broad stretch of rubble cluttered with parked cars and a few utility vehicles. A large puddle that covered half the road. Wooden shacks with stained corrugated roofs formed a topsy-turvy line. A couple of houses of concrete. On one wall, the paint faded by the rains, BUVEZ COCA COLA. And in the distance, the high, white city blocks rose up from the swamp.

"Pichon knew about Jerry Dupont all along."

"Then why didn't he inform us earlier?"

"Madame le juge, it was only the other day you asked me to look into the Dupont affair. I believe you saw Monsieur Carreaux." Trousseau paused. "Monsieur Carreaux of MANG."

"You knew there was a connection between the deaths of Hégésippe Bray and Jerry Dupont?"

"I'm only a greffier, madame le juge."

Anne Marie ran her finger along her upper lip. "But you're married to a white woman, I believe. Didn't you once tell me that?"

The dark eyes blinked.

"And you're an excellent greffier. The best I've ever known. The best and the kindest. Not just a greffier, Monsieur Trousseau, but also a friend."

He paused, took a deep breath. "A *Pied-Noir*—like yourself. A European born in North America."

Anne Marie frowned. "Who?"

"Dupont—that's not his real name. He'd grown up in the United States where his father was a security officer at the embassy in Washington. Jerry Dupont was bilingual." Trousseau tapped the dossier. "Pichon explains everything."

"Who murdered Dupont?"

"Murdered?" The idea seemed to amuse Trousseau. His shoulders began to shake. "That's the sort of simplistic thinking of the MANG." The laughter ceased. "There was no Jerry Dupont. You'd have thought Renseignements Généraux with all their intelligence officers could have managed to organize something a bit more sophisticated. But their plan worked and they found out what they wanted."

"What did they want?"

"The RG needed to know whether the students at the university and at the lycée were being manipulated by provocateurs."

"And?"

"Jerry Dupont gave them the information. His real name is Duchet—Jean Louis Duchet."

"Is?"

"Now with Renseignements Généraux in New Caledonia. Married a rich local girl."

"Then he didn't commit suicide?"

"No—unless his wife is a necrophiliac." He laughed.

More traffic lights. The wheels screeched as the driver braked.

"Renseignements Généraux were terrified of another '67 and more bloodshed in the streets. Probably acting on the instructions of the Préfet—who no doubt got his orders from Paris. They indulged in a bit of aggressive information gathering. And I don't blame them."

"Dupont was a spy?"

"In a manner of speaking."

"But they created a martyr."

"Apart from the MANG, who cares about Jerry Dupont?"

"I must read that file." The car went under the bridge and ran into the Boulevard Légitimus. "Put it on my desk, will you? I'll be in later today or tomorrow morning." She leaned forward and then tapped the driver on the shoulder. "I must get out here."

The driver nodded into the mirror and pulled the Simca into a line of parked vehicles at the traffic lights.

"I was hoping we could have lunch together, madame le juge," Trousseau said.

"Somebody I must see first." She got out of the car, and to her surprise, Trousseau followed her. "You have lunch, Monsieur Trousseau. Somebody I have got to see and then I'm going home. I didn't sleep last night at Trois-Rivières—perhaps it's the pills I'm taking for my hand. Incidentally, I spoke with the gendarmes in the Saintes. The father confessed to having helped Cinderella kill her baby. Her lawyer hopes to get her deported back to Dominica."

Trousseau touched her arm. "I wanted to speak to you in private."

"Perhaps later."

"It's about your husband."

"About my husband?" Anxiety in her voice.

The driver was watching them carefully. The midday sun was hot.

"I've heard about Monsieur Laveaud." Trousseau looked down at his shoes. "A rumor he was involved in the airport bombing. A rumor I've heard from several sources."

"Well?"

"I don't believe it—not a word. I know my opinion is of no importance—a humble greffier of Indian descent."

"What rumor?"

"Despite the rumors and all the unkind things that I've heard being said over the last twenty-four hours, I want you to know I don't believe them."

"Thank you."

"It is a deliberate attempt to sully your reputation—because you're efficient and because you do your work well. And because a lot of people would like to see you out of the way, madame le juge. I've seen judges come and go—but I've never seen anybody like you before—not even a man. You're hard working and you're honest. Some people say you're ambitious—but I know you're concerned about the people you deal with." He moved his shoe awkwardly. "I want you to know that it's not just me. There are other people at the Palais de Justice who know and respect you—and who like you, madame le juge. We will never allow you to be removed on a trumped-up charge against your husband. We will not allow you to be taken away from us just because alone among all the magistrates, you've had the courage to do your job—even if it means stirring up a political hornet's nest."

He raised his eyes and for a couple of seconds Trousseau and Anne Marie looked at each other. The Indian and the Pied-Noir, both stranded in a distant land. Trousseau was about to run a finger along the thin moustache when Anne Marie stood on tiptoe and kissed his cheek. "Thank you, Monsieur Trousseau."

She then darted across the road and entered the building. She stopped to look over her shoulder.

Trousseau had not moved. Nor had the driver sitting in the Simca. They were both staring at her.

She gave a small wave and then went over to the reception desk.

72

Truth

"I was just about to leave."

"I won't keep you long. May I sit down?"

The office was chill. Overhead, the conditioner hummed. On the wall, there was a poster with a photograph of Notre Dame de Paris.

The large desk was cluttered. Brochures, timetables, thick volumes of air ticket prices. And a Perspex cube which had been filled with various photographs. Anne Marie recognized the smiling face of Armand Calais in a snapshot taken in New York. Seeing the photograph, Anne Marie was struck by the likeness.

Madame Calais stood up. "I can't stay." She was wearing a black dress and a black cardigan draped over her shoulders. There were a couple of bracelets around her wrist. The freckled flesh had formed goose pimples.

There was an electric kettle on the floor. "I think you should. Perhaps you could offer me some tea—it doesn't have to be Fortnum and Mason. . . ."

"I'm meeting someone for lunch."

Anne Marie picked up the receiver of the grey telephone. "Give them a ring and tell them you're not coming."

"What on earth for?"

"Tell them you've just been arrested."

Madame Calais sat down again.

"What impressed me was your concern for Hégésippe Bray. You insisted he was innocent, you told me it was the MANG who'd killed your husband. And so I believed you. I believed you sufficiently not to associate you with the gun." Anne Marie smiled. "I now realize it was you who cleaned it and buried it. Admittedly, it would have been stupid to do otherwise. The gun must've been lying about your house for the last forty years—ever since Hégésippe Bray was sent to French Guyana and your husband took his land. Then with Bray back in Guadeloupe—and his name engraved upon the butt—you knew the gendarmerie would automatically accuse the old man."

"Am I right in thinking you're accusing me of the murder of my husband?"

"Have you noticed the way nobody's got a good word to say for your husband? A thief, a scheming politician, a blackmailer, a gangster—in fact, the only person favorably disposed toward him is you. Even your brother-in-law, Jacques Calais, has difficulty in hiding his distaste. But then, Raymond Calais was a distasteful man, and you did a lot of people a considerable service by destroying him." Anne Marie shrugged. "I hasten to point out that murder is a crime—and punishable in the last resort with the guillotine."

"I shall make some tea."

"A good idea."

Anne Marie leaned forward as Madame Calais plugged in the electric kettle. "I must say I like your bracelet."

"A friend bought it for me in Madagascar." Madame Calais set two cups on the table. "Milk or lemon?"

"Neither."

Later, as Madame Calais poured the tea, Anne Marie noticed that the freckled hand was trembling. The tremble was transmitted to the flow of amber liquid.

A bowl of brown sugar was placed on the blotting pad.

"Only your family could've had access to the gun. When

Hégésippe Bray went to French Guyana, he left no family in Guadeloupe."

"Sugar?"

"No thank you."

"An interesting theory—but not sufficient to convict someone with. You seem to forget, mademoiselle. . . ."

"Madame," Anne Marie corrected her.

"I'm a fairly wealthy woman. The best lawyers—I can get them from France, and I can pay for them." For the first time the mask of her face broke into a smile. "An argument like yours won't last five minutes in a court. You must realize that. If you really want to pick on the Calais family, I don't see why I should be considered guilty rather than Jacques." The eyes held Anne Marie's look. "It wasn't me my husband blackmailed. But he did blackmail Jacques Calais."

"Unlike Jacques Calais, your husband tried to murder your son."

The smile died slowly, leaving her lips hard set. There was a whiteness about the pinched nostrils.

"You see," Anne Marie said softly, her hand on her lap, "I am a mother, too."

73
Children

"A husband—you can never completely own him. You can love him, but you can never be sure he's yours. A child is different—a child is part of you; he's your own flesh and blood."

Madame Calais handed the thin cup and saucer to Anne Marie.

"After nearly forty years, perhaps I'd have done the same thing myself. Perhaps your husband deserved to die. But by deliberately rigging the evidence, you put the blame on Hégésippe Bray. That old man was arrested for a murder he'd never committed. He killed himself, and as far as I'm concerned, it was you who placed the noose around Hégésippe Bray's neck."

"He was going to die."

"He still had several years to live—years to live in the love of his family. After forty years in South America."

Madame Calais sipped her tea. "My husband was going to die. I was doing him a favor. A clean death—rather than the long, drawn out suffering and the antiseptic smell of hospitals."

"You murdered Raymond Calais because you hated him."

There was a long silence.

"I don't know whether I hated my husband."

"Why else did you murder him?"

"Raymond had lied to me. And he had stolen my child from me. Through no fault of mine but through his own stupidity, his own arrogance. Black skin—for Raymond Calais, it was the greatest dishonor imaginable—as if the color of our skin is going to make any difference when we come to meet our Maker. As if he didn't know there was black blood in the Calais family. One of his grandfathers was a mulatto—and on his mother's side, there were at least two octoroons. But of course, like all men, he could never admit his own responsibility." She laughed without humor and set down her cup. "The Békés are all convinced they're as white as the driven snow. They've got as much black blood as the mulattos—and they're no better than the mulattos." She stopped and looked at Anne Marie. "You're very shrewd."

"I'm a woman."

"When did you realize all this?"

"The day of the funeral—the day they buried Hégésippe Bray. I saw Marcel Suez-Panama walking with his mother—with the woman who'd brought him up. And behind them there was Armand, your son. I'd noticed something familiar about Armand—and I'd just assumed it was his likeness to your husband. The same jaw."

"You met my husband?"

"I saw the photographs." Anne Marie shook her head. "Then I saw Armand and Marcel—and there were only a few meters between them. By some coincidence, they were wearing similar clothes. It was inevitable I should see the similarity. But it took me some time before I realized that they were brothers."

"Brothers." For a long moment, Madame Calais sat staring at Anne Marie, staring without seeing. The eyes glazed over and started to water. "Brothers," the woman repeated, "and I could have gone to my grave thinking the little boy had died. My little boy." She wiped at her eye with a lace handkerchief. "What on earth drove Raymond to do that? I thought he was a man—but he was a monster. He was capable of coming between a mother and her child—just because the child didn't happen to have white skin and he was terrified of a scandal." She shook her head. "I'd always assumed the poor thing died at birth. That's what Raymond told me—and later, when the doctor came from Sainte-Anne, he told me the same thing. A couple of days later, there was the funeral. It was awful—awful. I was just married, you know—and had been married for less than a year, and for all of the next year, I wore black. Black for the child I'd lost—and all the time I thought it was my punishment from God. And Raymond was so cold with me, so cold and uncaring. It was as if he hated me, and he wanted to punish me. There were nights when I cried myself to sleep and wished that I could die—or be like these steatopygous Negro women for whom having children is second nature, a habit like straightening their hair with hot combs or sewing their clothes for the carnival. Raymond had other women, and I lived virtually alone on the estate. He refused to sleep with me. Young and innocent—and don't forget that I came from an English island where the whites never had anything to do with the local women. How was I to know why my husband was acting so strange?" She tried to smile. "Perhaps in his stupid, male pride, it never occurred to Raymond the poor child was his son, his own flesh and blood. I'm not an educated woman—but in Barbados, those unsmiling nuns had taught us about Mendel and his sweet peas. Perhaps Raymond really thought I'd been unfaithful. With some sweaty laborer from the fields. Or with Hégésippe Bray." A tear fell from the corner of her eye. "I was alone, so alone, especially after Monsieur Calais died. There was nobody to talk to. I felt so utterly rejected. Just nineteen—and in four years, I don't think that Raymond and I could have shared the same bed more than three times. During all that period, I could feel he hated me, and I didn't understand. I didn't understand he'd married me for my money. He was so hurtful, so unkind. The loss of the child—and then to be rejected by the man you love."

"Now you know the truth."

"But I am old. An old woman. Those forty years—I wanted him to pay me for them. I didn't say anything—but there was a look in his eyes before I pulled the trigger, and he must have realized. I hope he realized—but Raymond was so selfish and so self-centered that he could never understand I acted out of love. Out of love for the poor, sweet child he had stolen from me."

"Marcel Suez-Panama's in prison at the moment. He admits to having killed your husband. I suspect he's trying to protect his mother—his adoptive mother, because he thinks she killed Raymond Calais. On the Sunday that he died, Marcel and Madame Suez-Panama were both over at the Sainte Marthe estate, visiting Hégésippe Bray."

"The boy needn't worry. I'll get a lawyer for him. I'll make quite sure he's set free."

"Once you're arrested for the murder of your husband, Suez-Panama will be automatically released."

"Forty years—and I'd never have suspected a thing if the Salvation Army hadn't picked up that old man. And if his sister hadn't come to visit us." She shook her head. "Forty years—and I'd never seen him. Not even at his birth. There was no doctor, but the girl from Martinique gave me her magic potions, and I didn't understand what was happening. Then forty years later he was standing in front of me. My child. He had come with the old woman to ask about the land—and immediately I knew. It was like a flash of lightning. I nearly fainted. I knew he was my child." Her face softened. "My own child, from my body. Despite the color of his skin—the eyes, the jaws, the eyelashes. He was mine. I began to tremble and I had to leave the room."

"What did you do then?"

"What could I do? Tell him that this old white woman with the sagging chins and the loose flesh on her arms, tell him she was his mother? And although I knew the truth, I had to be sure. In my heart I knew—but in my head I was confused. He was black—how could I be sure he was my darling, darling boy?" She caught her breath.

"So?"

"So I did the only thing I could do."

"You asked your husband?"

"You think he wouldn't lie to me? He's spent all his life lying to me. He once told me he loved me—but that was before we were married and that was before he got his hands on my share of the family fortune. Raymond Calais was a liar. He lied with every breath he took."

"What did you do, madame?"

"Jacques was never like Raymond. Jacques is a good man—and if I'd had any sense, and if I hadn't been blinded by love, it was Jacques Calais I should've married. But in those days, Jacques was infatuated with a silly little mulatto girl from Basse-Terre. I went to see him in the showrooms. I knew Jacques Calais would tell me the truth—but by then, I'd guessed everything."

"The truth, madame?" Anne Marie placed her hand on top of the pile of brochures. "What truth?"

"Raymond Calais wanted to destroy the child. His own flesh and blood, the cement of our marriage—he wanted him killed. It must've been early morning when I went into labor. It came suddenly and unexpectedly—at least two weeks premature. There was nobody in the house, other than Eloise Deschamps. And my husband. Perhaps they were having an affair—I wouldn't put anything past her. She was an evil, scheming vixen, and she led her husband a fine dance. They say she was a witch. Perhaps she was—and perhaps she threw a curse on me. She knew all the magic potions. For me she made a herbal tea from tree bark. The pain—the terrible pain, a pain I'll never forget—began to lose its edge. I think I must've gone into a coma—because after that, I don't remember a thing. I don't even remember coming round when the little child was born. Later Raymond told me my baby had been stillborn—and I didn't even cry. I just felt empty—terribly empty."

"What did your husband do with the child?"

"According to Jacques, he gave it to the Martinique girl, and he told her to kill it. Of course, Raymond didn't have the courage to carry out his own dirty deeds. And the girl—perhaps she was a woman after all, and I must be grateful to her—she ran away and she took the baby to Pointe-Noire. I can only assume the Suez-Panama woman thought the child was the girl's. That's why she kept her secret—and that is why she bought the baby up as her own.

"And then the Martinique girl tried to blackmail your husband?"

"That's what Jacques told me. Eloise Deschamps was a grasping, evil woman."

"You were at Sainte Marthe at the time of the murder of the girl. You must know about it—you must know what happened."

"Monsieur Calais was already very ill. He wanted a grandson—and he was almost as upset as I was by the loss of my baby. He was very kind to me, and he didn't want me to hear anything or know anything that might upset me. He wanted to protect me—he had no idea that his son had left the marriage bed."

"Jacques Calais knew what happened?"

She nodded. There were traces down her powdered cheeks. Despite the nice clothes and the makeup, she looked a tired, old woman, and Anne Marie found herself feeling sorry for her. The sense of elation—and satisfaction—brought on by the woman's confession had now evaporated.

"Raymond knew the only alternative to being blackmailed indefinitely was to kill the girl. And that's probably what he did. He poisoned her."

"And the vials? And the magic ointments that Hégésippe Bray admitted to having tampered with?"

Madame Calais shrugged. "A coincidence—which most certainly suited my husband. During those four years that he refused to touch me, I thought it was because of the girl. I was convinced she'd put a curse on our marriage because my husband had killed her. I knew he'd poisoned her—the way he acted guilty, the way he grew angry when I mentioned Eloise Deschamps' name. And Jacques knew it, too—and instead of my husband, it was that poor, stupid black man that was sent to French Guyana."

"You did nothing to save him."

"I was nineteen years old, madame le juge, and I was in love with my husband."

"Something could have been done."

"What? What could Jacques do? He knew his brother was guilty—but if his father had known, it'd have killed him—and it would've been the end of the Sainte Marthe estate. A scandal—a terrible scandal with Raymond Calais denounced as a murderer. Jacques was ashamed of himself. Now I can see that's why he ran away to America."

"You don't feel guilty about inventing false evidence? You don't feel you're responsible for sending Hégésippe Bray to jail for a second time?"

"How did I know he was going to hang himself?" Her face broke into an unexpected smile, as if she needed to escape from her memories. "More tea, madame le juge?"

74

Boulevard Légitimus

Outside, beyond the blue-tinted window, beyond the hum of the air conditioner, there was a lull in the midday traffic along the Boulevard Légitimus.

"I will have to make out a warrant for your arrest."

"Arrest?" Madame Calais lifted the cup to her lips.

"For the murder of Raymond Calais, your husband."

Madame Calais shook her head. Then she drank.

"I have no choice."

"I know you have no choice, but I shan't be arrested."

"You are mistaken."

"It's you who are mistaken." Madame Calais set the cup down and poured more tea. Her eyes remained on Anne Marie. "You're mistaken because you don't understand Guadeloupe. You believe you're still in France. This isn't France, madame le juge, and I can tell you we don't behave in the same way here."

"Murder is murder."

"What would happen to your husband?"

"My husband?"

Her shoulders no longer sagged. "This is a small island and information travels fast. Very fast—particularly when you belong to a powerful minority. Do you really understand the Békés?"

"My husband has no effect upon the way I do my job."

"You won't be able to do your job—it's as simple as that. It is not you and it's not France that controls Guadeloupe. Guadeloupe is ours. France sends the money, but it's my people who decide how it's spent. Do you really believe that the Calais family and all the other families—you think they'll allow me to go to prison like a common criminal?"

"You've committed a crime." Anne Marie's voice was forced and unnatural.

"I've perhaps committed a crime according to your law—the law of France. Here in Guadeloupe, I'm in my own country and among my own people. Trust me—even if there were no solidarity among us whites, there'd still be no chance of my ever going to jail. Because the government—your government—needs us. Monsieur Giscard d'Estaing and Paul Dijoud and all the others—they need us because they need our vote. Without our active support, they know Guadeloupe will go to the Socialists. And that's the last thing they want in Paris."

"Party politics are not the concern of the judiciary."

"You're young and naive. Are you sure you wouldn't care for another cup of tea?"

Anne Marie stood up. She picked up her bag.

"Perhaps my husband was not educated—but he was cunning and he knew how to protect himself. And he always knew something could happen to him. That's why he told me all about the SODECA affair. I have most of the documents. Very compromising documents. Of course, the Chamber of Commerce and the bankers and even my dear friend the procureur—such a nice man—of course they're a little bit worried. The SODECA business could be most embarrassing for them. But they know that as long as Giscard's in power, there's nothing for them to be afraid of. A debt of fifty-three million francs?" She made an amused, dismissive gesture. "A mere bagatelle. The taxpayer can foot the bill, and within a year, it'll all be forgotten. Perhaps one or two discreet resignations—but nothing a quick whitewash can't cover up. But if you. . . ." Madame Calais smiled. "But if you decide to put me in jail—the wife of Raymond Calais—all my good friends know I possess a lot of information. Let the cat out of the bag—and in the process ruin several powerful families? You see, they're going to be annoyed. Not just annoyed . . . they're going to get angry. Very angry indeed." She paused and again she laughed, as if recalling an old joke. "Perhaps I've underestimated you, madame le juge. Perhaps you really do believe in justice. And perhaps you aren't afraid. But be warned."

"It's not for you to warn me."

The woman held up her hand. "Fifty-three million francs is a lot of money. And for a lot of people in Guadeloupe, your life—and the life of your son—aren't worth fifty-three million francs."

"You're threatening me?"

"Advising you, madame le juge. And my advice to you is to be very careful as you cross the road. There are a lot of bad drivers in Guadeloupe."

75

Bois sec

She climbed the stairs. Sweat ran down her back; even on the top floor of the Cité Mortenol there was no breeze. The white walls reflected the harsh sunlight.

Anne Marie unlocked the front door and let herself into the apartment. She picked up the telephone before she kicked off her moccasins and slumped down onto the divan. She had to dial three times—a flurry of electronic pips—before she got through.

"Gendarmerie, Terre de Haut."

"Le Bras?"

"Speaking."

"Le juge Laveaud here."

"Madame le juge, I rang about half an hour ago."

"I have just got home." She paused. "Well?"

Le Bras did not reply.

"My husband—where is he now?"

"Your husband's still taking lunch at the Hôtel Fontainebleau. I have a man there who is in direct radio contact."

"And my son?"

"The little boy's with his father."

"I don't want Fabrice—I don't want my son scared. Things are going to be hard enough for him as it is."

"Nothing to be scared about, madame le juge. It's best the boy stay with his father. There's nowhere that Monsieur Laveaud can go, and tomorrow I'll bring your son back to Pointe-à-Pitre."

"It's very good of you."

"Merely doing my duty."

"I worry about my son."

"I'll accompany him personally to the Palais de Justice. I am quite sure he'll enjoy the flight in our helicopter."

"You're very considerate."

"Part of the job, madame le juge. Au revoir."

"*Kenavo.*" Anne Marie hung up and waited a few minutes before getting to her feet. She went to the kitchen, drank a glass of chilled water and took two more antihistamine pills.

They had a soporific effect.

She went upstairs. The wooden stairs creaked in the empty apartment. Anne Marie took a shower, and then, still damp and with just a towel across her body, she lay down on the big bed. Within a few minutes, she fell into a dreamless sleep.

Outside, Pointe-à-Pitre returned to work after the midday hiatus.

The streets filled with fast, angry traffic. Cars honked and the Brazilian buses gave off fumes. The sun moved across the blue sky. The shadow of the flame trees, of the breadfruit trees, of the coconut palms, and the flamboyants inched slowly across the sidewalk.

Anne Marie was woken by the telephone.

"Ah."

She picked up the bedroom extension.

"Madame Laveaud? I've been trying to get through to you for the last half-hour."

"I was sleeping. Who's that speaking?"

"It's nearly half past five."

"Who's that?"

"Lafitte here. Glad I've got hold of you."

Outside the sky had begun to darken. A distant cloud was tinged with red.

"Madame le juge, I shouldn't really be phoning like this. I'm calling from the bar opposite the Palais de Justice. I could be getting myself into trouble. Serious trouble."

With one hand, she rubbed her eyes. "What's the matter?"

"Azaïs. He's got a search warrant, and he wants me to come round."

"A search warrant?"

"For your apartment, madame le juge. Cité Mortenol, 903. He wanted me to come round this evening with him—but I told him you wouldn't be at home and I managed to persuade him to put it off until tomorrow. Azaïs—I don't know, this is only my opinion— I get the impression he wants to incriminate you in the airport killing."

Anne Marie stared at her naked thighs.

"Are you still there, madame le juge?"

Her voice was weary. "Yes."

"I thought I'd better warn you."

"Thank you, Monsieur Lafitte." She rubbed her eyes again. "That's very good of you. I appreciate your help—and your consideration. Very much indeed."

"The least I could do." Perhaps he shrugged. Or perhaps the symmetrical features broke into a boyish smile. "You've always been very kind to me—better than a friend."

"Thank you," Anne Marie said softly and lowered the receiver onto the cradle.

She was tempted to go back to bed. She still felt sleepy, but instead she got up and showered, letting the cold water wash away the sweat and the sleep from her eyes. For a long moment she stared at her belly and she held her hand against the damp skin. Then she put on a cotton gown and went downstairs.

She found the phone number in her address book and she dialed. No answer.

Anne Marie sat on the divan and stared through the window as evening came to the city of Pointe-à-Pitre. The apartment was silent. From time to time, she looked at the photograph of Fabrice.

She dialed every five minutes and did not get through until nearly seven o'clock. By then the sky was quite dark.

"Hello?"

"Le procureur de la République?"

"Ah." A gentle laugh. "Do I recognize the charming voice of our young juge d'instruction?"

"Yesterday afternoon—at the supermarket—you suggested that you may be able to help my husband."

"He's in trouble?"

"You know perfectly well he's in trouble."

A long pause.

"You realize, don't you, madame le juge, you've not made life easy for me?"

"It was you, monsieur le procureur, who placed me in charge of the Calais dossier. You've only yourself to blame. You were hoping with a woman in charge you'd be able to control events more satisfactorily. Perhaps I've been unnecessarily stubborn, but I've tried to do my duty, and I'm now in a position to show Hégésippe Bray was innocent. Monsieur le procureur, Madame Calais has confessed to me. She admits to having shot her husband."

"Ah."

"She was jealous," Anne Marie said simply. "You see, it really was not necessary to kill Hégésippe Bray."

He laughed and over the line, his voice was harsh. "You still believe the old man was murdered in his cell?"

"I don't believe Bray hanged himself."

Another pause.

"Madame le juge, I can help you and . . . I think I can help your husband. The Cour de Sûreté de l'Etat—and particularly this man Azaïs—are kicking up a bit of a fuss. But don't worry. I still wield a certain amount of clout in the département of Guadeloupe." He stopped.

"Monsieur le procureur, could I take you up on your invitation?"

"Invitation? What invitation?"

"I could come round, and we could discuss these things. On

the veranda, over a planter's punch, enjoying the evening breeze as we watch the cargo ships sail out into the night."

"Sounds like a very good idea. Of course I can help you. You have my address?"

"I'll be around in forty minutes, monsieur le procureur—just the time to get ready."

"Excellent." He laughed contentedly and hung up.

Anne Marie put the telephone down.

The photograph of Fabrice stared at her.

"Eight years, two months and ten days. If you had to walk to the moon. You remember, don't you?"

It took her ten minutes to get dressed, to put on her makeup and brush her hair. More wrinkles—it was the sun that was drying out her skin. And a few more white hairs.

A drop of Van Cleef and Arpels to each wrist. She put on the new shoes; she also transferred her purse, her identity card and her keys to the new handbag. It was nearly eight o'clock by the time she was ready to leave. Just as she was about to go, she remembered the cigar tin.

She ran up the stairs—the new leather soles were slippery— and opened the drawer of the dressing table. She took out the tin.

Now that her finger was no longer swollen, the wedding ring slid comfortably back into its natural place.

Continue reading for a sneak preview of the next
Judge Anne Marie Laveaud novel

The Honest Folk
of Guadeloupe

I

Madame Dugain

Wednesday, May 16, 1990

"YOU'RE LOOKING for me?" The woman was attractive, but her face appeared tired, the eyelids dark. There were wrinkles about the soft brown eyes. She placed a pile of exercise books on the table, beside her handbag.

"Madame Dugain?"

"Yes, I am Madame Dugain. Your child is in which class?"

Anne Marie moved toward the table. "It's about your husband."

For a moment the expression went blank while the eyes searched Anne Marie's face. "I have already made a statement to the *police judiciaire*." Madame Dugain drew a chair—a school chair with a steel frame and a plyboard seat—towards her. "Several statements." She leaned against the backrest.

Anne Marie sat down on the other side of the table. On the Formica top there were a couple of tin lids that had been used as ashtrays.

The far wall was covered with pinned-up notices concerning the different teaching unions. Beneath the drawing pins, the paper rustled relentlessly; the doors to the staff room were wide open and a mid-morning breeze kept the air cool. Through the open shutters, Anne Marie could see a flame tree that had started to blossom.

"My husband is dead—isn't that enough?"

Anne Marie nodded sympathetically. "He died under strange circumstances."

"He was hounded to death."

"I don't think anyone hounded your husband."

Madame Dugain shook her head. "I'd rather not talk about these things."

"I understand."

The eyes flared with brief anger. "You understand?"

The two women were alone in the staff room of the Collège Carnot. There was silence.

(Somewhere children were singing. In another building a class burst into muffled laughter.)

"I know how painful it is to lose someone you love." Anne Marie held out her hand, "I'm Madame Laveaud. I'm the *juge d'instruction.*"

Madame Dugain took the proffered hand coolly. "I really have nothing to say to an investigative magistrate or to anybody else."

"I asked the head mistress for permission to speak to you."

Madame Dugain folded her arms against her chest. She was wearing a dress that went well with the brown, liquid eyes. A necklace, matching gold earrings. Black hair that had been pulled back into a tight bun. Her lipstick was a matte red.

"On Saturday, April twenty-first, three officers of the *police judiciaire* visited your husband in his offices in the Sécid Tower. They had a search warrant and they were seeking information concerning accusations made against your husband."

"Everybody accused Rodolphe."

"Accusations that as director of the Environment Institute, he had been misappropriating funds."

"My husband's not a criminal."

"Your husband received money from the government—from the Ministry of Employment—to recruit and train young people under the Youth Training Scheme. Six young people were working for him at the institute, and their salaries, funded entirely with government money, were paid into the Institute's account."

"I know nothing about my husband's financial affairs."

"Your husband's accused of employing two of the young people in his small business in Abymes and paying them with the government allowances."

Madame Dugain bit her lip. "My husband would never have taken money that wasn't his."

Anne Marie touched the woman's arm. "Now your husband's dead. I don't think any good can be achieved by continuing with the enquiry."

"Leave me in peace." The corners of her mouth twitched. "My husband and I were happy. We'd been married for nearly twenty years. My children and I have suffered enough."

Somewhere an electric buzzer sounded, followed almost immediately by the sound of scraping chairs and the scuffling of feet as the pupils left their desks at the end of the lesson.

"Just supposing that your husband was guilty of these accusations . . ." Anne Marie shrugged. "A fine—twenty thousand, thirty thousand francs. Not a lot of money for your husband."

Madame Dugain flinched. "Rodolphe was innocent."

"It's not for thirty thousand francs that an influential and well-respected member of the community decides to do away with himself."

2

Fait divers

France Antilles, April 23, 1990

Mr. Rodolphe Dugain, better known to most television viewers as Monsieur Environnement, died on Saturday, April 21, following multiple injuries and internal concussion after throwing himself from the fourteenth story of Sécid Tower block in central Pointe à Pitre.

If the rumour had been circulating for some time that the judicial authorities were making enquiries into the Centre Environnement, the sudden and untimely death of Monsieur Dugain, one of the major and most respected figures in the cultural Who's Who of our *département*, seems to have taken Guadeloupe by surprise. The ripples of shock can be still felt at the university where Monsieur Dugain held a lectureship in natural sciences as well as along the corridors of the RFO television station where he regularly broadcast his popular nature programmes.

On Saturday morning, three officers of the Service Régional de la Police Judiciaire presented themselves at the offices of the Centre Environnement. According to eyewitnesses, Monsieur Dugain appeared his normal, jovial self, not allowing his good humour to be affected in any way by the presentation of a search warrant. He is believed to have offered a drink to the three men then while the officers were looking for documents and other information—the nature of which as yet has not been revealed by the *parquet*—Mr. Dugain managed to slip from the room. Once on the far side of the steel door, he locked the police officers inside and, taking to the stairs, Mr. Dugain climbed from the third to the fourteenth floor of the tower block. On the top floor, he went to the observation window and from there jumped to his death, landing on a car parked on the sidewalk of the Boulevard Chanzy. Mr. Dugain died immediately from the impact. The vehicle was badly damaged and several people were taken to the nearby *centre hospitalier universaire*, suffering from shock.

A crowd of onlookers gathered around the macabre spectacle. Yet again in Guadeloupe, the lamentable behaviour of rubbernecks and passers-by hindered the fire and ambulance services in the execution of their duty.

Monsieur Dugain, who was a Freemason and an ex-secretary of the Rotary Club, was born in Martinique fifty-seven years ago. He leaves a wife and two children, as well as two other children from an earlier marriage.

A memorial service at St. Pierre and St. Paul will be held on Tuesday at ten o'clock. The inhumation will take place at the municipal cemetery at midday.

3
Public trial

"I need to know why he died."

Madame Dugain raised her eyes. "Is that important?"

"You said he was hounded to death by the police."

"It doesn't matter any more."

"It matters."

A moment of hesitation. "You don't believe my husband was innocent?"

"Innocent or guilty, suicide is not a normal reaction."

"The SRPJ threw him from the fourteenth floor."

"Unlikely."

"I must be going." Madame Dugain took up her bag and stood up. She was in her late thirties, a trim girlish silhouette and attractive brown legs. She ran a hand along her hair. "It's been nice meeting you."

"When somebody's pushed through a window, the victim hits the ground close to the building. Somebody committing suicide jumps—and the car on which your husband landed was nearly four meters from the entrance to the Tour Sécid."

Madame Dugain stared in silence at the clasp of her handbag.

"Nothing else you can tell me?"

"Else in what way, *madame le juge?*"

"Was anything worrying your husband?"

"What more do you want, for heaven's sake?" A hard laugh. "His name in the papers? The accusation of cooking the books?

The police coming to search his offices? His probity and his reputation were being called into question. My husband was being put on public trial—no, not a trial but a public lynching. The telephone never stopped ringing."

"With a good lawyer, he could have . . ."

"My husband needed to be left alone. He didn't need a lawyer just as he didn't need being dragged through the mud. The mud his enemies wanted. That the police wanted. That's what you've now got and I hope you're satisfied."

"Satisfied?"

"Rodolphe's dead."

Anne Marie caught her breath. "Who were his enemies that you talk about?"

"I've nothing further to say."

"You really don't want to help me set your husband's record straight?"

"You couldn't care less about my husband's reputation."

"I care about the truth."

"Your truth." Madame Dugain picked up the pile of books, turned and walked out into the sunshine. As she passed beneath the flame trees her heels clicked on the stone pavings.

4

Headmistress

"Liliane Dugain's my cousin."

It used to be the *lycée*. Then in the mid-sixties, a new school complex was built at Baimbridge on the edge of the city to accommodate the increase in the number of pupils. Consequently the old colonial Lycée Carnot, with its courtyard, its mango and flame trees, its airy, wooden classrooms, stranded in the heart of Pointe à Pitre, was transformed into a *collège*, a junior high school.

The two women walked out of the staff room and across the yard, between the trees. A breeze rustled through the leaves, and the pendulous, mangoes swayed gently at the end of their long stalks. Other mangoes had fallen to the ground and split their bruised skin.

(Anne Marie was reminded of her school years in Algeria.)

"I got the impression she was more angry than upset."

The headmistress raised her shoulders. "Liliane'd been married long enough to know what Dugain was like."

"He was fond of women?"

"You know a man who isn't?"

Anne Marie glanced at Mademoiselle Salondy as they stepped into the school building. "That's why you never married, Lucette?"

"One of many reasons." The headmistress put her finger to her lips and nodded to the closed doors of the administrative offices.

The muffled sound of a typewriter.

They went up the wooden stairs and entered an air conditioned

8

room. There was a large desk. A photograph of President Mitterand hung on the wall between a poster of the Declaration of Human Rights and a calendar from a local garage. The cables leading into the light switches were unconcealed and had been tacked into the wall with staples. A telephone sat on the desk and beside it, a plastic cube containing various pictures of Lucette Salondy's relatives. In a small glass jar, there was a solitary anthurium.

"Madame Dugain's your cousin?"

"Sit down, Anne Marie." Lucette Salondy had a smile that formed wrinkles at the corner of her bright eyes. "Who isn't a cousin on this island?" She was a large woman whose dress could not hide the matronly hips.

"You know her well?"

"Liliane's more than twenty years younger than me, and when I came back from France in '66 she was doing her philosophy baccalaureate. A bright girl and the youngest in her class." She tapped the desk. "That was when the *lycée* was still here, before they built the concrete jungle on the ring road."

"I shouldn't discuss things that have been told to me in confidence."

"Then don't."

Anne Marie squared her shoulders. "Liliane Dugain was acting out a role—that's the impression I got."

"Liliane's too old to act. She simply needs to be left alone."

"That's what she said."

"Perhaps you don't understand Guadeloupe women here. They hide their suffering."

"Do you ever talk to her?"

"My prison." The headmistress gestured to the office, the walls painted the pale grey of France's tropical public buildings and beneath the opaque louvers, the potted dieffenbachia, the leaves yellowing at the edges. "No time for idle chat—there are at least three new teachers this year whom I've never spoken to." She pulled a blue cardigan from the back of the chair onto her shoulders. "Headmistress? I'm just a cog in a big, faceless administration. My job's to sign bits of paper or phone the Rectorat in Martinique to sort out problems of their making. I am afraid our cousins in Martinique are notoriously incompetent."

"You're talking like a racist."

"Perish the thought. Put simply, in Martinique they don't understand our problems in Guadeloupe because those gentlemen of Martinique prefer not to understand. During the revolution we set up a guillotine here in the Place de la Victoire and we chopped off the heads of all the whites who hadn't run away. For eight years we were free while over in Martinique the English protected the slave owners. So they like to think of us as peasants."

"The gentlemen of Martinique fail to understand the honest folk of Guadeloupe?"

"My word! I see you've done some studying, Anne Marie." She smiled. "The nobility of Saint-Domingue, the gentlemen of Martinique and the honest folk of Guadeloupe. Except that now in Guadeloupe and Martinique we run around in SUVs while the immigrants from Haiti cut our cane in the fields."

Anne Marie smiled. "You don't have time to talk to Madame Dugain, but you find time to talk with me."

"First time I've seen you since Léonore's wedding." She stretched a plump arm across the desk and squeezed Anne Marie's hand. "I rarely get out of this office."

"You've just been out."

"I went looking for you, Anne Marie Laveaud because I want to talk to my sister-in-law before she scurries back to the law courts."

"Sister-in-law, Lucette?"

"I'm your father-in-law's daughter—remember? Which makes me the half-sister of your husband."

"My ex-husband." Anne Marie gave a terse smile. "You still have your apartment on the beach at Le Moule?"

"I was there yesterday. I had to take a couple of hours off to drive over to les Alisées. Someone renting it—and the lavatory is blocked up." Lucette Salondy shrugged. "A couple of hours I could ill afford to waste on private business. I just don't get time for myself. My weekends are taken up with administrative work. Perhaps when I retire."

"You'll never retire, Lucette."

The large woman sighed. "So many things to do, and never a moment to spare. I can't wait to retire." She added, "She was Dugain's second marriage, you know."

"They weren't happy?"

"Liliane Dugain has two lovely children."

"Why wasn't she happy?"

"My cousin married someone who was seventeen years older than her. That kind of age difference's common here in our islands but Liliane's an educated woman, and she wanted a friend, and in the end she married somebody who could've been her father. She wanted equality, and she found a man who never treated her as an equal. Someone who gave her two lovely daughters but who went elsewhere for his pleasure."

"Other women?"

"I don't know why you sound so surprised, Anne Marie."

"Not the sort of thing I'd expect."

"What do you mean?"

"When there's a big age difference, men are supposed to lose interest in philandering."

"Are they?"

Anne Marie shrugged. "Or so I am informed."

"Men in mainland France—but not here in the islands," Lucette Salondy said, folding her arms. "Dugain appeared on television. He was a public figure, the kind of person to appeal to women, to our groupie mentality. We're attracted to the dominant male." She clicked her tongue, as if reproaching herself for something. "Dugain probably didn't go out of his way looking for women— but they were there. There are always women." She sighed. "You haven't learned that about Guadeloupe?"

"Who?"

"Even a headmistress and a spinster locked away in her office hears things." She got up and went to a small filing cabinet. She turned the key. "Care for a drink? A white rum at fifty-nine degrees from Marie-Galante can work wonders."

"No thanks."

"Let me tempt you. I often wonder how you manage to stay so slim, Anne Marie, but I suppose I shouldn't. So slim and so young." Lucette Salondy poured herself a thimbleful of white rum into a small glass. She took a slice of green lime from a small refrigerator. "Worry about my figure at my age?" She sipped and winced. "The great thing about being old is you don't have to try to please any more, and the strange thing is, it's only when you've stopped try-ing to please men that they actually start noticing you. Not for your body, for your figure, for what you can do in bed—they actually notice you for what you are." She smiled wistfully. "I was thinking about your husband only the other day, Anne Marie."

"My ex-husband."

Another sip. "How's your son?"

"Who were Dugain's women?"

"Tell me about Fabrice, Anne Marie. We were all sad when he moved on to the *lycée*."

"Fabrice?" Anne Marie flushed. She was about to say some-thing bitter but instead she chose to relax and allowed herself to sit back in the tubular chair. "Wind surfing, most of the time. And probably about to repeat his year in the *première scientifique* at the *lycée*. Fabrice is quite hopeless at school."

"He can't be too hopeless if he's in *première scientifique*. Bril-liant when he was here and always top of the class—but never conceited."

"Hopeless in everything except English—because it's the only thing he's willing to put his mind to. He's so stubborn, never wants to be helped."

"Stubborn like his father." Lucette Salondy frowned. "Where is that ex-husband of yours now?"

Anne Marie looked at her hands. "Fabrice's lazy. If he's not interested in something, then he just can't be bothered. He spends his time watching the American channels on the satellite dish. Understands everything in English—but refuses to work at school. I mustn't complain, though. He's a good boy and very affectionate. Just dotes on his little sister."

Lucette Salondy's face broke into a broad smile. "And Létitia?"

"The apple of her mother's eye."

The headmistress took the plastic cube and pointed to a photograph on one side of it, a photograph taken outside the church in Pointe à Pitre. Children in white dresses, holding flowers and squinting into the sun. Létitia stood in the centre of the group. Her dark hair hung in short, beribboned plaits. The soft brown skin of mixed parentage. She was wearing a white dress, and she looked at the camera with her head to one side. She was holding a bouquet of flowers. Inquisitive, self-assured eyes.

"The apple of her aunt's eye, too. An aunt who doesn't get to see her enough."

"Létitia just loves church—goodness knows why. Perhaps it's the dressing up she likes." Anne Marie touched the cube with her finger, "I thought I was too old to have a second child, and when I found out about Létitia, it really wasn't the happiest of times, and I even thought about an abortion. When I now think I could've spent the rest of my life without Létitia . . ." Anne Marie looked up at the older woman. "You could've had children, Lucette."

"Instead I've got an entire school. Before long, you'll be sending Létitia to us—only by then, I'll be long retired."

"You love this job too much to retire."

Somewhere a bell rang.

"Why are you interested in Liliane Dugain, Anne Marie?"

"It's her husband's death I'm interested in."

The headmistress folded her arms. "He jumped from the top of a building."

Anne Marie remarked, "There are a lot of nasty rumours."

"Rumours concerning the *police judiciaire*?"

Anne Marie gave Lucette Salondy an unblinking stare.

"Dugain had a lot of enemies, Anne Marie."

"Arnaud doesn't believe it was suicide."

"Who's Arnaud?"

"You don't know the *procureur* here in Pointe à Pitre?"

"Arnaud is his given name?" Lucette Salondy held her glass motionless in mid-air, and the room seemed suddenly chilly. With her other hand, she pulled the cardigan tight against her large shoulders.

"Dugain had a mistress?"

"You really want to know?"

"It's my job."

"Perhaps you ought to change jobs."

Anne Marie pointed to the poster on the wall. "There's no republic without justice."

"I thought it was me who was supposed to teach philosophy."

"There's no justice without truth."

An amused laugh, lubricated with white rum.

"Never underestimate the Lycée in Sarlat." Anne Marie grinned with pleasure. "I won the *prix d'excellence.*"

"You were a swot." The headmistress put down the glass of rum and sighed as she took a pen from the mahogany inkstand in front of her. "Everybody knew it was a mistake. Liliane should never have married Dugain. Few people will miss him—not even his groupies. Forget about justice and, in your position, I'd certainly forget about Monsieur Environnement." She jotted something onto a piece of paper then folded the paper twice, firmly, as if she wanted to have nothing to do with its written contents. "A womanizer and a fraud."

"You're not in my position." Anne Marie took the slip of paper, without glancing at it.

"But like you, I'm a woman."

5

Trousseau

Trousseau had been putting on weight. It pushed at the cracked crocodile belt of his trousers.

"They told me downstairs you were here, *madame le juge.*"

Lucette Salondy smiled brightly. "Please enter."

Trousseau took a hesitant step into the office. He held a brief-case under his arm, and Anne Marie noticed that beneath the white shirt, the narrow shoulders ran down to a bulging belly. His eyes darted from one woman to the other. He smiled nervously and straightened his tie. "I wouldn't have . . ."

"Come in and sit down, Monsieur Trousseau." Anne Marie gestured him to the chair beside her. "Nobody's going to hurt you. Just two old ladies chatting."

"We're in a bit of a hurry, *madame le juge.*" He stood with his dark hand on the handle of the open door. "I've just come from the Palais de Justice."

"Monsieur Trousseau, you know Mademoiselle Salondy?"

He moved reluctantly towards the desk and shook the out-stretched hand, while his eyes remained on Anne Marie. "There's a plane waiting for you, *madame le juge*, at the airport."

She laughed. "My children are waiting for me."

"You're wanted in Saint François."

"On Wednesdays I have lunch with my children. This after-noon I'm taking them to the beach."

"It's very important."

The laughter left her eyes. "Why a plane, Monsieur Trousseau?"

He smiled nervously and edged back towards the door.

"To think that I chose this job." Anne Marie looked at Lucette Salondy. "A functionary of the state," she sighed before getting wearily to her feet. "Come and see us. Létitia would love to . . ."

Lucette held Anne Marie's hand. "I'm retiring at the end of the year. I'll have plenty of time to visit you then."

Trousseau was fidgeting and again he pulled at the dark tie. "The *procureur* insisted on an escort."

"Give my love to the children, Anne Marie. Kiss the lovely Létitia."

"If ever the *procureur* allows me to see them."

The two women embraced and Lucette Salondy squeezed Anne Marie's hand.

6

Gendarme

The officer helped Anne Marie from the military helicopter and accompanied her to the waiting car—a dark blue Peugeot that glinted in the sunshine. Trousseau followed, muttering to himself and wiping his forehead with a handkerchief.

"We'll be there in a few minutes." The gendarme spoke with an educated accent. He belonged to the new generation of West Indians that was now beginning to reach the positions of authority. There was about him the faint odour of expensive eau de cologne and self-assurance. Anne Marie got into the car, and he closed the door behind her. He went round the back of the vehicle and climbed in from the other side, a smile playing at the edge of his lips.

Trousseau sat beside the uniformed driver. He held the battered attaché case on his knees. He was now wearing his threadbare jacket.

"To the Pointe des Chateaux." The gendarme removed his kepi, revealing a high forehead and the short, curly hair that had begun to recede. He was good looking, but slightly chubby. "Capitaine Parise," he said.

"Anne Marie Laveaud."

The lips broke into a wide smile. "I've heard much about you." He held out his hand; Anne Marie noticed a gold wedding ring. "A pleasure to meet you, *madame le juge*." The intelligent eyes watched her carefully.

The car took the road from the small airport, went past the Méridien Hotel and the bright flags flapping from the high staffs, and out onto the road toward the Pointe des Châteaux.

Tourists were swinging golf clubs on the green of the golf course. Caddies lolled in the limited shade of the motorised buggies.

The sky was cloudless, the sun directly overhead. The car was air conditioned and the windows tinted. Only the slightest hint of humming as the Peugeot travelled eastward. Thin dancing mirages played on the surface of the tarmac.

"I don't envy you."

"What?"

"The Dugain business. You're making a lot of enemies within the SRPJ."

"Why the helicopter, Commandant?"

Parise coughed. "The *procureur* wanted you as soon as possible. Over the coming days, I'm afraid, you're going to be rather busy. Good job it's not the high season."

"High season?"

"The high season for tourism."

"Does that matter?"

Parise glanced at Trousseau's neck. "A nurse, *madame le juge*, aged twenty-three or twenty-four. She was on holiday here."

The unmarked Peugeot went past the new restaurants—low, concrete buildings with grey-green corrugated roofs—specialising in lobster, conch and other sea food. The restaurants were doing brisk business beneath the hot, midday sun. Rented cars with their stencilled plates were parked along the narrow highway.

Another day in this tropical paradise.

"A tourist from Paris who was raped and then murdered, *madame le juge*."

Trousseau was humming softly.

AUSTRALIA

LONDON, ENGLAND

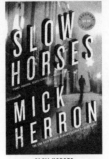

THE DRAGON MAN
GARRY DISHER
ISBN 978-1-61695-448-2

SLOW HORSES
MICK HERRON
ISBN 978-1-61695-416-1

BATH, ENGLAND

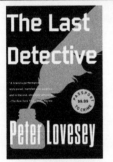

AMSTERDAM

HOLLYWOOD

THE LAST DETECTIVE
PETER LOVESEY
ISBN 978-1-61695-081-1

OUTSIDER IN AMSTERDAM
JANWILLEM VAN DE WETERING
ISBN 978-1-61695-300-3

CRASHED
TIMOTHY HALLINAN
ISBN 978-1-61695-276-1

SWEDEN

SOUTH KOREA

BRAZIL

DETECTIVE INSPECTOR HUSS
HELENE TURSTEN
ISBN 978-1-61695-111-5

JADE LADY BURNING
MARTIN LIMÓN
ISBN 978-1-61695-090-3

BLOOD OF THE WICKED
LEIGHTON GAGE
ISBN 978-1-61695-180-1